The Lighthouse Keeper's Daughter

The
Lighthouse
Keeper's
Daughter

Cherry Radford

urbanepublications.com

First published in Great Britain in 2018
by Urbane Publications Ltd
Suite 3, Brown Europe House, 33/34 Gleaming Wood Drive,
Chatham, Kent ME5 8RZ
Copyright © Cherry Radford, 2018

A CIP catalogue record for this book is available
from the British Library.

ISBN 978-1-911583-64-6
MOBI 978-1-911583-65-3
EPUB 978-1-911331-90-2

Design and Typeset by Michelle Morgan

Cover by Michelle Morgan

Printed and bound by 4edge Limited, UK

URBANE

urbanepublications.com

Cover image designed by David Izquierdo Arispón (www.izkaris.com)

The Lighthouse Keeper's Daughter

To me, the concept of distance is not important. Distance doesn't exist... and neither does time. Vibrations from love or music can be felt everywhere, at all times.

Yoko Ono

The Lighthouse Keeper's Daughter

MUSIC PLAYLIST

Link: **spoti.fi/2AJZEVl**
Create a free account on Spotify and listen to some of the novel's music.

The Lighthouse Keeper's Daughter

The Lighthouse Keeper's Daughter

The Lighthouse Keeper's Daughter

CHAPTER 1

FRIDAY 30TH AUGUST, 2012
The South Coast, England

The day it happened, she'd come out of the lighthouse and seen the car – shining in sudden sun – hurtling up the hill towards her. She was filled with a sense of fate, a feeling that her life was about to change.

That's how her novel could open.

If she ever started one.

In reality, she looks out of the lighthouse through a wet window, spots Ewan's Jeep in a line of cars making their awed way along the Beachy Head cliff road, and reckons she's got five minutes. She goes to her tiny round bedroom and brushes her hair, softens the pitiful tidiness of the living room with a tossed sweater.

Something comes to her from the builders' ghetto blaster below, so she stamps down the stairs and yes, it's Don Henley singing *Heart of the Matter*.

'Look I'm sorry, *no music*, I thought I explained,' she directs at Del (Dale?).

'Ah yes, sorry love.'

Ewan calls her about the gate.

'Sorry, thought I—'

'The one to get onto the drive, yes, but now this massive…'

She presses the button by the front door and the gate judders open to let him through. She sadly realises that unless her son's keeled over on the back seat like he used to as a sleepy tot, he's not in the car.

Ewan gets out, groaning and stretching his long arms – never a one to let a good deed go unnoticed. His hair might have a little more grey at the front, or might be lightened by a couple of weeks at his parents' villa with Madd-*ie*. He's wearing a leather jacket she doesn't remember. A yellow shirt a full spectrum away from his usual… his previous colour preferences.

She wonders whether they're going to do that kiss on each cheek thing, but they go into a polite hug.

'Can't *believe* it about the Fiat,' he says, as if its demise after three years is more astounding than that of their marriage after eighteen. He lets go and holds her by the shoulders. 'But look, I've been thinking – this isn't a loan. Just had a birthday haven't you? Call it a late fortieth present.'

'I'm forty-*two*.'

'So you are. But this can make up for all the birthdays I've forgotten. Anyway, I've had my eye on the Mercedes four-by-four, and Ollie needs a manual to learn in, so it's no good for him.'

'You sure? That's… great! Thanks!' She puts a kiss on his cheek. 'And where is Ollie?'

'Stayed over at his mate Will's.'

'Oh. Didn't you—'

'So how are you enjoying living in a giant knob?' he asks, looking up at the lighthouse with a smirk. 'And… *Je*-sus.' He's walking up the slope, staring at where the garden wall tumbles into the air. 'Talk about driving someone to the edge.'

'Ha-ha. But no nearer. It can crumble at any time.'

 2

He's still contemplating that unfeasible grass-sky interface, shoulders hunched as he braces against the wind. 'Fuck me, how d'you *cope* with this?'

'Well, I don't have to topple over any more than you have to stroll onto the A3. Anyway, I tend to look *this* way.' She waves an arm at the gently tipping hills of sheep-dotted pastures, farms sitting snug behind clumps of trees.

A pat on her back encourages her to keep doing that, or maybe he just wants to speed up the visit. 'Come on, guided tour.' He looks up again at the grey brick tower and the boxy cottage with non-matching windows stuck on the front of it. 'Not exactly a looker, is it?'

'Well I like it.'

They go inside.

'The keepers' cottage attached to the tower was originally one floor, but the previous owners added another and put the kitchen upstairs,' she finds herself informing him.

'But now there'll be one downstairs again,' he says, exchanging nods with the two builders when they look up at him from their sawing.

'Yes. Aunt Dorothy's got to have one-floor living sorted before she comes home, a bathroom with rails and stuff.'

'I don't remember you ever mentioning an *Aunt Dorothy*. Oh no – hang on, was she the old bird you met up in London a few months ago?'

'Yes. Hadn't seen her or my cousin since I was about twelve and then Anthea suddenly sent me a Facebook message.'

'So you must have come to this lighthouse as a child?'

'A couple of times. My father used to visit his sister on his own – Mum couldn't stand her. Anyway, she and my uncle hadn't had the place long before my father...'

He crosses the hall to the rounded wall the other side. 'So what's this door? The entrance to the lighthouse? How exciting.' He pulls at the handle, but it's locked.

'No. Well not nowadays – I think it's just storage.'

She follows him up the spiral staircase and watches his gaze pass over the sagging sofa and blue Formica to the view of the Seven Sisters cliffs from the living room, the slope and rise up to Beachy Head from the kitchen area.

'Wow.'

'Even better from up here,' she says, opening the door leading to the winding stone steps of the tower. She climbs up before him, holding onto the rope handrail, until they come up through the ceiling into the glare of the glassed lantern room. Sitting down on the curved sofa, she bends over to move some of Dorothy's old boxes of paint tubes to the side so that he can open the door and walk round the gallery, his exclamations lost in the whine of the wind.

He comes back in. 'God! Why don't you work up here? Amazing!' There are questions about the Seven Sisters, but she doesn't want to recount her efforts at walking along the undulating cliffs, the earth dropping and swaying beneath her until she had to lie down on the damp grass to recover.

She leads him back down to the living room and watches him pull open the door to her bedroom.

'God, you never said you sleep in the actual *shaft* of this thing.'

Had he always been this crude? But then apparently they were working all hours on the script for the new series of smutty footballers and their women in *Playing the Game*.

'Oh – brilliant!' he says as he finds her tiny shower room under the bunk bed. 'Although if you were an inch taller it would be daily concussion.' Now he's looking out of the narrow window above her desk. 'Doesn't that *bother* you?'

He could mean the profile of the Beachy Head cliff, but he's probably referring to her father's lighthouse in the sea below it.

'Doesn't it bother *Dorothy*?' he asks.

'It's empty now, and a long time ago.'

'Why did they build a second lighthouse there anyway?'

'This one was no good – you couldn't see it in the fog.' She moves towards the door. 'An early lunch? There's a nice Thai in the village.'

'Another time. Just a quick coffee and a sandwich, if you wouldn't mind.' He follows her and sits down at the kitchen table. 'Anyway, I thought you'd gone off restaurants.'

'It's all the competing conversations, but this one's—'

'When are you going to see somebody about your hearing?'

'How many times… I'm not wearing a hearing aid just because people can't be bothered to repeat themselves sometimes. I'm *fine*.'

She puts coffee into mugs, takes cheese and tomatoes out of the fridge. Just when she can't remember if he has one or two sugars, she's visited by a replay of a hilarious picnic in the garden with a small Ollie. How quickly so much is forgotten, yet other things too much remembered.

'*Are* you fine?' he asks when she joins him at the table. 'Up here all alone on a precipice?'

'I'm not alone. You're my third visitor in a month.' Like the other two – wives of their friends – she suspects that now he's satisfied his curiosity, he won't be down again anytime soon. Then a warm hand covers hers and she's alarmed to feel the sting of possible tears.

'And are you sure you're managing? Didn't you say the local *Fun for Families* mag is going to pay you even less than the Surrey one?'

'Well, without rent to pay…'

'And of course being part-time gives you time for The Novel.'

'Hm. Still not coming up with any ideas. Maybe it's just not the right time.'

He sips his coffee, puts it down. 'Come on, you could do something based on what happened to your father at the Beachy Head lighthouse. What did you say on the phone? Dorothy wants to send you some photocopied entries from your father's diaries? The novel would write itself! But only, of course, if you really get *stuck in.*'

She's forgotten about that sneering curl of the lip. The way he always assumes she won't quite come up to the mark.

'There's no way I'm writing about my father. How could I possibly get into his head? A few jottings about his life on the lighthouse aren't going to do it. He gave half his life to that thing, and then, just when I needed him most, he let the sea take the rest of him.'

'Imogen! It was an accident, wasn't it?'

'How can we really know? Anyway, he'd never be happy with what I wrote – he'd be turning in his watery grave, coming back to haunt me.' She takes a bite of her sandwich and knows she won't be finishing it. 'Shouldn't we be talking about Ollie? I really thought he—'

'Ollie's okay. He's busy getting his holiday homework done before starting back on Monday.'

'I thought you said he was staying with Will.'

'Well… both. Look, I'm sure he'll come down and see you before long, give him time. We all need time to get through this.'

Get through to where? But they are soon in the car and he's showing her the Jeep's controls, because he seems to have forgotten that she used to drive it occasionally. He turns some music off, waves his hand dismissively, says she can have that too. Now he's

 The Lighthouse Keeper's Daughter

saying something about making it official, paperwork, and her heart stops until she realises that he means the *car*.

⚔

She watches him disappear into Eastbourne station and is suddenly weighted with tiredness, desperate to get home. Home: how quickly the lighthouse has unexpectedly become that. In a way that she never felt about the sulky little flat in Weybridge, from where every emergence was a painful encounter. Or before that, the house with Ewan – for some years an uncomfortable space with hidden boundaries and sudden, raucous confrontations. She drives off.

For some years. How many? How far back in time would she have to go, to re-write the story of their marriage? To before Maddie joined the cast of *Playing the Game* – although of course there may have been other Maddies before her. To before Ewan's writing *finally* took off, making him swell with the indignant pride of the long passed-over. To before Ollie became a teenager and only needed his father – but no, he'd always been like that, because he'd been brought up by Daddy who stayed at home and made up funny stories for grown-ups (even if nobody read them), while Mummy was *always* out writing stuff for the magazine about what fun things you can take your children to (even if she seldom had time to take him). So yes, she would have to go way back – in fact, to around the time of that all-afternoon picnic in the garden, with 3-year-old Ollie's Early Learning plastic cakes mixing in with the salmon sandwiches and strawberries. She closes her eyes and approaches them – the younger, more sensitive Ewan, her own slimmer and more carefree form, the irresistibly soft and golden Ollie – and says *listen, you'll never believe it, but this isn't going to work out.*

A car beeps behind her; the lights have changed. She makes the square bonnet move forward. A friendly shape, she thinks, remembering a much-loved green Jeep in Ollie's old basket of cars. She was going to feel safe and cared for driving around in it.

She drives up the steep wind out of Eastbourne and along the Beachy Head road, sees a sign to the Sheep Centre and thinks how much Ollie would have liked it, as little as five or six years ago. Then pulls over into one of the tourist car parks and gets out her phone.

'Thanks SOOO much for the Jeep, I'm driving it with a grin on my face. It was good to see you, even if briefly. Come again soon, bring Ollie and we'll have time for the Thai place and a walk... We can get 'through this' as friends. Thank you again. Imo xxxx'

She isn't expecting an immediate reply – he'd mentioned a dinner with his agent – but it buzzes in her hand.

'No problem.'

She stares at the words. Tries to scroll down, but that's it. Just: *no problem*. No problem delivering the car, seeing her briefly, and letting Ollie refuse to see his mother any more than three times in five months. Certainly no problem *getting through* this – as long as he doesn't have to commit to making plans for ex-family outings.

She starts typing *'Is that all you can say?'* but deletes it. If only she could delete her own message – because of course they're not going to spend the day together, and she wouldn't want to. It's over. She's on her own. She's been on her own, and wanting to be, for five months. In many ways, for longer than that. But sometimes time swings around and confuses her.

Dorothy's lighthouse shimmers with her tears. It's just five minutes away, but she doesn't want to take these feelings home. The tissue packet in her bag is empty. Nothing in her pockets. She reaches over to open the glove compartment and, struggling with the catch, bumps her elbow against the car stereo button.

A fading chord, then silence.

Out of the corner of her eye, as she lifts out a tin of sweets and a small torch, she sees the track number flick to twelve. There's a dusty little box of tissues at the back of the compartment, just a few left.

A guitar chord that doesn't sound quite right, then twang, twang... and down to another discord.

She'll blow her nose and then turn it off.

There's further chordal pondering, followed by an exotic waterfall of sound.

It's... flamenco. But not the happy clappy type she and Ewan used to—

Rising from the desolation, the beginnings of a melody. Not a full line, just uttering, like somebody saying a few incoherent words. Then back to those strange chords, hesitantly, as if making it up as the mood takes him.

Take your time, *hombre*. She looks over at the lighthouse. Nobody's waiting for me, carry on.

He does. His phrases more plaintive, yearning.

She pulls out another tissue, her throat aching; she didn't know the guitar could *sigh*.

Now he's showing her something faster, an elaborate crystal of musical images, tumbling over one another for her attention, beautiful but becoming unbearable when that melody starts to speak over the top of it all, and then he's speeding up towards... a shocking crash of strings.

She sits in the swirling after-glow of the chord. How had she never understood the anger in sadness?

Now he's bent over his guitar, spent, back to those bleak ruminations.

Is this how it ends? She looks at the stereo display, 06:22, 06:23... There can't be much more. Don't do this to me.

He doesn't. Rising phoenix-like from the misery of those chords there is a new, questioning melody. Quiet but insistent, sharing the last word.

Silence.

Track One now, a dark but rhythmical number with a low, low bass guitar.

Who is this? She ejects the CD, stunned by the sudden emptiness of the air around her.

Santiago Montoya.

Montoya, Montoya… seems familiar. She checks the pockets in the car doors, the glove compartment: no CD case.

The gates take ages. So do the door and the stairs. She switches on her laptop and types *Santiago Montoya + guitarra*.

It's all in Spanish, but he was one of the members of that band that did the *Tangoza* song that Ewan kept playing in Marbella. There's a more recent shot of him, much more filled out. Another that doesn't look much like him at all, playing a long-haired guitarist in some film.

She puts the CD in her laptop and lets the first track fill the little room. She'll have to buy some speakers. She takes out her emptied and almost-Oxfammed iPod from the back of the bottom drawer, starts charging it up. Tomorrow she'll buy one of those things you stick it in. Really is time she started listening to music again. She rests her head in her hands, closes her eyes, smiles to herself.

Then she opens them again and goes into Twitter. For once it might be of some use. He's there. *Santiago Montoya, Madrid*. His profile picture probably his album cover, looking slightly uneasy as he peers out over his guitar, black curls carefully arranged by someone round his wide, sculpted face.

She types in Spanish – no accents, but probably about right.

Today my life stopped when I heard the last thing on your album. It stopped and started again.

She looks again at the photo – eyes a bit frightening or fearful, it's impossible to tell, but his mouth has a gently comical expression. She bends forward for a closer look.

He stares back at her.

Thank you Santiago.

CHAPTER 2

FRIDAY 31ST AUGUST, 2012
The South Coast, England

Imogen finishes a flapjack at a table from which she can observe the whole of the new Hippomania soft play centre while hopefully being out of range of the ball pit. All done: photos, leaflets about the party deals and the Halloween special, and a page of notes. It's basically an agreeable padded cell for pre-schoolers intent on damaging themselves; and mothers needing to flop down and eat very good cake without having to get up every few minutes to check their kid isn't being strangled in the underworld of a play frame. Some of this assessment will go into her one-fifty-word review, although the jaded tone appreciated by the Surrey *Fun for Families* isn't going down as well on the Sunshine Coast.

She used to interview families in these places, but nowadays she'd never hear a word above the background hum of the inflatables and the excited squeals. For the same reason, it's very unlikely that anything will ever come of the exchanges with friendly lone fathers – such as the lovely chap who just helped wipe up her spilt tea.

There are some *very* shrill little girls in here. You'd think reduced hearing could have its moments, but her ears seemed to

The Lighthouse Keeper's Daughter

have become simultaneously dull and acutely irritable. There's no doubt about it, she is no longer – was she ever? – writing for the right magazine, but she's not exactly getting snapped up by any others.

⁓

The Arndale centre is full of even noisier kids; small ones on shoe and pencil-case missions with Mummy, and hordes of laughing, pierced teenagers enjoying the last few days of mindless freedom. All those years of naming new uniform, sorting out crayons and maths sets, hunting down black Velcros in 4F, 5F, 6F and eventually clomping great car-tyre shoes in size 9… Now Ollie's term will start without any help from her – except for the few words of encouragement he allowed her in last night's brief phone call.

Curry's has a family of five enjoying television demos. She unhooks some higher priced earphones, and then – having confirmed with little more than sign language that the speakers she's chosen will work with her iPod – joins a queue to pay. Same old shops: Next, Holland & Barratt, Smith's – all best dealt with online these days. There's a make-your-own-bear shop like the one where Ollie's Taekwondo Teddo was born. Specsavers: sooner or later she'll have to have an eye check and succumb to reading glasses – and it turns out that you can have your hearing checked there too. In maybe less than ten minutes she could have a hearing aid in her bag, next to the speakers and earphones – she could go home and hook them all up together, ha! But it's not funny. None of this is funny. Fun is not to be had in a shopping centre, with all its crowds, noise and strange previous and future versions of oneself looking for different things.

The builders are there, and the boss one seems to be going into a tedious explanation about why they've managed to come up today after all. 'It's good, 'cos we can finish off the tiling,' he concludes with a smile.

'Ah – okay, great.' She rushes on upstairs.

The ghetto blaster. It's still there on the living room table. Perhaps he'll think he left it at home.

'Er… Imogen?' A grinning shaven head appears at the top of the spiral stairs. 'Have you confiscated the radio?'

'No! But sorry, I did borrow it.'

He's coming up the rest of the steps. 'There's no music player up here?'

She shakes her head. 'Not working. I had a CD I needed to play. I'm really—'

'No, no. I'm relieved. Worried about you, stuck up here.'

She puts her bags down on the sofa. 'I'm fine, it's lovely and quiet for getting on with my work.'

'And when you're not working?'

'I… need a new collection.'

'Ah. Memories, eh?'

Exactly how much has Aunt Dorothy told him? 'Anyway, I've just bought a speaker for my iPod, so I'm all fixed up now.'

'Right.' He's smiling and nodding. The other guy can be heard clattering around downstairs, humming something. 'Nobody should be without music.'

She picks up the ghetto blaster and hands it to him. 'Thanks.'

'Any time.' He seems about to say something else, but turns to go downstairs.

'Oh wait. Dale? Shall I bring down some tea for you two?'

He comes up again. 'It's Dyl. Dylan. We've brought our own, thanks.' He reaches forward and takes the CD out of her hand. 'This is what you needed to listen to?' His rough hands turn it over with surprising care. 'Santi-ago Monto-ya. I like a bit of Latin – got a warmth, hasn't it.'

'Yes. Well, thanks again.'

It's too precious, she needs another copy – and it would be interesting to see the case. She sits down at her desk. Not available on Amazon. Damn. But actually – good. She can ask Santiago how to buy it here, see if he answers.

Dylan is back at the top of the stairs. 'Think you missed this,' he says, holding out a letter. 'Jersey postmark, must be Dorothy.'

'Ah, thanks.'

She sets up the speaker on her desk and puts her iPod on to Santiago's album. Twists the volume up until it sounds like his guitar is in the room – well, louder probably. Lovely. It might be fun to read her father's diary pages in the lantern room, glancing over at his lighthouse, so she puts the volume up even further.

She pulls open the heavy door and climbs the steps, round and round, her feet in time to Track One. Then there she is, squinting in the sun; there's so much light up here, it's as if the long-gone Argand lamps have left an afterglow.

Inside the envelope there is one piece of folded A4. Nothing else. No 'isn't this funny/sad/ interesting?' or 'I'll look through and send you something else soon, love, Dorothy'. She unfolds the sheet. Her mouth opens at the sight of the neat loopy handwriting; she can almost hear the scratching of one of his skinny yellow BIC biros.

'Fri 14th Aug.'81
So they've given us a date. 28th June 1982 she'll be fully automated

and we won't be needed anymore. Heck knows how they can be so precise, but that's the Corporation of Trinity House for you.

And the day we get this news, it has to be my turn for the Middle watch, doesn't it. I get a pat from Len, an egg sandwich using the last fresh tomato from Bill – because we all know if there's anything on your mind it's bloody hard staring out alone from the top of a lighthouse for four hours in the middle of the night.

Just checked the light, then found myself out on the gallery, leaning over and listening to the crash and hiss of the waves in the darkness below, walking round with my hand on the cold wet glass of the lantern room like I'm stroking her or something.

Then it was downstairs to do the 3am weather log (without touching Bill's polished handrails): visibility poor, gallery temp 52 but barometer's dropping, overcast / drizzle, weather-vane NW, wind on cheek Force 5. All the time wondering how I'll compare to the automated readings. This is how it'll be from now on, everything we do seeming too little or too much.

Len says block it out and carry on, but he's been a Principal for 23 years and happy to retire, looking forward to joining the amateur dramatics group. But Bill's got a kid on the way and doesn't know what to do – so he's spent the day joking and calculating: 152 more days on duty, 21 more Columbos from our Parker Knolls, possibly 3 more chuck-ups over the side of the relief boat.

Trinity might find us other posts of course, but it's the beginning of the end, they'll all be automated soon, so why play a game of musical lighthouses? Better to go out on a high, the three of us together. Start looking at other things. Maybe something at Newhaven port. But oh God.'

She looks over at the lighthouse and imagines him standing there with a battered leather logbook in hand. Poor chaps, can't have been easy.

 The Lighthouse Keeper's Daughter

'Back upstairs, looking out at the flashes of water. The thing is, I need the sea. I need the sea between me and others. Somehow the sea creates a distance that's more than physical. Yet sometimes it can draw you closer, like the magical refraction of light.'

What? It certainly didn't draw him and Mum closer; she hated 'that bloody Channel.'

'Done my letters:

BERYL - Giving her the news. She'll already have had it from the other wives of course, but I need to look like I'm sharing it with her on the day it arrived. The <u>news</u> that is, not my horror of the idea of going ashore for good.

IMOGEN - Eleven! Asked how her birthday went, told her next year I'll be there for it.

DOROTHY - It's all gone through, they now own the old cliff lighthouse – we'll almost be able to wave to each other!

S - While writing the letter, beginning to understand what I have to do.

How will it be, the 28th June? Balmy summer evening, sea like a lake. A last look out from the gallery, then winding down through the service room, to the bedroom with the banana bunks we'll never sleep in again, to the kitchen where nobody will get on to the r/t anymore to report people in trouble on the cliffs or trapped by the tides on the beach, through the store rooms to the lobby, and out down the dog-steps to the set-off – with somebody turning to shove that heavy door closed for the last time. But it won't be me. I'll already be gone.'

The horror of coming ashore for good. God. A punch in the gut, and an irritation that has her glaring back at the lighthouse for an explanation. Were she and her mother really so awful? Mum was a bit of a nag, but did everything she could for him when he was home. And as for her... well, by that age, she was sitting around daydreaming or curled up with a book most of the time – not exactly a nightmare. Maybe he was just dreading leaving a life he'd known for so many years.

But then there's the all-important letter to 'S'. Who the fuck is that? And why did they seem to be advising that he should already be gone before the last day at the lighthouse? S. She doesn't recall any of his friends – all in the lighthouse service – having a name beginning with S. And anyway, why just 'S'? Surely there are only two reasons for putting an initial instead of someone's name in a private diary: they are either a close family member, or a person you're too embarrassed or scared to name, *even to yourself*... Ha! She's been reading too many books; this is her sensible Dad.

She stands up. Grass, sea, horizon. She waits until the green-grey-blue feels as harmless as a child's painting. Then, humming along with Track 3, she unlocks the door and goes out on to the gallery for the first time, walking right round it, not holding the metal rail, but running her hand along the wet glass walls. Like her father did at his lighthouse. Did he like its curved perfection, or just the hours he could devote to reading and listening to music inside it? Can you *love* a lighthouse? Maybe it felt like an impending bereavement. Maybe 'S' was some kind of counsellor – if they had such things in those days. Or someone somehow fulfilling that role, like... a penfriend. Nothing wrong with that, if it was helping.

She goes back down to her guitar-filled room and wonders if Santiago has answered her. He has. You can get it here, English flamenco lady, he's said in Spanish, giving a website address.

'Thank you,' she writes, but then notices that he was on here

                    The Lighthouse Keeper's Daughter

just ten minutes ago; maybe he's still at his computer or looking at his phone.

She turns off the music so she can concentrate, Googles some words and then writes in Spanish: 'Your second track puts me on a new level. But today in the car it put me on the wrong road – look what you made me do!'

She's sounding a bit star-struck, but it's completely true; music this entrancing shouldn't accompany the operation of machinery.

She jumps as a 'jajaja' laughter appears, followed by something like 'Of course, because the track is called Two Roads!'

'I didn't know! At the moment I've only got the CD, not the box!'

She types in the next box that she's sorry, she forgot to write in Spanish, did he understand?

'No!!!' comes back at her, so she translates.

Then he seems to be suggesting that whenever she says something to him, she could always write it in both languages, to help his English.

An invitation to send further messages. She feels her cheeks burn. 'Of course! / *Claro!*' she writes with a smile.

The narrow window above her desk has a perfect view of her father's lighthouse, now forlorn in a flat low tide, no boats in sight. Nothing wrong with having a penfriend.

CHAPTER 3

FRIDAY 31ST AUGUST, 2012
Madrid, Spain

What was he doing chatting with this woman on Twitter? Now she'll be pestering him about his English, and probably – like Mad Marta or that fragile drama student girl – getting hurt and stroppy when he doesn't tweet back; he doesn't want to go through all that again. But… his track stopped her life and started it again. That's quite something. Maybe she's old and lonely. Or ill. Shit.

He taps on her profile. A wrapped up character with a healthy grin, a frothy grey sea behind her. Brad, as in Brad Pitt. Maybe @ImoBrad is a *boy*. He opens the website: seems to be some kind of journalist. Ah, and female. Imo-gen Brad-field. Not old, and not too bad a looking woman – despite her long reddish hair and narrow little face – so surely she won't be lonely for long.

Anyway, good on her for buying another CD. He breathes out heavily and looks over at the dusty pile of boxes of them in the bedroom. Why did he put them there, under the photo of Tangoza celebrating their album release? He goes over to look at it. It's not the best time for Tangoza to re-form, but why else would his sister and brother-in-law *need to talk to him about something*? There was

The Lighthouse Keeper's Daughter

that drunk chat about it in the pool in Ibiza, but not a word since coming back to Madrid.

Lunch at three, his sister said. She performed at Casa Patas last night, and Fran, flying back from the States, was going to guest on her last set; the meeting will be laden with their own wearying success. That radio show including Tangoza in a game about one-hit-wonders said they were an unusual example of a band that turned out to be *less* than the sum of its parts – kindly ignoring the small size of his own contribution.

But then there's his acting. He picks up the script and covers up the highlighted block. Stares out of the window at the washing hanging up over the attic terrace opposite. Tries to ignore the vacuuming in the apartment below and a tiff outside Café Kiki on the corner. No, it's not there. He starts reading it out loud again, but stumbles – if Miri was here she'd be furious and insisting on helping, sitting on the bed in her Cine shop's clapperboard t-shirt.

If it's not his girlfriend going on at him, it's his manager; they both have a ridiculous belief in this New York film audition. He runs his fingers through his hair, closes his eyes, has the usual hollow-stomach feeling that follows the mere thought of it. And wasn't Ignacio supposed to be getting back to him about the Madrid gig? He picks up his phone. It could be a voicemail, an email, WhatsApp or even a Twitter message. He finger-paddles through the wretched river of tweets, the direct message tributaries. Briefly visits the near dried-up riverbed of his Facebook 'Actor' page. Then it's over to the texts. A barely remembered school friend is congratulating him on his small scene in last week's episode of *La Universidad*. Then there's Ignacio: *'Don't forget your English class today – if you don't turn up this time you'll lose your place.'* Followed by: *'Looks like you've got just four months to read up, shape up and improve your English – the screen test will be in the new year. Just for now, put the guitar DOWN Santi.'*

≍

During the sweaty drive to Esme and Fran's, he can't help imagining writing together again in their air-conned basement studio. As the car judders across calle Arturo Soria and that orange signal comes up again, he also imagines the possible change to his finances. Once he didn't have to be at the studio for early calls, maybe he could move over here. Not to the pressured footballer dormitory where Esme and Fran live of course, but a small place in one of these quiet roads. Handy for his daughter's school and nearer to her mother's place. He'd start seeing her during the week for pancakes at VIPS. Now she's older, she'd understand about the touring. He passes the road to the Cultural Centre. Nearer to the English class too – he'd need it for the tours, can't leave Fran to do all the talking.

He wills the car up the hill, phones Esme to open the gates and parks next to Fran's Porsche. She's standing between the pillars grinning and waving her hands about, draped in a flowing white top with ludicrous gold bits. 'Sant-*i*! Come here, my gorgeous little brother!'

She calls upstairs to Fran, who comes down smiling but heavy-eyed, wearing one of his loose shirts but his long hair now cut short and whipped about. They go through the house to the terrace by the pool, where their handsome Romanian nanny is putting the final touch to the table with roses from the garden.

They talk about their exhausting tours and his nephews' basketball, ask how things are going with Miri, and laugh about how his daughter now calls herself 'Tricia' rather than Pato. Santi

The Lighthouse Keeper's Daughter

sinks into his chair; it doesn't look like Tangoza's rebirth is on the agenda, and all he has to do now is play the scene moment by moment, as the teacher used to say in acting class. You know what's coming, but you still have to *listen*, remember the bridge between stimulus and reaction, always be aware of the *bottom line* – which in this case is that he really wants to be in the band again, and it's fucking hard and hurtful that they don't feel the same.

'How's the weight loss going?' asks Esme, offering him some more salad. 'And any news on the film?'

'Don't know. But I should be getting some more gigs soon, and I'm trying to get ideas together for the new album.'

'Some *songs* this time, Santi,' says Fran. 'The company might have a point, a bit more… upbeat. Hey, the country needs a *lift*, okay? Don't get me wrong, you know I love your stuff, but you need to widen your audience.' He looks over at Esme, and maybe she gives a little nod. 'But what about the acting? Even if this Lorca film doesn't come off, surely you'll get another series after *La Universidad*? With your… what did they say in that article? Your special *intensity*.'

'Ha! What they're seeing is pure terror. It was different with *Flamenco Academy*, a one-off. I'm a musician for God's sake.'

'You can be both! Listen to you; an American film, two popular drama series, and you still think you're a beginner!' He finishes his wine and glances at Esme again. 'But look Santi, we've got to tell you… We'd both be happy to be on a track on your next album if you like, but there's not going to be a new Tangoza.'

'No of course, it's a busy–'

'Because… I'm going to the States. I'll be over frequently, but… I'm buying a house, it's where I need to be.'

Santi looks over at Esme. 'The boys! Have you told Mamá? She'll be devastated!'

Fran looks down at the table, but Esme gives him a wry smile. 'We're staying here,' she says quietly.

'But… Oh… God, I had no idea.' He looks over at Fran and back to Esme; his own experience of marriage break-up is all to do with thundering rows and crying on the floor.

'Fran and I have been living almost parallel lives for a long time. Have you really not noticed? Don't worry, we've got it all worked out.' Fran nods in agreement. 'But we know how you feel about Tangoza and wanted to tell you first. We're really, really sorry.'

The Lighthouse Keeper's Daughter

CHAPTER 4

FRIDAY 31ST AUGUST, 2012
The South Coast, England

'I'm sorry dear, we're closing now.'

'Of course you are, sorry.' Imogen finishes the last of her tea from the little faded cup and pays a bill suggesting that the Victorian Tea Room hasn't turned a calendar page since nineteen eighty. Actually, that's about when she was last here, she realises, and smiles at the enormous old chandelier as she walks past it on her way out back onto the decking. She's now rather glad that those forgotten print cartridges made her come into town again, drive along the seafront and suddenly want to go on the pier.

Heaven knows why her parents used to like bringing her here so often – her father already spending half his life suspended over the sea, her mother usually preferring places with more substantial retail opportunities. The three of them would stroll round it, Imogen talking to the seagulls, her mother proudly hanging on to her father's arm as he nodded in reply to people greeting him like a minor celebrity. Then her parents would settle down in a couple of deckchairs next to these blue ironwork railings, while she went off to spend a heavy pocketful of pennies on the game with the little race horses in the amusement arcade.

In the old Sweets and Treats shop she half expects to see the lovely lady who used to deal with all the jars. She comes out with a paper bag of Flying Saucers and wanders along towards the domed pavilion at the end, its white paint glaring in the sun. Spreading herself along a curved wooden bench, she looks back over the sea at the sedate Victorian seafront.

This is the town where her new start begins. Here of all places. Although her father's death was an accident, it is still somehow the place where the first man in her life let her down. A place of happy but also painful and puzzling memories. It is also a town apparently peopled by the very old and the very young; her chances of ever meeting someone here must be next to nil. She should probably move to Brighton. But for now, it somehow feels like where she needs to be. It's a long away from Ollie, but it wasn't much easier communicating with him when they were living in the same town.

A flyer on the pavilion catches her eye: once a week they do a club night for sixteen to eighteen-year-olds. She gets out her phone and as soon as he answers she's telling him about it.

'So send me a photo then, Mum.'

'I haven't got my camera.'

He groans and might be saying something about smart phones.

'Perhaps you'd like to come down with Will one weekend and go to it.'

There's a lot of background noise at his end. A plaintive seagull at hers. She can't hear what he's saying, but it sounds disjointed and non-enthusiastic. Then he probably said he had to go, because he is no longer there.

She's suddenly had enough flying saucers, and the breeze is getting cold. Driving home, Santi's track feels in sympathy with her resentment, telling her story. After seventeen years of her care,

   The Lighthouse Keeper's Daughter

Ollie seems to have little further need of her company or support. Worse, he seems irked by the inconvenience of her departure, rather than having a little sympathy for her – even though surely he can see that the Maddie thing finally made it inevitable? How did she raise such a thoughtless boy? Or maybe she just doesn't understand the male teenage mind. Or any male mind, for that matter.

Back home, she tries to write a Facebook message to Ollie but deletes it. Wonders if she should write to Ewan about Ollie, but she's already done that. Reads a patronising job rejection email from some complete dick at the Sussex Countryside magazine. Looks at her father's diary page again. None of this is doing her any good. She is here to hibernate, regain, re-ravel. Ah... and sometimes have a bit of fun. She was about to switch the laptop off, but goes into Twitter and clicks on @Santi_Montoya.

'What are you doing? / *Que haces?* (In English!)'

CHAPTER 5

FRIDAY 31ST AUGUST, 2012
Madrid, Spain

Juan Sanchez, the English teacher a couple of Ignacio's other clients have recommended, turns out to be a camp, little strip of a guy, with small whirly handwriting (on the note he hands him about Essential Books) that instantly jumbles. Reverting to his twelve-year-old self, Santi takes a seat at the back of the classroom.

'So Santiago, welcome. Everyone calls me Johnny – as in Johnny Depp...' He writes J-O-H-N-N-Y on the board and says something in English about introductions.

Ten or so faces turn to Santi – and he can see that the two middle-aged women on the next table are already whispering about him being that awful gypsy boyfriend guy in *Universidad*. He's really not in the mood for this.

'You missed the introductions on Monday,' Johnny repeats in Spanish, 'can you tell us a little about yourself, and why you need this intensive English course?'

'Well, I'm a musician, I want to improve my English because...' Why? As a musician he's unlikely to need it any time soon – Tangoza is now definitely dead, and his new little band are struggling to get *local* gigs. 'Because I'm also an actor and... you know, I might need it...'

Johnny grins, coaxes this muddled sentence into English, and uses it as a starting point for a class discussion on Spanish actors in English language films. A smart old gentleman in the front row manages something about how he read that Penelope Cruz had difficulties with English while filming *The Hi-Lo Country*, while a couple of the women argue about whether Javier Bardem learnt English quickly by having two months of daily lessons or by just dating his teacher. Ignacio was right, conversation practice is much more fun in Lower Intermediate; it would have been deathly doing a third Beginner's course.

Then it was time to open the grammar book.

A girl in a tight red t-shirt and green nail varnish is asked to move her chair closer to his so that he can share hers. They're already on *Unit 8: I am doing (present cont...?) and I do (present simple)*. But it's *not* simple, because apart from *do* and *do-ing*, Johnny is talking about "duz", which he can't see anywhere. His eyes flit down the page, the words in bold floating out above it so that all he can see is *'m... ing... 's... DON'T*.

They're going to have to give examples of their own. He starts again at the top of the page, leaning over and putting a finger along each line. The girl appears to be intrigued by his no doubt troubled profile, but it's just too bad. There's a sentence about the guitar in one of the boxes. He's now being asked for the present simple, the one without *ing*, so he puts his finger on the first word and replaces it with *I*.

'I do-es play the guitar.'

><

I do play the guitar. *Do* can be used for emphasis, Johnny explained. It wasn't *that* wrong, and it wasn't that funny. I *do* play the guitar, and I *do* play in a group, he thinks to himself. It's not Tangoza, but there's a good energy between them, not unlike what he felt in the early days of Tangoza. Except it's all so much harder these days.

A text from Pato: *'Papi, can we make it nine instead of eight?'*
'It's eight NOW and I'm sitting in the car outside your apartment!'
'Sorry. OK, I'll be there in half an hour.'

Half an hour is definitely more than he wants to spend with Anita in the apartment; he'd rather get on with his homework. He opens the book. Words with *–ing* are okay, but jumbling in front of them are *I'm, is't, itn't… are* and *are-nt…* Fuck.

Twitter dongs the arrival of a tweet. It's the English woman again. Wanting to know what he's doing – in English.

He looks at the page. He could write *I'm learn-ing English* – she'd be delighted with that. In fact… he flicks through the pages and smirks as he picks up the notepad. *What are YOU doing? What are we wait-ing for? We are in bed.* He chuckles. *I'm work-ing hard. Are you feel-ing good?* And oh God… He snorts like a schoolboy. *Are you com-ing?*

The phone ringing makes him jump.

Uncle Pedro. 'How are you doing, Santi?'

'Esme told you.'

'I think *confirmed* would be the word. But really, you don't need Tangoza.' A crowd of yelling teenagers stumble past on the pavement. 'My God, where are you?'

'Doing English in my car while I wait for Pato to turn up.'

'You do realise that Lorca didn't actually learn any English in New York?'

'Really? Ha! That's got to be good news. But unfortunately the film's *in* English.'

'Oh dear. Well best of luck with that. But meanwhile I need some flashy guitar for this high energy TV Sports album I'm working on, and the arthritis is playing up. Quite a few bits actually – two days' work for you.'

'Great!' A *sports* album. How could Uncle Pedro stand this crap after his years of touring sold-out concert halls? But he had a way of needing him exactly at the moment when Santi needed a boost in finances or confidence. 'Thanks, I'll call you when I get home.'

Pato arrives, carrying shopping bags.

He opens the window. 'Can we go now, Pato? I've got plans.'

'It's Tricia, *please*,' she says. 'I'll just pop in and get my case.'

I've got plans. She used to like it when he said that. Back in the days when a weekend with her was a large stretch of non-existence unless you gave shape to it with plans for the duck pond, the Teleférico ride, the zoo, Retiro Park, the puppet theatre on Sunday morning. Nowadays her visit was squeezed into a mere kernel of a weekend, her friends and school commitments eating away at either side of it.

Tricia gets in. There's that renewed shock of the eyeliner and puffed out hair.

He gives her a hug. 'Please, I've said it before, just be there when I turn up, OK?'

They drive off. He learns that her friend's birthday party was fine. Also fine were school work, the boy she was 'seeing', and last week's trip to the coast with her mother. She's sick of VIPS, but the Italian restaurant on the corner would be fine.

Now they're in the apartment. At least, he is; Pato-Tricia is in her phone, tapping away with two little thumbs.

'Tell you what, let's have no phones at the restaurant, okay?'

'Mamá says I should always have it on me.'

'Well, they'll stay in our pockets then.'

They go to the Italian. There won't be time for the cinema now, but she's already seen REC3 anyway.

She looks at him across the table and smiles. 'Sorry I was late.'

He pats her hand. 'Okay. Anyway, next weekend I'll be taking you home from the match, so—'

'Er... no. I'm quitting the basketball team.'

'What?'

'I'll play at school, but the Saturday matches have got to go. I've sort of grown out of all that, you know? Saturday's for seeing my friends.'

'And shopping.'

She raises her eyes to the ceiling. 'Oh I just knew you'd be like this.'

Santi sips his wine. No more basketball, cheering her on, chatting about it afterwards – another change to accept. 'I just think it's a shame, that's all.'

Then she starts suggesting that maybe sometimes the two of them could go and watch her little cousins play instead, and it starts to feel like the evening might be fine after all. Until she mentions the school skiing trip again.

'Pato, I told you – and Mamá – it's a lot of money, and not a good time for me.'

'All my friends are going, and they won't believe we can't afford it, when you're on the telly every week!'

'Until the end of the series, or maybe before... Don't make me go through this again, okay?'

When they get back, she goes to bed. Or at least she goes to her phone, no doubt Facebooking her grievances. As he is, in texts to Anita – who denies having discussed it and 'can't really talk now'.

He sits in the living room with a second bottle of Rioja. Gets up to close the blinds on an argument on the terrace across the road. Sits down again and lets that releasing warmth spread through him. Then picks up the guitar and lets his fingers walk out a whingeing melody – interspersed with thrashing *rasgueado*. He hums a melody over an arpeggio figure, sings something about talking… about not listening… Ha! Pato can hear it but doesn't know it's about her. Pausing for a moment, he hears his phone announce a tweet.

The English woman again. 'I listen to the track Dos Caminos like a story / *Escucho Dos Caminos como una historia.*'

'It IS a story,' he replies in Spanish.

'Whatever I want it to be. Today about my son / *Cualquiera que yo quiero. Hoy sobre mi hijo.*'

'I just played a story song about my daughter!'

Is Pato on Twitter? He made a profile for her some while ago but has never seen her on here. He finishes his glass and, without thinking too much about it, clicks ImoBrad's Follow button and sends her a private Direct Message.

'Is no isi wihth the hija (17)', he types.

'Santiago in English! Well done! Better: it's not easy with the daughter ('dota').'

Then another message from her: 'It's not easy with my son (17 too!) either. He thinks only of himself / *piensa solo en su mismo.*'

'Exactamente! Mi dauhgter to.'

'My = *mi*, ToO = *tambien.*'

'Yes, my daughtre too'. Oh no. He types again. 'Ufff… DAUGHTER!!!'

':-D It's difficult to talk to them / *Es dificil hablar con ellos.*'

'Everything "fine" until they can't have what they want ☹,' he writes in Spanish.

'When will they speak the same language again?! / *Cuando volveran a hablar el mismo idioma*?!'

Good question.

'Papá?' She's in the kitchen. 'D'you want a hot chocolate?'

He doesn't, but she's trying to say sorry. 'OK!'

'I am going now,' he writes. Correct! But maybe it sounds a bit abrupt. The title of the bilingual book on Lorca catches his eye. He taps the two words into the box. 'Back tomorrow.'

The Lighthouse Keeper's Daughter

CHAPTER 6

WEDNESDAY 5TH SEPTEMBER, 2012
The South Coast, England

*Un*believable. Apart from that jazzy piano guy, there are no other English names among the 48 people Santi follows. He's taken on an English penfriend-teacher; they could say anything to each other now, he would be back tomorrow...

But that was five tomorrows ago.

Chin in hand, she scrolls down her Direct Messages: 'Will you be back today?! / *Volveras hoy*?! Haha', 'Santi, you are late (*atrasado*) for your class!!!' And then this morning's sickeningly confident invitation: 'Do you fancy an English breakfast?! / *Te apetece un desayuno ingles*?!' How stupid it looks, an unanswered hour on.

She closes the Direct Messages and allows herself one more look at his Twitter profile. No tweets or re-tweets today or yesterday. What's happened to him? Although up until Monday night he was of this world, replying to a succinct bullish individual who could be his manager, exchanging admiration with another *fenómeno* musician and giving flowery fits-all affection to several *guapísimas* – gorgeous women. Back to the Direct Messages, even though the absence of a blue blob tells her that no messages have arrived. And... no messages have arrived.

She groans and clicks on the OTHERMAGS spreadsheet, with its ever increasing proportion of browned-out magazines. This is what she should be mulling over today, not the likelihood of a couple of tweets from an amiable but adulated guitarist.

The phone in the living room rings. She glances at her watch and wonders how she could have forgotten.

'Dorothy! How are—'

'Just checking that you've remembered, Imogen.'

'Of course! I'm looking forward to it.' Three hours as a volunteer in the local Visitor's Centre. 'Oh, and thanks for sending me the first of Dad's—'

'Have you been there to introduce yourself?'

'Well no, I was going to go, but—'

'That's a pity. It's very important that you take this job seriously. If you aren't satisfactory, they'll have to take on someone else and won't keep the post open for me. You do understand, don't you?'

'Yes of course. Please don't worry. I'll—'

'You better skip along dear, you mustn't be late.'

Imogen pulls on a navy linen skirt likely to make her feel at home with her presumably ancient fellow assistants and dashes down to the car. On comes Santi's only upbeat track, but she switches it off.

Down the hill, then up to the highest point on Beachy Head where the fog is thickest. There it is, between the pub and the Coastguard office. She parks the car and braces herself for a shopful of Dorothies: tall, formidable creatures with the hollowed bone structure and French buns of former beauties, heavy lines extending from disapproving mouths. A picture coloured in by what she recalled of her mother's dislike of the woman. Marriage to an eminent doctor had lifted this former nurse to a life of engagements too important for her to have time for her lonely sister-in-law; why was a voluntary job selling postcards to tourists so important to her now?

She walks into the shop, accidentally buffeting a bookmark stand into rotation.

'Oops. Hello I'm Imogen, Dorothy's—'

'HE-*LLO*!' cries out an ample woman in pink coming through to the till from the office. 'Annie. And this is Frank,' she says, tilting her bobbed grey hair at the grinning, wiry old man beside her.

'Sorry I'm a bit late, I—'

'You'll have to speak up a bit m'dear, we're both a bit Mutt and Jeff,' says Frank.

'No problem – I'm tired of having to try and keep my voice down! My ears aren't too good either!'

'Join the club! Pop your bag in the back here, dear, and Frank'll show you round.'

She hangs it up next to a window overlooking undulating fields of cows and follows a beckoning Frank.

'Sheep things. Lighthouse stuff. Fridge magnets. Stationery—'

'Ooh I need some of these!'

'Ten per cent discount. Twenty-five per cent on the fudge,' he adds with a wink. 'And over here… Well, we're a gift shop too so we've got this kind of, er…' He winces as he points out a china bulldog in a Union Jack basket.

'Pony and trap?'

They chuckle and move over to the entrance to the museum, which is guarded by a person-size model of the Beachy Head lighthouse that will flash its light for 10p in a slot.

'Oh!' She tries to fix the tiny broken rail outside the lantern room.

She sees Frank suddenly looking serious; Dorothy must have told them about her father.

'I love this!' she says, and sees Frank's smile return. Then they have fun with the interactive displays of seagulls and shepherds.

'I can see I'm going to have to watch you two!' Annie calls out. 'Come and show her the till, Frank.'

She learns which buttons to press and takes money from the customers while Frank bags up the items. At one point she has a quick look at her phone and finds that there's no signal; even if she ever gets a mobile with internet on it, this place is going to be a healthy mid-week Twitter time-out.

A large, cheery man in a red polo shirt buys one of the big fudge tins and says something about money. He and Frank start chatting about the fog while he empties the Beachy Head Chaplaincy Team collection box into a bag.

He turns to her when he's left. 'That's Ben. He and the others get *fifty* per cent discount on the fudge. Wonderful job they do. People don't realise.'

'They talk to those who're about to…?'

'Yes. What did that author say, the one that wrote *Captain Corelli's Mandolin*… "This beautiful place openly invites you to die."[1] Trouble is, the poor coastguard chaps have to go down the cliffs and risk their lives to pick up the bits… And then you get those who survive – in bits.'

'Oh God. How do people do it?'

Frank shakes his head. 'The world can be a lonely place.'

A woman is also buying fudge.

'Maple Walnut. An excellent choice, m'dear,' he says.

She delves into a pink bag with a matching monkey key ring, blonde hair falling over her face.

'Gorgeous bag!' Imogen says, but the woman doesn't look up.

---

1   Louis de Bernières. (1996). Fatal Attraction. Independent, Saturday 10 February 1996

Then two small boys come up to the till and start complaining about something in the museum, so Frank goes off to investigate.

'Anything else?' Imogen asks, turning back to the customer.

She shakes her head, gives Imogen a five pound note and puts the change in the collection box before leaving.

Frank comes back to the till. 'The bottom-feeders in the tank weren't moving about enough for them, didn't realise they were in a show. Oh – whose is this?' He has stumbled into a bag by his feet.

'Oh! I know...' Imogen rushes out with it.

She calls out to the woman, hoping to catch her before she crosses the road to the bus stop.

'Thanks!' She has red-rimmed lids and flushed cheeks – just like Imogen in the hayfever season. She smiles but seems to be hanging on to the car park wall.

'Are you alright?'

'Yes... Just need a bit of sustenance.'

'Me too. D'you know if this pub is any good? Thinking of having lunch there.'

The woman looks down the hill – presumably for the bus – and then back at Imogen. 'Hearty stuff. Not a bad idea, I might do the same.'

'Well I better get back and finish, might see you there later.'

'Thanks again. I'll be by the window with the old lighthouse view.'

Imogen walks back to the shop. She's just arranged to have lunch with a stranger. Now she's got into Twitter, she's becoming used to making unexpected little friendships. There's the chick-lit author in Cambridge with an un-retweetably outrageous sense of humour; a graphic designer in Seville with whom she shares YouTube flamenco clips; an artist friend of his who has a thing about lighthouses; and the Spanish, anglophilic wedding photographer who seems to be a cousin of Santi's in Australia.

'You caught her. She all right?' Frank asks.

'Yes. Very grateful.'

'Good. Because they do that you know, try to leave bags with us.'

'*They*?'

'The jumpers.'

'Oh God no, she's just a bit low blood-sugared.'

'As *you* might be – one o'clock Imogen, and well done. We'll see you next week then?'

※

She finds her in the corner, studying her phone. The fog has given way to a pale blue sky; the view over to her lighthouse is stunning, but she won't mention it.

'Hello. Are you getting any signal?'

She looks up. 'Hi. Not really. Join me if you like – or you won't get a window. I'm Jules.'

'Thanks. Imogen.' She sits down. 'Phones are no good here.'

Jules puts hers away. 'They're no good anyway. Even with the best technology, you still have to deal with the random brainfuckery of the person at the other end.'

Jules would get on well with her Twitter friend @DudessofCambridge. 'Neurological noise.'

'Unreliable receivers.'

'You never know which emotional extension you're being connected to.'

They grin at each other.

'Anyway, there are better things to do.' Jules picks up the Specials sheet. 'Especially on Homemade Pie Day! Wine?'

Fun work at the Visitor's Centre, her first local friend and possible jogging partner, and the sun has come out; the day is going well – something she needs to remember if he hasn't replied. She sits down at her desk.

He hasn't replied.

Why would he? He'll be working. As she's going to be, after an hour in the garden. But first, a call to Dorothy.

Her cousin Anthea answers, and says Dorothy can't come to the phone, could she take a message.

'Well, just to say that Annie and Frank at the Visitor's Centre send their love. And that I really enjoyed my first session – I've even volunteered to help them out with some extra dates.'

'That's great. I'll let her know.'

She shouldn't have said the last bit, letting on that she knows the Centre is desperate for volunteers and there is clearly no need for Dorothy to worry about 'keeping her post'. Why would she make that up? It doesn't make sense.

But then, none of it makes sense. On hearing that she'd separated from Ewan, Dorothy invited her to stay with her at the lighthouse – but avoided speaking to her for more than a few minutes on the phone. Then, while Imogen was taking too long deciding whether she could face living with Dorothy, there's a call from Anthea about how her mother's had a fall while staying with her in Jersey. But when she asks for the hospital's address so that she can send flowers she's told not to – and there's a lot of vagueness about when Dorothy will be back. Then there are her father's diaries, inexplicably stored in Anthea's loft. Why doesn't Dorothy just send the whole lot over? Or at least a bundle of photocopied excerpts, rather than a one-by-one drip feed.

She gazes out at The Beachy Head lighthouse, sitting in a wispy blue-grey sea today. Fishing from the set-off… the unpredictable currents… freak waves… bodies can be washed out to sea. Her mother could seldom be persuaded to talk about it, but she'd read the reports: suicide ruled out after interviewing the other two keepers, just a tragic accident. Why Dorothy wants to remind her of all this, is anyone's guess; she'll just have to go along with it.

She changes into shorts and takes a mug of tea outside, settles herself on the wooden bench that's been pushed against the garden wall to keep out of the wind. Looks out over the tilting green fields dotted with little wind-bent trees that greeted her father when he came ashore after being 'off' on the 'light'. She remembers her mother telling her to shush all the time and let him sleep; apparently he had to adjust to normal hours after the shift patterns. Then he would emerge, pale and weary. Look at her school work and make suggestions. Tell a few funny tales from the lighthouse. Then, in what seemed like no time, he'd be busy getting his provisions together before being off again – halfway through a book with her, missing the school play.

Certainly he'd had a more exciting life in his youth; before meeting her mother, he spent five years floating around the Med as a deckhand on that rich Greek guy's yacht. Sometimes he told stories of dolphins, turtles… Once, before her mother could stop him, there was one about saving a drunk actress from drowning – which might explain the grateful wad of euros enclosed with every Christmas card from 'the old Greek'. Thinking about it now, it's hard to connect this free spirit with the quiet, respected lighthouse keeper he became.

She lies back on the plank and closes her eyes. It must have been a difficult time, with just a month until the completed automation of the lighthouse would make him and the other keepers – and

The Lighthouse Keeper's Daughter

their profession – redundant. But apparently he had a handyman job lined up in a good hotel in Eastbourne, and a holiday in the Lake District had been booked. The reading and listening to classical music he enjoyed when off duty in the lighthouse could have continued at home; her mother was happy fussing with the house, and she was an undemanding eleven-year-old with similar interests of her own. In fact, he might have spent more time reading to her – and helping with her stories.

Santi makes up *musical* stories.

She opens her eyes. Where had that come from? Santi has walked into her brain. She looks at her watch. Half five, half six there; what time does a soap actor get home from work?

Where was she? Books with her father. An image of them companionably reading together comes to her. She's got *The Diary of Anne Frank*, and, looking over and seeing a similar layout in his book, asks whose diary it is. He says his is *like* a diary, but it's twenty years of letters between friends who never met, beautiful writing. Maybe this is what he hoped to have with 'S'.

It's getting cold. She goes in and makes tea and toast. She doesn't hear her computer twang to announce the arrival of an email notifying her of a tweet, but when she sits down at her desk there's a blue blob by the Twitter Direct Messages envelope.

CHAPTER 7

WEDNESDAY 5TH SEPTEMBER, 2012
Madrid, Spain

'Cut! Let's do it again, Santi.' A dramatic wipe of the forehead; they are already behind schedule. 'Ah, here's Tania, that'll help.'

Tania's back in position next to the camera, patting at her blonde hair while she sips an iced coffee; if she's bothered by Santi's dialogue uncannily repeating what he said to her six months ago, she's not showing it. But then, she's an actress.

The sound crew have a problem, so there's time for the sickening fear that he's going to forget the words. He does forget the words, missing out two hard-learned lines – but gets a thumbs-up anyway.

'Cut! Print it. Prepare for the two-shot.'

After some lines about not being able to commit to a relationship, he will soon be kissing her and laying her back on the sofa. Just as he did in real life. Except that in the drama the speech will come *after* the seduction; they're only filming the shot in this more moral order to save time on lighting changes. Someone from make-up removes the sweat on their faces and combs out Tania's ruffled curls. They get into position.

'Action!'

The body is your instrument, as they say in acting class. Her instrument duets with his, probably with a similar mixture of embarrassment and unwilling arousal. He has to *be* rather than *act*, so he's remembering her pale hair on the cushion, her lithe, freckled body – while trying to forget how much adoration and hard work she needed, and the annoying American twang of her gasps. Then his phone starts vibrating in his pocket, and suddenly the English woman is in his head – and trousers – with *her* freckled body… What?

'Cut! Print it. That was great Santi.'

><

Pleased to avoid a post-coital *cafelito* with Tania, he is soon speeding away from the slit-eyed, concrete face of the Faculty of Communication.

The air-con's barely working; he's sweating and smells of Tania's floral perfume. But there's no time to go to his apartment for a shower; he needs to get to his English lesson early and finish the homework. A sign flashes thirty-two degrees. But it isn't just the heat, he wants to wash the whole day off: the rushed rehearsal, the static filming, the crappy dialogue. It's no fun being an instrument when you're being played by an idiot. It was different with Flamenco Academy; his few words were meaningful, and they welcomed his input when he had the courage to give any. If he does Lorca – well, it was going to be the young guy who's won an award for that Civil War drama, so hopefully…

He parks in a shady corner of the Cultural Centre car park and groans with the effort of grabbing his books from the back seat. Opens the door. Sips from a lukewarm water bottle and feels both slightly nauseous and still strangely aroused.

His phone rings. 'Hello gorgeous, am I seeing you tonight?'

'Miri… We said Thursday, my love.'

'But I'm at a friend's in Arturo Soria, you could pick me up after your lesson.'

'I've got an early call.'

'I know but… I've been shopping – believe me, you won't regret it!'

'Okay, okay…'

He leans back in the seat and closes his eyes, wondering if he has the energy for whatever Miri has in mind. Just sometimes it would be nice to have a short, sharp shag.

Now that he's going to be tied up for the evening – hopefully not literally – he checks his phone. There's a message from Uncle Pedro saying he's thinking of him today. Of course, it's the anniversary of his father's death. Thirty years. How could he have forgotten? But then that's what happens when you fill your day with crap. He imagines his uncle reminiscing about their adventures on tour, the crash, his father desperately holding on to life because he didn't want to leave his family. Well, at least his father doesn't have to see his son playing a stereotypical gypsy on the TV.

Then there's the English woman again, inviting him for an 'English breakfast' this morning. It's worrying that she seems to be sending a message *daily*. He tries out various replies (I take breakfast at 05:30! / Yes! / Jajajaja!) and deletes them, but he presses on the website link and goes to the page where she can be seen sitting next to a computer and a pile of papers. An awkward, slightly toothy smile. Hair something between peach and chestnut. He feels bad about briefly ravishing her in his mind; she doesn't look like she'd appreciate it. She'd probably rather sit outdoors with a big hat and have tea with him, like in that *Importance of Being Ernesto* film they were told to watch.

A text from Miri flashes up: her friend's address and a grinning face with a tongue hanging out. It's followed by one from Tania congratulating him on his performance – exclamation mark, exclamation mark – with the same emoji; what in hell was that supposed to mean? He closes their text bubbles and enlarges the picture of the English woman until her speckled face and jumpered small breasts fill the screen. She's not exactly sexy, but having her would be like the simple, divine joy of tucking into a real-strawberry ice lolly.

⁂

It's a telephone-themed lesson. They're watching a film of a rock band called E-L-O performing 'Telephone Line'. The music has that British dignity about it, but it's also sensuously harmonious. After the '*Hello, how are you*' he's mostly lost, but clearly the girl isn't answering, you can tell that from the music. The singer hides behind a guitar and sunglasses; a backing singer with long hay-coloured hair stands next to him, swaying to his music, ignored.... He finds it on YouTube and saves the link in his phone.

The smart old guy in the front row is asking Johnny to put it on again; he went to one of their concerts in the eighties. The two middle-aged women nod approval, while Green Nail Varnish raises her eyes to the ceiling.

'Do you know it, Santiago?' Johnny asks.

'No, but I like.'

'I like *it*.'

It comes on again. Half way through, drunk with the sadness of it, Santi sends the link to the English woman with a 'Mi teacher plays it in the English class. Very good. Know it?' No reply. 'Hello, how are you, have you been all right? Jajaja ;-)'

Johnny has put on another film. English people talking much too fast on an office telephone, a red Doctor Who type telephone box, a brick-sized mobile.

Maybe she doesn't have Twitter on her mobile. Or maybe she's cross that he hasn't replied for a few days. 'I sorry I no anwser. I learning much mierda words for drama of the televisión, very tried :-('

It occurs to him that until today, he hasn't admitted to anyone – even himself – that his dialogue in the series is shit. And he's never told anyone else that he finds Pato so difficult. English is hard and slow, but somehow he can say things to this woman without it mattering; it's like being extravagant abroad with a foreign currency.

He finds the song lyrics on the back of the *Using the Telephone* hand-out and copies out *Pick up that telephone!* But no, no – that sounds desperate. He turns the sheet over again, smiles back at Johnny, who has noticed that he's stopped watching the film.

She needs to get an iPhone. She needs to get used to him not answering every single message, fuck's sake. He spots a phrase in the hand-out. 'Sorry. I hung up on you :-/'

CHAPTER 8

THURSDAY, 6TH SEPTEMBER, 2012
The South Coast, England

Another very thin envelope. She sits down at her desk to open it.

'Fri 4th Sep.'81

No chance of Vince's boat coming today, not in this sea. Won't he be pleased. I can just see the bugger: post bag on his sticky kitchen table, mouth all curled up on one side as he fingers the London post-marked letter. I don't think he ever believed that S was a distant cousin who'd become a penfriend, but I should have stuck with that. Things have been a lot worse since I tried to explain the quantity of letters by making out the cousin is giving me <u>French lessons</u>. Like last week, when Len told him to moor up and come in for tea, and he <u>sniffed</u> her letter before handing it to me, a leery look on his face. I could have slapped him. I could have slapped him right out of the kitchen, down the stairs and into the sea.'

She stares at the handwriting: yes, it's her Dad's. But she doesn't recognise this testiness. What's going on here?

'Len says I'm over-reacting; remember he's a lonely guy waiting a

few more years to be evicted from the home he was born in before it follows the other Birling Gap cottages and falls onto the beach. And now he's going to lose most of his livelihood. He reminds me that there's no knowing why he was turned down by Trinity House those years ago – although I can think of a few reasons – so you can't blame him for feeling jealous sometimes. Well actually Len, you _can_, because you and Bill are keepers too, but don't get his endless jibes. Ah well, at least Vince and his bloody boat are one thing I won't miss in this job.

S would argue that it's just another reason to move on from letters. She wants to _talk_. She must have had my response for more than a week. Maybe she's hurt. Cross. But the thing is, I'm no good on the telephone. Never have been. To talk to her, after two and a half years of writing… OK we talked when we met, but about Fauré, Debussy, what we felt about the music. It was a chat between concert goers, not two people who've spent – what – more than a hundred hours in each other's company.

I know what she means by the problems with writing – the mismatch of time, a late night letter reaching a bright early riser. The lack of instant feedback and the post-posting paranoia. But God, I'd rather _meet_ than go into a bloody phone box and try and make blind sense to her.

Not that we ever say that much, not really. It's weird, we must have covered all our feelings and fears – our love of impressionists, the Beatles, ELO, Fowles, Du Maurier, 84 Charing Cross Road of course; my dislike of Thatcher; her concern for Princess Di; our problems with large dogs, underground trains, clothes shopping, sarcastic people and very small children; our failure with contact lenses; our skills at boat handling – even if hers have only been tested doing schoolgirl dinghy sailing on a Sussex reservoir; a shared talent for baking; an equal determination to improve our French – everything, in fact, other than our feelings about each other and the

The Lighthouse Keeper's Daughter

impossibility of doing something about them.

Writing, talking. If only there was something in between that we could move on to: messages we could send back and forth to each other – like a written conversation, but with a few seconds to think about what we're saying before we write it. I don't know, a sort of small portable telex machine – that would be helpful at this point.'

So 'S' is a penfriend. *She* is a penfriend. But one who wants to move on to *talking on the phone.* Why, when it's 'impossible to do anything about their feelings'? Her father was losing touch with reality – and should have been writing more to Mum, not this fantasy lover.

She puts the sheet down and looks out of the window at her father's lighthouse, then at her laptop's Twitter page in front of her. But then, everyone likes a little fantasy sometimes, don't they? Perhaps they started out like her and Santi…

'No?' Dylan calling out from the living room.

'No.' She leaves the frozen Twitter and checks Google again. 'No, still no internet.'

'This router's crap. You should've picked up a new one when you were in town.'

She goes through to him. He's back at the kitchen table, his shaved head bent over her new iPhone and old pink mobile.

'Ah – but I think you're in business here.' He looks up at her with his light blue eyes, pulls out the chair next to him. 'Come on then, you'll want me to show you round.'

'Please.' She sits down, watches his boyish profile as he concentrates on some final adjustments. If he'd just let the light fuzz on his head grow into hair, he'd be quite attractive.

He's talking about 3-G and tapping through some settings to show her what he's done. It's all a bit tedious.

'Great, thanks so much.' She can see a Google icon and wants to get onto Twitter.

'Then there's the apps,' he says, paddling away from Google to an icon on the next page. He pushes his mug towards her. 'Bit stronger this time. I'll get Facebook and Twitter for you. What else... WhatsApp?'

'What's *what*?'

'WhatsApp. Messaging app, it's the new thing.'

'Huh? Oh no...'

'And you'll have to get iTunes going on here. How's the iPod filling up?'

'Great.'

He's sitting where Ewan sat – facing away from her – because it's impossible not to position yourself for the view. Even though he's probably a local and grew up with these colossal images, blocky cliffs in his school paintings.

'Okay, that's them downloaded.' He chuckles. 'And I'm afraid you're going to get my band's gigs in your Facebook stream... but you can always 'Unlike'!'

'Oh! What d'you play?'

'Bass. You should come along to one of our rock nights in Pevensey Bay. You know the pub on the beach? Great crowd – even if you came on your own, you'd soon be part of the family.'

Imogen smiles. *Family*. Both her families have collapsed like three-legged stools. 'Sounds great, but I'm not very sociable at the moment, lot of work to do.' And it would probably finish off her remaining hearing.

'But second Sunday of every month, okay? If you change your mind.'

⁂

Alone again, she checks Twitter from the comfort of the sofa and finds Santi's messages from his English class on Wednesday night. Good God! What are the chances of Santi discovering her father's blessed ELO?

'Of course! / *claro*! I love *(me encanta)* Telephone Line!' she replies. 'I have been ALL RIGHT thank you!' she adds, and corrects his English. Poor guy, stuck in some crappy soap when really he should be making music. 'Can you change *(cambiar)* it?' she asks, leaving him to wonder whether she means his dialogue, show or profession. She smiles and leaves the 'I hung up on you' uncorrected, then lies back on the sofa, her phone on her chest like a new baby.

She picks it up again. 'I've got *(tengo)* an iPhone now! So there's English anytime you want it *(cuando quieras)*!' Damn, that was way over the top.

She jumps when the phone rings in her hand. 'Imogen? It's Frank at the Centre. Betty can't make it – any chance of you getting down here?'

'Oh. OK, I'll be right there.'

Then there's a call from Jules. 'Listen, you know you said you wanted to walk to the lighthouse? Well there's a very low tide this afternoon and the weather's clearing... Can you be at Cow Gap at half four?'

'Ooh yes! I'll come straight from the Visitor's Centre.'

'I'll pick you up from there. You'll need walking shoes, gloves...'

※

Frank watches Jules wander into the museum room while they're cashing up. 'Isn't she that dopey woman who left her bag here?'

'Well yes, but she's great, makes me laugh. And she's done the walk before.'

'Hm. I'm just going to double-check she's got the tides right. There's a list at the Coastguard's next door. Back in a tick.'

※

'What did he think I was doing, luring you to your death?' asks Jules, catching her breath.

'I'm afraid he remembers you being a bit vague in the shop.'

'Oh. Fair enough. I wasn't doing well that day.'

They're at the top of the hill, looking back down at the Eastbourne seafront glittering in the sun before going down the steep steps towards the beach.

'So how old were you again? When your father died?'

'Eleven.'

Jules pats her arm. 'I'm sure he'd be right chuffed that you're visiting his lighthouse.'

'Yeah, he probably would.'

'What makes someone want to be a lighthouse keeper?'

'Well he grew up to it I suppose, his father was a keeper. But it was actually *me* who made him one, when I came along unexpectedly and he felt he had to marry Mum and get a secure job. What's your excuse for the lighthouse fixation?'

'I used to do this with my ex – weather, tides and childcare permitting. He was a bit of a lighthouse nerd… God, we're fucking nuts! We should both hate the damn thing!'

'Uh… these steps are doing me in.'

'Ha – wait till we're on the beach! Man up woman, it's going to take at least an hour and a half of hard clambering to get there.'

They are now on a grassy path above the beach; apart from a woman coming back with a bag of shells, there's nobody about.

'So now he's a lighthouse nerd in… Oxford, did you say? Must

The Lighthouse Keeper's Daughter

be difficult seeing the kids.'

Jules jumps down the last step onto the pebbled beach. 'I don't.'

'What?'

'They're not mine remember. I just looked after them for six years. And they're teenagers – they've got someone else to wash their favourite trackies now.'

'And he doesn't encourage—'

'No. I'm no longer in the plan. But hey, I've got a seafront apartment, plenty of time to sit and mope – I mean, design jewellery. I tell you Imo, that free Jeep might just be the start.'

'What?'

'You need to go up to Weybridge and try and take him out again soon. Take Ollie out for dinner that is, not shoot Ewan. Although that could help.'

'You're right.'

'Okay, time to concentrate or you'll break an ankle. Put your gloves on, the rocks can be sharp.'

The stones have been getting larger and larger; they are now scrambling between chalk boulders up to their heads. Imogen looks up at the cliff face. There are washing-powder white areas where chalk has recently fallen.

'If people could see this they wouldn't stand so near the edge.'

Jules doesn't answer – or she does, but Imogen can't hear her; the wind is getting stronger, filling her ears.

They clamber on until they reach an area of golden sand.

'Gorgeous! Wish we had time to swim,' Imogen calls out.

'It's called Fallen Sands,' Jules shouts back.

'Because it's under where most people choose to fall?' She looks up again, this time at the tufts of grass at the top of the cliff over five hundred feet above them. And the ledges and crevices on the way down, from which people often have to be rescued.

'Come on, still a way to go.'

It's true; up ahead, the lighthouse doesn't look much nearer than last time she looked. They enter another stretch of boulders.

Imogen steps into yet another quicksand-like pool, up to her ankle. 'Oh for—'

'You just don't learn, do you!' Jules says, taking off her gloves to take a photo of her – and dropping one down a crevice. 'Fuck!' She takes off the other glove, but within seconds it's blowing away over the boulders.

'Nor do you!' Imogen says, laughing.

They carry on, laughing and shouting about ears hurting from the wind, blisters and knotted hair.

'Uh – what do we want with this over-sized bath toy anyway?' Imogen calls out.

'Damn this candy-striped dick!'

They rest for a moment in the shelter of a boulder. Jules looks at her watch.

'We must be nearly there. In fact…'

They come out of the jungle of boulders and are blasted with a screaming, salty wind as they step onto flat rocks covered in seaweed – and there it is. Just fifty yards away, rising up high into the sky. From the cliff top, it was an endearing, little red and white striped ornament; on the beach it is shockingly tall, its colours majestic, a sad and mysterious presence.

They battle forward against the wind, stepping over twisted rusty chains, an old numbered door. Imogen reaches the steps leading up to the square 'set-off' – where boats used to deliver the keepers. She looks at Jules, who nods uncertainly.

It's easy to climb the steps going up the side of the foundations, but at the corner she has to hang on tight as she goes up the second flight against the wind from the sea. At the top, she crawls onto the

The Lighthouse Keeper's Daughter

set-off, afraid of being blown to the rocks some thirty feet below. She looks at the rungs going up to the red door with its Trinity House emblem. There's a shout from Jules below; she's shaking her head. She's right. It's too dangerous.

This is where he died. He put himself at risk, or put his own problems first; either way, he let her down and left. From here. The wind, as if remembering, is intent on pushing her off too. She hunkers down, pushes herself towards the lighthouse. Pressed against its rounded wall, she's protected again from the wind and can tilt her head back to look up at the red gallery, the lantern room. Imagining him there. Then she looks over towards her squat little grey lighthouse on the cliff in the distance. It always seemed like he was waiting for her to grow up; he just didn't wait long enough. Her throat tightens. She wipes her face with her glove. Jules has come half way up and is beckoning to her. She crawls back against the wind and down the steps.

'Sorry, being a complete…'

'Come here you,' Jules says, and pulls her into a hug. 'Now let's get back before Frank calls the Coastguard.'

※

Maybe Santi went out with friends straight from the television studio – with the blonde @TMurphyMendezOficial girl, for example, who's always sending kisses and seems to be in the show with him. He's also got quite a family; surely not all the chaps he calls '*tío*' can be uncles, but two youngish-looking ones are Montoyas and looking forward to Santi's mother's paella at the weekend. As are his sister – the one who used to play keyboards in Tangoza – and nephews.

She flops onto the sofa with her phone, presses on Facebook

and types the name of her only remaining close family member. Oliver Anderson. There he is. He's on it fairly often, moaning about homework, sharing World of Warcraft and other games. Shouldn't he be coming out of that computer-cocoon now? Sweet that he's still friends with two girls from junior school, but where are the photos of crazy parties that she should be worrying about?

Aha, more like it: a line of cocktails. But no: it turns out that he made these *at home*, something to do with his Art 'A' level. Marbella: Ewan, Maddie, Ollie and his mate Will as a perfect beaming family of four in a fish restaurant. Then at the villa: Ollie laughing, having just fallen out of the hammock, and Maddie beside him – a fucking concerned hand on his shoulder.

She taps 'Message'.

'Hi Ols, how's it going? Thought I'd come up this weekend – would you like to go to Giovanni's or the Thai place? Lunch or dinner, either day – just let me know. Love Mum xx'

The phone announces his reply with a surprised pop.

'Hi Mum. Sorry but I want to stay at school this weekend. Maybe half-term? Ol x'

Six or seven weeks away.

'I could pick you up and take you back afterwards.'

Facebook informs her that this message was seen at 21:32. She sits through Ollie's ten minutes of distraction or deliberation. *'I can't, said I'd go to stuff.'*

Stuff more important than seeing her.

A further pop. *'How are you?'* he is remembering to ask.

'Fine thanks, but missing you. It's beautiful here, you should come down, bring your sketchbook.'

'I went to Seven Sisters on a school geog trip.'

'I remember. You came home cross that you couldn't go to the Sheep Centre while you were there.'

The Lighthouse Keeper's Daughter

No response.

'*It's just down the road! I'm going to be writing a review of it in the spring.*'

'*Mum! I'm not eight!*'

'*And there's Brighton – the pier, the crazy Royal Pavilion, that new wheel thing.*'

'*But we don't like heights!*'

'*Let me know which weekend you would like to come down, ok? Fun for us.*'

Fun for us: the title of an early reading book that had stuck with them. Surely he hadn't forgotten.

Seen 21:54.

She waits.

'*Sorry Mum, I've got to go. Bye xx*'

The green spot by his name disappears. She reads back the conversation. Still no plans, but a great improvement on the half-heard mumblings she gets in telephone calls.

She turns off the laptop and gets into her pyjamas, puts her phone on charge by the bunk bed. Of course, Santi might not have gone out with friends; and despite the loving family – and maybe even a wife – he might be pottering around at home feeling as despondent as the guitar in his last track. About his demeaning acting role, his difficulties with his daughter, his English classes…

She climbs the ladder to bed, lies down under the low ceiling and turns out the light. The wind whistles and groans outside her window. In sweltering late summer Madrid, you would probably be glad of a good breeze.

She picks up the phone and types. 'What are you doing?'

CHAPTER 9

FRIDAY 7TH SEPTEMBER, 2012
Madrid, Spain

What was she doing, asking what he was doing at half-eleven last night? But he probably smirked as he tapped out possible replies, because Miri – returning to bed with a bowl of ice cubes for one of her less successful ideas – also wanted to know what he was doing.

Now he's sitting at the bench table in the shade behind the Faculty of Communication Studies, with a Solero pressed on him by Maria from the kitchens, feeling somewhat anxious about what he's just done.

It's sort of her fault, the English woman. *Can you change it*. Has she seen episodes on YouTube? As a writer, she'll see the flaws in the plot – if her Spanish is up to it.

His phone. The AD. 'Santi I've had a word and we'll get back to you next week, right? Anyway, we won't need you any more today – in fact not until Thursday or Friday next week – so have yourself a break, OK?'

'Oh. And you'll email me the changes—'

'Yes, yes, yes. I'll let you know, OK? Gotta fly. *Ciao*.'

Maria patted his arm. 'All right love?'

'Yes. Well, hopefully… Thanks for the lolly. You're an angel.'

He does a cap-pulled-down purposeful walk to his car; the last thing he needs is some smart-arse media students interviewing him about Diego. Once inside, he switches on the engine – but the phone keeps tinging. There's a whole page of texts from Tania. He turns off the sound and swigs from his water bottle.

What he asked wasn't unreasonable: why would a gifted American student come to study in Madrid and, in her third year, risk all by having a fling with a druggy gypsy guitarist who's quite obviously a complete bastard? Diego's redeeming features – the honesty and humour about his past failings – have somehow been forgotten among the changing team of writers. There are other minor characters to develop; all they've recently done for Diego is remove his clothes more often.

Now his phone is vibrating and groaning.

'Tania. I just asked them to change it a bit so that he looks sorry for what he's done. He should get back with the girl who—'

'I don't know why you're doing this, Santi.'

'I don't know why you're taking this so… *personally*. It's best for both of our characters, can't you see that?'

'Well listen to you – a *screenwriter* all of a sudden! Let me guess, your girlfriend has been talking to film buffs in the Cine shop and passing on ideas—'

He cuts her off. Women: if you've had sex with them they just have to keep patting and scratching at you – even when they're now apparently happy with someone else. And oh no, here she is, coming out with her phone in her hand. He drives off, realising with relief that he never gave her his new Argüelles address.

At the roundabout he starts worrying about Miri seeing him drive into the underground car park and wondering why he's back so early; bad plan having a girlfriend who both works and lives in your road. He swerves into the parque del Oeste and parks by the fountain.

Tucking the English book under his arm, he heads for a bench underneath one of the giant conifers. It could be where he played guitar for Anita, where she flushed with pride as a little crowd formed – just before Tangoza was signed. Miri prefers the drama of the area with the Egyptian temple up on the hill. The English woman would probably prefer the neat roses in the Rosaleda.

He opens the book. Ah yes, *I have been… He has done… She has just…*

The English woman *has been* very well behaved today; she *has done* no messages and it's three o'clock. He picks up the phone and goes into Twitter. She *has just* haha'd to a tweet from some guy called Jules. Something about a lighthouse – with a picture of her looking windswept and uncertain in front of a rather splendid striped one. He presses on Jules' leopard profile picture and finds that he *has just* started Twitter and – what an oaf – has used the 'fuck' word in most of his ten tweets.

Back to the English, filling in answers to the exercises until *I've just finished work* brings the studio back to mind. He shouldn't have cut Tania off; they've got a lot of work together next week. There's another message from her.

'Sorry. Bad time at the moment. You may be right about the scene :-/.'

'I'm sorry too,' he types. *'Take it easy.'*

'Kisses.'

Back to Twitter. Now the English woman has just answered some guy in Sevilla about the latest Vicente Amigo album – and corrected him on his future tense.

'What are you doing?' he types in the Direct Message box, and waits for a reply. She did say *English anytime.* English woman –

 The Lighthouse Keeper's Daughter

why does he call her that? What's her name again? Imagen. No, I*mo*-gen. Like the word for picture, but slightly wrong. Pacture. Pocture.

A group of excited boys are clambering up the grass slope towards him. He gets up and makes his way to the Teleférico for eleven minutes of solitary peace in one of the little cable cars. But as he swings out over the railway line and the *Manzanares* river he realises that the guy pointing at his book while giving him his cable car has played a joke; the car is introducing itself and describing the sights in English. What a strange, quacking comedy language it is – and a damn difficult one; even knowing what it's probably saying, he can barely understand a word of it.

The cable car arrives with a jolt. He makes his way to the café, and takes a coffee out on to the terrace. Beyond the tree-dotted yellow grass of the Casa de Campo hills, there's the zoo that Pato used to start going on about at this point in the outing. Now they're playing that Ketama song they used to like, Pato singing along with the chorus – 'Where are you going?' – as if she was questioning all his trips to Granada for filming Guerra, and later his move out of the home…

He needs to get on with the book. It looks like he's left out a chapter – one called 'I was doing… I did.' Ha! He needed this last night: *I was do-ing sex when you did send your message.* He stifles a chuckle.

Ah – Imogen has written 'What are YOU doing?'

'I am in a cafe, looking at the *vista* of the Palacio Royal… *Vista* – what is?'

'I'm in my garden (*jardín*), with a VIEW (*vista*) of the sea.'

'I love the sea!! Describe me it, is good for *vocabulario geográfico* jaja.'

'There are lots of green hills (*colinas*), and then an enormous cliff (*acantilado*)... In the sea below, there is a lighthouse (*faro*).'

'!!!!!'

'You must be happy there,' he writes in Spanish, wondering if she'll mention the Jules chap in her reply.

'Yes.' A minute passes. 'Well, not completely happy. My father died (*murió*) at the lighthouse when he was working there.'

So she also lost her father as a child. 'My God. What happened?' he writes in Spanish. Then adds 'I'm sorry, maybe you don't want to talk about it.'

'He was fishing (*pescando*) from the lighthouse, they think a big wave (*ola*)...'

'*Ay*... How old you were?'

'Santi! You say 'How old WERE YOU?' I was eleven.'

'I was nine when died my father. In a car.'

'Oh. I'm sorry.'

'Tomorrow we have fiesta family for his live after died 30 years,' Santi writes.

'To CELEBRATE his LIFE after he died 30 years ago. How lovely.'

'Yes but not much for me, I no remember him and I feel bad.'

'Ah. I know this feeling (*sentimiento*). Feeling bad that you don't have enough feeling. Do you understand?'

'I think that yes. My mother likes talk of him, and thinks I remember things. And with you mother?'

'No – the opposite (*contrario*)! My mother didn't want to talk about him, and said almost nothing about the accident. She married (*se casó con*) another man when I was 15.'

'You should ask her,' he puts in Spanish.

'She died some years ago.'

'*Ay*... ☹'

A minute passes, and she's written 'You should ask = *Deberías preguntar*.'

 The Lighthouse Keeper's Daughter

'Thank you teacher.'

'I'm slow (*lenta*) because I have to look for (*buscar*) the words in WordRef. Uh my Spanish… ☹'

'Your spanish is *maravilloso*! But if you need practice I will help!'

'*Por favor!*'

'OK,' he writes in Spanish. 'Tell me what you're doing this weekend.'

'I don't know that last word, "*finde*".'

'= Fin de semana. Weekend. You have to talk like a *madrileña* (Madrid woman) ;-)'

'Hahaha! OK. I go to Jersey, I have sexual relations there,' she writes in Spanish.

Santi bursts out laughing. The elderly couple on the next table stare at him. 'WHAT?! *QUÉ*?!' he taps out.

'What *que* what?'

'Look it at WordRef app, woman!!! Jajajajajaja :-D'

After a while there's 'NOOOO! I wanted to say I have RELATIVES there!'

'No sex?? / *relaciones*??'

'NO!'

'What a shame!' he writes in Spanish. 'It would be more fun, no?' He's chuckling. 'Poor little thing ☹.' He puts a hand over his mouth. 'Maybe soon!!! ;-p Hahahaha.'

Three minutes. *Five.*

'Imagen! Don't be angry with me! :-o' Where has she gone? Is she really offended? 'Hello hello?' No reply. He puts ':-(' Then ':-((' This is crazy. 'I-MAAAA-GEN!!!' he types.

'It's ImOgen.'

She's back. 'Ah *sí*. I know. Imogen. It sound like picture in Spanish – *imagen*.'

'No. g like j. English J.'

'And that is what?'

'J like in JAM (*mermelada*).'

'Like in Spanish ham / *jamón*.'

'No! A different sound…'

'ImoYen? ImoCHen? Ufff.'

'Sh! I'm trying to think…'

':-#'

'Ah! Like John Lennon of the Beatles! Do you know him?'

'Of course! John. ImoJohn. ImoJen. But difficult, I have to hear it. I need to HEAR English. Maybe one day we speak in Skype ☺'

He waits. Finishes his coffee. He's gone too far, *again*. What the hell did he put that for? But now that he has, she could at least answer. He looks at his watch. 'Uff I'm sorry I have to leave you – English lesson. We are doing Past Continuous + Past Simple ??? :-(('

'What in hell (*infierno*) are they?!'

He grins; she's still on board. He glances back at his book to check. It's the other page that he's stuck on, not this one, but he can't confuse things by trying to explain that now.

'I was doing, then I did… :-o'

'I could help you with some examples?'

He says yes please and gives his email address. 'Kisses and many thanks. Until tomorrow ☺☺'

CHAPTER 10

SATURDAY 8TH SEPTEMBER, 2012
The South Coast, England

Two pieces of paper in the envelope. She sits down at the kitchen table.

'Sat 12th Sep.'81

How's it going, I ask Imogen. She looks up from her bending of the menu card over the edge of the table – but at her mum. Two weeks into secondary school, you'd think she'd have something to say. Top group in English, Beryl puts in. I say that's great, but Imogen just gives me that closed-mouth smile she has these days. I ask her if she's made some nice new friends. Again she looks over at Beryl - you'd think we were using a bloody interpreter.

Then Beryl says there's been a bit of teasing. I say not to worry, we can now go ahead with the orthodontist, but Imogen scowls and looks out to sea as if she wants me back there. Apparently it's not that. Or not <u>only</u> that. They've started calling her <u>Gracie Darling</u> – the history teacher having mentioned the heroic daughter of a lighthouse keeper during a class on the Victorians.

Then while Beryl moans on about the school drop-off parking, Imogen gets a book out of her bag. It has a pair of t-shirted teenagers with *First Love* stamped over them in crimson relief. Beryl must have seen my face and says she didn't get *Watership Down* as I suggested, Imo's too old for bunnies. I try to explain that it's about more than that but she says, can't I see Imogen's growing up?

There was a time when I was waiting for her to grow up. Imogen as a colicky baby and easily-troubled toddler didn't register with me. Then at about four she arrived: an imaginative, funny little person. Laughing at the voices I gave to characters in her books. Drawing stripey lighthouse pictures. Switching her bedroom lamp on and off at night and being convinced I was signalling back to her when she could see the lighthouse beam from her window. I was two months off and one month ashore in those days, missing more than half of her childhood, but she could see where I was and accepted it.

Then we moved here and she grew up a little more. So did the children around her. It used to be just nudges in assembly when the hymns had words about shining lights, but after a while it was questions about whether I had another family somewhere, or preferred to live with <u>men</u>. There were no more lighthouse pictures (although I did once catch her looking through one of my books about them). She only wanted me to read alternate paragraphs in her books, discuss the characters, and accelerate her escape into fiction. Where did you go, Imogen?'

Where did I go? Where did *I* go? I was always here. Half my childhood waiting for you. She wipes away another tear before there's another smudge on the photocopy, blows her nose on a piece of kitchen roll. But... sometimes it took me a day or two to get used to you being back, that's all. Not always. There were times at that café when you made us laugh telling stories of domestic disasters on the lighthouse, or Mum and I would give you ten guesses at something we'd bought for the house...

The Lighthouse Keeper's Daughter

She braces herself for the second page, wondering why they are paired.

__Fri 25th Sep.'81__

Went to see Dorothy in her old cliff lighthouse! Beautifully done up. Great views from the lounge-kitchen. I started teaching her Morse and semaphore, so we can speak to each other when I'm off! She said again that the old keepers' little bunk room is mine if things get too difficult with Beryl.

Another week like this last one, and I'll take her up on that. Beryl's on and on about why I won't accept the Principal job at the North Foreland land light – especially now Bill's wife's described the attached cottage in the minutest bloody detail. I told her there's no point, it too will be automated – just months after ours for all we know. I want to see out my keeper days with the best guys I've ever worked with, it's all going to be upsetting enough. But she doesn't listen. She __never__ listens. Or maybe she does, but we speak such a different language these days, she can't understand me.

Dorothy and her husband __do__ speak the same language, she says, but they're seldom together to do so; Clive stays at his London club during the week, and is always flying off to medical research conferences. Anthea's at Edinburgh University now and hardly ever home. So she says she's recently become involved in research – supporting an American writing an article about the lure of Beachy Head after his cousin lost his life there. He needs a __lot__ of support, she says, and looks at me. Then says, Hughie, I'm trying to tell you that I'm having an affair with him. I'm actually rather shocked, but, given a few minutes, rather impressed. Then she sits me down with a coffee and says, __tell me more about this penfriend, Sophie.__

She gets up for a glass of water. Sits down again with the two pieces of paper in front of her, side by side. Any normal person would have paired this sad account with a happier entry about her, but for some unfathomable reason it's come with this hideous revelation of her Aunt's cheating on poor old Uncle Clive. Her father might have been impressed – for God knows what lurid reason – but she is definitely not. They're dated the 12th and the 25th, not even consecutive days. Why is she filtering the diary in this way, distorting the truth? Enough of this.

She told Santi she was going to her Jersey relatives for the weekend; how appalled he'd be to learn that she'd actually just planned a day trip with a self-invited drop-in-for-tea arrangement with them – which she was about to cancel for fear of behaving very badly if she went through with it.

She picks up her phone. 'Anthea? It's Imogen. Can I speak to Dorothy please.'

'I'm just taking her to the chiropodist, we've got a busy morning. Can it wait until—'

'I'm not coming. Sick… I've got a sick bug.'

'Oh dear, I'm sorry to hear that. Another time.'

'But listen, these extracts… Why can't she just send the diary?'

An odd few seconds of silence. 'It's very precious.'

'I could collect it.'

'And quite a… Look Imogen, my mother's just trying to help.'

'Well it's *not* helping,' Imogen manages, trying to control the wobble in her voice. 'I need to see all of it, not just –'

'He didn't write every day. And you have to remember, he's only writing what he felt at the time, nothing is an absolute truth. Eventually you'll see the bigger picture.'

'Which is?'

'You need to see it for yourself. But listen, my mother's still in

The Lighthouse Keeper's Daughter

Christmas card contact with Bill, one of Hugh's fellow keepers. Would you like to have a chat with him? I could ask her to give him your number.'

Mr Trewitt. Nice man, keen to be a father himself, always made an effort to talk to her. 'Yes. I'd like that. Thanks.'

Perhaps she should have gone to Jersey and had it out with Dorothy – but then her aunt could always just decide not to give her any more pages at all.

She slumps down on the sofa with her phone. Maybe concentrating on the email to Santi will calm her down.

Subject: *I was... and then...*
Hola Santi
*Think of it as a situation (situación) going on for some time...
and then somebody (alguien) changes things*
1. We <u>were</u> (éramos) young when our fathers <u>died</u> (murieron)
*2. My friend and I <u>were</u> (estábamos) in Marbella when we <u>bought</u>
(compramos) the Tangoza CD*
*3. I <u>was feeling</u> (me sentía) tired in my car but then I <u>heard</u> (oí)
your Dos Caminos.*
I hope this helps!
Imo

Better without the pathetic sentence about how she hadn't been listening to music for some while – and he doesn't need to know that it was Ewan who bought the Tangoza CD. There's nothing wrong with using examples from their... little boxed friendship. *Amistad encajonada.* Even if they ever manage Skype, that's still what it'll be, just a bigger box; it would be madness to entertain the idea of it ever being anything else.

But she already has.

It was his fault, making such a thing about her Spanish blunder. The trouble is, once your mind starts making its way down this kind of path… He comes over here for a concert – a small venue in Brighton perhaps. They meet afterwards, he's always wanted to see inside a lighthouse… And oh God, last night's dream; they didn't actually have *relaciones*, but there was a vague pushing up against one another, unmistakable warmth, then lying in his arms… Heavens, it's a fun daydream; no harm in it.

Fun. She's not going to be on a golden Jersey beach today, so she should at least take herself down to a pebbly one in Eastbourne – the one with that café above it.

She just gets herself comfy on the towel when his email arrives.

Subject: Re: *I was… and then…*
Imo!!! Thank you guapa, I will learning from this.
I am going to party of family, with mi daughter.
A kiss
Santi

Subject: Re:
Have a good time!
But Santi: I WILL LEARN (no 'ing'). Problems with the future too?!
A kiss
Imo

Subject: Re:
Yes! Help! Where are you?

She emails a photo of a groyned beach with a huddle of white huts and a bit of Eastbourne-blue Victorian railing.

The Lighthouse Keeper's Daughter

Subject: Beach!
The best beautiful beach!! Jesrey?

Subject: Re: Beach!
The MOST beautiful… No, I'm not going to JERSEY now. This is a beach near me.

Subject: Uff
Uff wait momentito…

He sends a photo of two lines of traffic waiting behind a couple of zigzagged cars, two irate drivers and a gesticulating policeman.

Subject: Uff
On no, what WILL YOU DO? Hahaha

Subject: Re: Think thought
When I <u>am</u> at the party, I <u>WILL think</u> of you. Is correct? :-/

Subject: Re: Think thought
It's perfect! ☺

CHAPTER 11

SATURDAY 8TH SEPTEMBER, 2012
Madrid, Spain

Santi slows his running machine and presses the Stop button. 'Fuck this, let's do some lengths.'

'*Lengths*?' His cousin does the same with his and looks out at the small communal pool shadowed by the surrounding apartment buildings. 'Shouldn't you be going to a proper gym?'

'If I've got to do more than put running shoes on or take a lift it just doesn't happen.'

'How buff d'you have to get?'

'I don't know. It's all bollocks – Lorca wasn't the least bit athletic.'

Joselito takes off his t-shirt and gets into the water; he's ten years younger and has inherited Uncle Pedro's small wiry frame. Santi joins him and they start to swim up and down.

'Ignacio still working on getting us more gigs?' Joselito asks.

'Apparently.'

'That's what you said last time.'

'I know mate, but what can I do? I'll ask again on Monday. But he just goes on about getting ready for this audition.'

'Oh yes, and your *English*. This Twitter woman that's helping, what's she like?'

The Lighthouse Keeper's Daughter

Why on earth did he mention her? 'Very… *English*. Ten, I think.'

'She's a *ten*?'

'No! I think that's ten *laps*.'

'Blonde?'

'Sort of pale red.'

'Oh no! Don't think I could cope with a red bush.'

'Well thankfully she doesn't put it on Twitter.'

'So even if she came over here, you wouldn't give her one.'

Santi tries to imagine Imogen's shy freckled body on his sofa. No, no, it would have to be in a bed. Surely only the ones with *very* red hair have…

'Santi? Oh my God, you're having a *Two*mance!'

'Fuck off!' He splashes him in the face. 'She's just brilliant for my English, that's all. You've got a one track mind, we need to find you some sexy little lady *soon*.'

'True. But hey, if you've had enough of Miri—'

'What?'

'Well, you said you're not taking her to the party.'

'Only because it's such a family thing. But actually she *is* coming – Fran bumped into her in *Gran Vía* and not only invited her but said he'd be near *plaza de España* later and could take her.'

'What? That's a bit much. She should go with you and Pato.'

'No, I've got to go early to help move things around, and Miri's doing overtime this afternoon. Anyway, I think she's pissed at me and likes the idea of arriving with Fran.'

'So what about Pato?'

'She's shopping with Miri and then helping her with the stock-take for a bit.'

'So she'll go with Fran too?'

'No. She's refusing to speak to her ex-uncle now she's heard that he and Esme are no longer a "proper couple".'

'*Women* – so bloody complicated.'

'Yeah. Your dad told me there's some kind of spat going on between our mothers about the paella for God's sake!'

'Fifty I think. Is that enough?'

'Definitely. Let's go up and I'll play you the new track.'

'What are you *doing*?' Pato asks.

'Same as *you're* doing,' Santi says, but moves his phone to the other side of the steering wheel.

Pato puts hers down and puffs up her hair. 'I'm getting all *sweaty*.' She starts fiddling with the air con control.

'Leave it, it's already on max.'

'I'm going to look like a *rag* before the party's even *started*.'

'What? Your job is to sit with your feet in the pool chatting to Grandma so she sits down for a bit.'

'Yeah I know but… It'll be *hours* before anyone's there.'

Anyone meaning persons under the age of twenty-five. 'Hm… well your luck's in darling – doesn't look like we're going to get there anytime soon.'

The drivers are still arguing with the policeman, cars are starting to bleep. Why can't the English woman say where she is? He taps out a rhythm on the steering wheel. Ah – she can – and he's oddly pleased to learn that, *relaciones* or not, she's not in Jersey.

'What are you grinning at?' Pato asks, leaning over.

He closes his phone, and sees he's being waved forward. 'Ah. I think we're getting somewhere.'

The Lighthouse Keeper's Daughter

Santi stops playing, Joselito silences his guitar strings and puts a hand to his mouth. 'Fran it's *sol fa* there,' Santi says. 'And… there should be more space in the bass part.' He said he liked the album, but has he ever really listened to Dos Caminos?

Fran puts down the bass. 'Look I haven't time for this, somebody's calling me back from the States… And it's just for the folks for God's sake, this isn't *Casa Patas*.'

'Yeah but I'm just saying—'

'Boys, boys!' Uncle Pedro picks up the bass. 'Fran, grab the *cajón*, ok?'

Fran sits on the box and flutters his fingers on it.

They start again. Uncle Pedro must have listened to every nuance of the track – just like Imogen had, letting it draw her out of one life to another.

Then car doors are slamming in the drive, and there's Mamá's sister's twittering voice followed by that of her gruff husband and grumpy children. Through the window he can see the people carrier of Uncle Pedro's older son from Aranjuez, who will have brought his elegant wife, three sons, daughter, son-in-law and grandson. Joselito pulls up behind him and gives Santi a sympathetic wave. He's been charged with collecting the two grandmothers – gypsy and non-gypsy – who, even after all these years and descendants, don't look too happy to be in a car together.

So now there'll be the sangria and endless questioning about his record sales and what he's going to do when *La Universidad* ends, heaps of paella and sticky puddings he needs to go easy on, over-excited children, under-excited adolescents, a very drunk uncle, an appalled grandmother or two. Until the music starts, with Santi's little group as the inevitable warm-up act for Esme and Fran's well known numbers, followed by a jamming session and favourite *bulerías*, with anyone not on a guitar or a *cajón* taking to their feet… If only they could cut straight to that.

He disappears to the bathroom and takes out his phone.

'Why you not stay whith the '*relaciones*'?!' he writes to Imogen. 'What did happen? Good past tense, me :-))'

'No, it's 'What happenED'.'

'Imogen! I haven't got time for this, I'm in the bathroom at the party!!!' he writes in Spanish.

'What?!'

'What relatives they are?'

'Aunt and cousin / *prima*.'

'You have no more?'

'My son.'

'Only 3? My God, Imogen :-(I have 2 grandmothers, mother, 3 aunts, 2 uncles, a sister, 8 cousins, my daughter, the cousins' children… and they are almost all here,' he writes in Spanish.

'Santi! Go and join the party!'

'I no enjoin the partys, only the music.'

'I don't ENJOY partIES either. Poor you. Bye bye (adios) now, maybe I will see how you are later ;-)'

'Bye bye!'

He leaves the bathroom.

'I didn't know where you were!' Miri shouts above the Barbería del Sur album someone's put on. She's accustomed to meeting famous people from the film world in the Cine Shop, but she's looking anxious about his relatives.

'Don't worry, they're all either lovely or completely mad anyway.' She smiles, watches him put his phone in his pocket.

'Anita about the arrangements again?'

'Yeah… wanting to know if we can drop Pato back early tomorrow morning. Crazy. I said no.'

The rain has stopped, so everyone has gone outdoors and already nearly every seat he put out there is taken. They grab a drink at the bar and do the rounds. *She's beautiful and clearly loves you* whispers one aunt, *you even look alike* says another. His mother has warmed to her more during chat over the salad preparation, and his father's mother *just knew* that Miri has a bit of gypsy blood. Male family members, of course, are enchanted.

'See? Told you it would be fine.'

They sit down with Esme to eat their paella.

Santi looks over at Pato. 'Good, she's stopped flirting with your au pair now her cousins are here.'

'Flirting? She was just being friendly,' Esme says. 'She only has eyes for Miguel.'

'He's just the boy she's "seeing" as they say.' He looks from one anxious face to another. 'Ah. So he's now a *boyfriend* is he?'

Esme puts a hand on his arm. 'She *promised* she'd talk to you.'

'Maybe she just hasn't found the right moment,' Miri says.

'Talk to me about… Oh *no*, don't say…'

'I know it can't be easy, but it couldn't be a nicer chap,' Esme says.

'You mean she's… *Bloody hell*, she's too young for this! And why am I the last to know? I haven't even *met* him!'

Miri puts her hand on his other arm. 'Don't worry, she's been to the doctor.'

'Fuck! Uff, I mean… I need another drink.' He starts to get up, but Pato is coming towards him with her phone in her hand.

'Mum. She—'

'Why didn't you ask if your *boyfriend* could come?' he asks her.

'He's at a wedding,' she replies calmly. 'Papá, it's Mamá on the phone, she wants to know if it's okay for me to stay Sunday night too? She wants to change her flight, she's having such a good time.'

'Er... yes, of course.' Santi takes the phone, but it's hard to concentrate on what Anita's saying when Miri is looking at him in horror as she hears from Pato that Anita is in Tenerife.

Pato, in one of those rare moments of teenage empathy, reaches up and kisses him on the cheek before taking her phone and bounding off.

Esme gets up. 'I better help Fran with starting to get people together for the photo.'

He turns to Miri – but she's not there. The back of her little red dress is just disappearing into the side door of the house. He follows her, through the kitchen and an argument between his aunt and a drunk uncle, through the hall and a negotiation between one of his cousins and her bolshy son, and up the stairs.

'Miri!'

She gets to the end of the hall and turns. 'Why don't you just *tell* me?'

'Tell you what?'

'Santi! Why would Anita want Pato home in the morning when she's not even in the country! You *lied* about that call, it was someone else!'

'No, no.' He shakes his head.

'That's why you didn't want me here, why you're pushing me away. You've met someone else. Just admit it, *please*.'

He tries to put a hand to her stressed little face. 'I must have misheard Anita earlier, that's all.'

'Locked in a *bathroom*?'

'I don't know, it wasn't a good line... *Please* sweetheart, come on, there's nothing to be upset about.'

She wipes a finger under each eye and sniffs.

'I'll get you a tissue.' He grabs a box from Mamá's bathroom and comes back to her. 'And I don't "push you away". You know I need space, but that doesn't mean I don't love you. Come on my Miri, everything's fine.'

It is, for a moment, but then he discovers that he forgot to switch his phone to silent.

'Who *is* this person who keeps calling you?' she asks.

'It's just a message.'

'Messaging you then.'

'Well actually it's just a tweet.'

'A *tweet*.'

'I should switch it to silent; it can wait.'

She sighs. 'You've changed, Santi. I don't know why, I'm not sure when, but you're… distant. And… oh, I don't know, but now, for instance, the guy who used to hate his phone… is desperate to take a look at it.'

'I'll switch it off.'

'So you're not denying it.'

'Denying what? Miri!'

'That you're desperate to read that… *tweet*.'

He raises his eyes to the heavens.

'Let me see it.'

'Oh for fuck's sake.' He forces a laugh. 'This is ridiculous.'

He takes out his phone. Two unread tweets. They could be from anybody – Tania asking about going for a drink; Diego fans; old school friends he barely remembers; the guitar shop retweeting his earlier compliment; Ignacio about a number of things; maybe even a saucy one from Joselito about another cousin's new girlfriend – but Imogen said she was going to ask how he was doing, and never lets him down. Miri taps the icon.

'Okay, I've dealt with my relations (*he manejado mis relaciones*), how are you doing with yours?!'

There's a further tweet, apologising profusely for making a mistake with the word *relaciones* again, but Miri doesn't wait to read it.

The Lighthouse Keeper's Daughter

CHAPTER 12

SUNDAY 9TH SEPTEMBER, 2012
The South Coast, England

'Good morning Imogen ☺' Santi has written.

She rubs her eyes. 'Buenos días. Have you survived (*sobrevivido*) your relatives?'

'Yes.' Then he writes: 'No.'

'What happened?'

'Pato. I learn all the world know she has boyfriend but not me. Why she not tell her Papi? Like I am no part of her life.'

'☹. But hombre, it is because you are the most important person to tell! She was waiting for the best moment, you'll see.' How does she know? By the time she had her first boyfriend – that sweetly poetic dopehead in First Year at uni – her mother and stepfather could only disapprove from heaven.

'Thank you *guapa*. I have to leave. Kisses.'

Maybe he's off to choose a new sofa with his wife, or take a new girlfriend to one of the many big patches of green she's seen on the internet map of Madrid. Of course, he could be wondering whether she's preparing a big Sunday lunch for her husband's parents, or spending the day in bed with a new lover. Their little friendship exists in a pure two-dimensional form, unshadowed by the people – present or past – around them. Heterosexuality has been proved by the existence of their seventeen-year-olds, but how these offspring have come about is yet to be discussed. Are they deliberately not discussing partners, or have they just not got around to them in their jumbled languages?

The phone in the living room. She stumbles down the vertical ladder from her bunk and rushes over to it. A number she doesn't recognise.

'Is that Imogen?'

'Yes?'

'It's Bill Trewitt here, Dorothy gave me your number, said you'd like to talk to me. I was on the lighthouse with your father when he had the accident.'

'Oh!' She takes the phone back to her room and sits down. 'How kind of you to call.'

'It's a long time ago now love.' A wheezy cough. 'But if there's something you want to ask?'

'Well... Can you remember how he'd been the days before it happened?'

'Ah.' He clears his throat. 'He sometimes kept to himself, your father. Don't get me wrong, he was a great bloke, but he had his reading and his music.'

'And writing letters.'

'We all wrote letters, it was what you could do for the family.'

She sees her mother at the kitchen table opening bills, the booklet from the Church, the weekly *Woman's Realm*... She thinks she remembers a weekly envelope that included a letter for her.

'Imogen, as I said to the police at the time, he might have seemed a bit down in his diary, but there was *no* way that... that it was anything but an accident. It was a hard time for us, but your father had a job lined up, he was okay. He just fancied a bit of fishing. Len took him his tea, and then, what, fifteen minutes later he went down to tell him lunch was ready and… he'd gone.'

'Just *gone.*'

'Yes. No sign of him. And can I tell you something? I always wish *I'd* taken the tea; perhaps I would have persuaded him to come up. But Len said *don't worry, you carry on with what you're doing.* I was checking the supplies you see, always had a bit of a thing about it. And your father and I had had a tiff about what was left, it looked like we hadn't brought enough with us. The awful thing is that after the accident, maybe after a few days, I checked again and he was right, everything was there, nothing for me to fret about. I don't know how I made the mistake. I felt bad about that, arguing with him about nothing just before…'

'I'm sure he'd forgive you. But wasn't it a bit foolish, fishing from the set-off in that weather?'

More coughing. 'We all did it. There was a bar across the door you see, but… there must have been a fault. I'm sorry Imogen, about your father. Terrible thing. For your family, but also for us. Principal Keeper for twenty odd years, Len, seen some things in his time, but a good friend of your father's and took it bad.'

'Oh God, I can imagine. I remember him.'

'But Imogen, Dorothy tells me you're living in the old cliff lighthouse, you write for a magazine and have a son – I'm sure your father would be proud. He was always talking about your reading, how well you were doing at school, the funny things you said…'

'Oh…' She bites her lip.

Loud coughing. 'I've got to go now, okay? You take care love.'

She looks out at her father's lighthouse, today surrounded by tell-tale white horses. A whack of his head on the set-off or the rocks below, a gulping down of swirling water. A brain – full of books he was going to read, Debussy records he had on order, things he was going to share with his penfriend, a sense of duty towards his faultless wife and smart but plain little daughter – that got switched off.

She remembers her mother tearfully sitting her down and telling her, and finds herself wondering how long it was before the penfriend found out. Probably heard it on the local radio news, in between their favourite songs at the time. She has a sudden wish to hear that music, as if it could conjure an understanding of this strange relationship he was having with Sophie.

She goes into YouTube. Stevie Wonder's '*Lately*' is a bit miserable, but his earlier '*Signed, sealed, delivered I'm yours*' might have made them smile. Earth, Wind and Fire's '*After the love has gone*': why on earth has she clicked on that? They were having an 'impossible' fantasy relationship, it never had to go – or so they thought. She lets the heaving waves of misery tumble over her anyway. Then there's Randy Crawford's '*One Day I'll Fly Away*' – they would have liked that. Hang on, what is she doing here? Why does she care what this woman felt? It's probably her fault that her father *had* the accident, his head full of nonsense about her... But she's already clicked on an early recording. Randy, dressed in a ball gown, is on a glittery TV show – but she's not there; eyes are almost closed, she's totally immersed in the song. In the need to get away. She felt this once, herself – for at least a year or two – and then she flew.

A tri-tone from her phone. 'What are you doing?' Santi is asking.

'I'm listening to some old songs. Uh... too much sadness / *tristeza*.' She sends him the link to Randy's song.

After a few minutes he writes 'I know this'.

'The song is known in Spain?'

The Lighthouse Keeper's Daughter

'No. I know what says the song.'

'Well done!'

'Imogen!! I know what the song… I want to say, I have felt this,' he continues in Spanish.

She hesitates; wandering if she can ask him about it. 'Me too.'

':-('

':-('

':-(('

':-((((haha.'

Her mobile rings. Dylan. 'Hi. Can you hang on a minute?' she says into the phone.

'I have to go, Santi.'

'OK. Kisses / *besos.*'

'Besses.'

'Kissicos.'

Dylan is saying something about grouting and the internet.

'Yes, of course.'

He must have been almost at the gate, because she just has time to have a quick shower and pull some clothes on and he's calling up from downstairs. He's shinily tanned from Bournemouth, Weymouth or wherever he went.

'Good break?'

'Great. Are you ok?'

'Me? Yes.'

'But you didn't go to Jersey.'

She only decided to go while he was away, didn't she? Perhaps she mentioned it before.

'I've got the new router here,' he says.

'The what?'

'The box for the internet, Imogen. Dorothy wants a new, state-of-the-art one fitted. Aren't you a lucky girl.'

'Good! Look I've got to pop out.'

'Oh?'

'To the village, or you won't have any coffee.'

⚞⚟

Coffee, bread, cheese, two types of locally grown cherry tomatoes. She picks up the last bottle of washing up liquid, and there are no washing machine capsules; cleaning materials aren't a strength of the village shop, unless you count the extensive collection of hand-made soaps.

She queues to pay. In front of her, the old guy from the Post Office donates a half-smile to the forty-ish woman stuck up alone in the lighthouse. A small child in a party dress stares at her with inexplicable hatred while her mother buys flowers and her father honks at them from one of the parking bays. Behind her, there's the squelchy sound of kissing between a young couple wrapped up in each other.

Now there's some young thing with a breathy voice singing on the radio. Quite enjoyable in a four-square poppy kind of way, but the girl in the song is considering her chances with this guy who keeps flashing up on her phone…

A hand waving in front of her face. 'What are you grinning at?' asks a laughing Jules, her shorts and trainers suggesting that she's taken yesterday's advice about running for seeing off the blues.

'Oh! Just this shop and its identity crisis.'

'Don't knock it – where else can you get locally-grown lavender bags in an emergency?'

'So where are you off to?'

'I went for a run that slowed to a walk and then ended up in the Bear Inn.' She looks at Imogen's bag of shopping. 'Any chance of a lift? A coffee in your lantern room?'

'Hop in then. You can meet Dylan.'

'Dylan? Dylan Thomas, Bob Dylan…?'

'Dylan the friendly builder. Actually I've got a theory that Dorothy pays him to spy on me.'

'Ooh-er, that sounds fun! Is he any good? I've got a whole load of things need doing.'

※

Jules on the phone. 'Imo, you've *got* to come tonight.'

'Where?'

'The Pevensey Bay pub to see Dylan's band. Weren't you listening?'

'You know I hate pubs, I won't hear a damn thing.'

'Nobody will – we'll all be blasted with rock. Why didn't you *tell* me about him? What a lovely guy. I said we'd be there before they start playing at nine. Sorry, I'd have asked you earlier but he's only just left.'

'Good God, he's been with you for… six hours? What *have* you been doing?'

'Well the estimate of course, a coffee, then another, a stroll to the bandstand, Tesco Express and a spag bol.'

'Jules! Okay, if you need me to come along… Shall I pick you up on the way? I'll be as quick as I can.'

※

Jules is waiting for her and bounds out of her apartment, gets into the car and gives her a hug. 'You're a star. And look at you, didn't even take time to put on any make-up!'

Imogen drives off.

'Or brush your hair! Have you really got *no* interest in meeting someone?'

'Of course I have.'

'I suppose the Twitter romance with the Spanish guy keeps you going.'

'What? We just chat a bit and improve our languages.'

'What d'you need Spanish for then?'

'I *like* Spanish.'

'And him.'

Imogen hesitates for a moment. 'Well yes, it's like having a friend in my pocket.'

'I take it he's also cute.'

'Oh I don't know.' She doesn't want to start poring over photos of him with Jules. 'Anyway they're all really short, aren't they.'

'Well, go over there and have a look!'

'Jules! Why on earth would I do that?'

'Because it would be fun for us both to be in love with guitarists!' Jules says, waving her arms around playing air guitar. 'Ah, just turn left here.'

The car crunches into a shingle parking area. They get out and can hear the sea sucking at the beach, the multi-coloured pub lights reflected in its dark expanse.

'Do I look okay?' Jules asks. Tight jeans, a red blouse. Imogen pats her arm and nods.

The pub has put on Bon Jovi's 'Living on a Prayer' to get people in the mood – as if they weren't already. Almost everyone, young and old, is either in leather or – like the band in their poster on the door – an animal print onesie. The band is setting up at the far end of the room, but Dylan puts down his bass and comes over to say hello. His tight leopard print emphasises his neatly toned body; he's probably not even thirty. About this time yesterday,

Jules called to ask how she had so messed up her life. Now look at her. But she needs to keep some perspective; you should never let your entire happiness depend on a man – especially one who's at least ten years younger than you.

The band starts. She's never been interested in these old rock songs, but now she's enjoying their power and joining Jules in singing the choruses of 'Here I go again' and 'In the name of love'. Then eventually the band takes things down a bit, and their eyes water with Queen's 'Who wants to live forever'. After the break it's all full on again, and she starts to worry about what the volume is doing to her ears. Jules gets up to go to the Ladies', so her mind turns to Santi. As if by telepathy, her phone buzzes against her hip.

'Now what you listen to?'

'HIGHWAY TO HELL! Because my friend Jules has taken me to see a heavy rock band in a pub :-O'

'Jaja yes, ACDC grupo I know it. Why he taken you there?! *Pobrecita* / poor girl :-('

'Because SHE is in love / *enamorada* with the man playing bass guitar!'

'Jajaja! :-))'

Dylan is looking over at her with a grin. She's about to put her phone away when it buzzes again; Santi has sent a link to ELO's Mr Blue Sky, with a 'Look it, I fond for you :-)'

She stares at the words. He means *found* of course, but she won't correct it.

It's finished. Dylan is taking Jules home, so she gets back into the Jeep on her own. There's a queue to get out of the car park, so she takes out her phone. Before she goes back into Direct Messages, she notices Santi in her timeline, replying with a smiley face to Fran from the old Tangoza band and his cousin @Lily_Lopez in

Australia. She scrolls up. Lily has retweeted Fran's photograph of a lot of people in a garden, and regretted not being in it. She clicks on it for a better look; how interesting, it must be a picture of Santi's family from the party last night.

Then her heart misses a beat.

She taps the CD player off. Enlarges the photo. It's definitely him, and there can be no doubt about the *relación* he has with this curvaceous young beauty he is whispering to and wrapping in his arms.

It's always in the stomach. Why is that? These kind of feelings should affect your sight or your hearing. But hang on – why is this affecting her at all? *Nothing's changed.*

She drives off. After some wrong turns in Eastbourne – just like that time she was listening to *Dos Caminos* – she finds herself at the Beachy Head car park she pulled into when she first discovered Santi's album.

She gets out her phone for another look. Checks their hands for rings… Oh for heaven's sake, what *is* she doing? Does she want Santi to be alone? He deserves to be happy. It's not as if she's about to fly off to live with him in the middle of Spain, even further from Ollie, unemployed, struggling to hear and understand him, and eventually being kindly but firmly rejected for… well, such an exquisite member of his own kind.

Oh no, is she really going to cry? *Jesus.* And why park here, of all places. She gets out of the car and walks up the grassy slope in the light of a big moon, slows as she approaches the cliff and sits on a comfy bench of grass five steps from the edge. As many a sad solitary person has done before her.

From below, the lighthouse winks its light at her. And again. And again. How much did her father know about *his* penfriend? Wink. Wink. Winking just like he used to at home, when he

The Lighthouse Keeper's Daughter

cracked a joke. She'd forgotten about that. It's like he's telling her how ridiculous she's being. How ridiculous they're *both* being.

CHAPTER 13

MONDAY 10TH SEPTEMBER, 2012
Madrid, Spain

Imo-gen Brad-field: if she knew what she put him through this weekend.

He orders a coffee and stretches out his legs under the table, looks over at the old monument with its marble lions, imagines jumping into the reflections in the cool glassy water of the lake. He should come to *El Retiro* for his morning runs whenever he's not shooting during the week. Which, this week, is most of the week.

He pulls out his phone and checks all the possible means of communication: still no message – or script – from the studio. In fact, strangely little communication at all this morning. Then it rings in his hand.

'Little brother! Just wondering how the rest of your weekend went. Did you manage to calm her down about this Twitter girl?'

'Uff, what a fuss. But she seems to be okay with it now. And then I get Pato starting up when I was driving her to college this morning, explaining the importance of trust in a relationship – like she's the expert these days!'

'I hope she talked to you about Miguel too.'

The Lighthouse Keeper's Daughter

'Eventually. I've said he can come here next weekend with her – but sleeping in separate rooms.'

'Fair enough! Oh – got to go. Just wanted to check you're okay.'

Twelve. Back for a shower and then surprise Miri by turning up at the shop to take her out for lunch. Odd that she didn't suggest it, knowing he wasn't at the studio today. He checks his phone again; no, not a peep from her. Nor from Imo-gen Brad-field.

※

He should love this shop. A film buff's paradise. He wants to be a film actor doesn't he? No, he *is* a film actor – or at least *has* been, once.

Miri's not in the book section or the café area. He edges past a glamorous woman he should probably recognise looking at books about Audrey Hepburn, a young guy looking at a hardback about Almodóvar's films, and a couple pointing out Javier Bardem and Anthony Minghella among the letters stuck to the shop's pillars.

She's not round the corner in the poster and quirky gift section either, and all the staff are busy, so he picks up a book celebrating the film *Blancanieves*.

'Hi Santi. *Snow White*. Beautiful, isn't it. My favourite of the year.' Part-time actress and boss Leticia, noticing him from behind the till.

Santi nods. He hasn't actually seen the film; Miri got impatient with him and saw it with girlfriends, and Pato wasn't having anything to do with a silent movie. He goes over to pay.

'Mireya's popped out I'm afraid – your manager was passing and took her for a break. Should be back soon.' She puts the *Blancanieves* book in the shop's clapperboard plastic bag. 'Take a seat. Coffee on the house while you're waiting.'

'Great, thanks.' He sits down; it's better than browsing through the books, watching the words jumble, wondering why people want to write about films rather than watch them. This *Blancanieves* thing is a one off: a book with few words, about a film with no sound. Other than music, of course. Dialogue in small boxes, uncrowded, necessarily to the point. Like Twitter.

'Santi!' Ignacio's resonant voice. He's standing there with a hand on the doorframe like he owns the place, white shirt brilliant in the sun. Miri is grinning beside him. They come over.

'Sorry, took your ladylove for a quick pancake,' Ignacio says, then leans towards him and lowers his voice. 'She's fixed me up with Ariadna Alonso.'

'Who?'

'You know, the new actress in *Hospital Central*. What with Antonio last month, she's becoming quite a little scout!'

'Actors come in here for a bit of a chat and a moan sometimes,' Miri says, wide-eyed. 'I was just trying to help.'

'Well keep it up darling!' Ignacio pats her shoulder.

Santi wonders if Ignacio hasn't already got more clients than he can properly look after.

'Look Santi, we need a meeting. Can you do… let's see…' He gets out his phone.

'Now?'

'No, no, I've got to fly. Five? Ah…' He's moving his phone diary around with his finger. 'Yes. That bar we liked in Salamanca, near Velazquez metro, OK? You can go straight to your English lesson afterwards. You *are* still going?'

'Oh yes,' Miri says. 'He's taking his English *very* seriously these days, aren't you Santi.' She gives him a nudge and a half-smile.

'Well I have to. That's fine. Is there some news then?'

'Gotta dash. I'll tell you later okay? Ciao!' He strides out of the shop, people moving out of the way to let him pass.

Santi turns to Miri. 'I was going to take you for some lunch.'

'Oh, sorry love, I haven't got time. But have one of our wonderful salads here, and I'll try and sit down and have a juice with you.'

'No, I'll let you get on.' He gives her a kiss.

'I'll make you something tonight then.'

'I've got the guys coming round for a rehearsal. I'll call you.'

※

His scripts, the books on Lorca… He reads regularly and never gets any faster. But this book that Imogen recommended is different. Neither banal nor profound, and nobody's waiting for the results. He's sitting on the terrace with a Diet Coke, moving the Casa del Libro bookmark down the page to isolate each line, as he was shown to do years ago at school. Unbelievably, the story is carrying him along. He'd rather be playing the guitar or listening to his new Pitingo album, but this is quite enjoyable.

He finishes the page, grins to himself and picks up his phone. Of course, it's not just the story; he's also wondering why she chose *The Time Traveler's Wife*. The girl has red hair! The couple are frequently separated – although by time, not just distance. An impossible relationship, really. Did their friendship remind her of this story?

'I buyed the book. Is very wide but I have enjoyed the start :-)'

A few minutes pass. Five. Ten.

'No – how bad. IT is very wide :-D'

'…LONG!!! Uff.'

He imagines Imogen hearing her phone pealing three times in her bag.

But there's no reply.

Her Twitter page: a couple of exclamation-marked tweets that he can't understand between her and the Jules woman; a Spanish thank you to the *sevillano* graphic designer who has now introduced her to the albums of Diego El Cigala... and an English reply to someone who liked something she's written – *just fifteen minutes ago*.

He puts the phone in his shorts pocket and goes to the kitchen. Ha – she'll soon be sending vibrations to his groin hehe. Meanwhile he makes a virtuous small tuna roll and takes it and the last of Miri's fruit salad out on the terrace, turning on the iPod as he goes past. He selects Mr Blue Sky, but it doesn't conjure a reply. She's probably out somewhere and run out of battery, she'll reply later. In fact, she'll have to, because he now realises that 'buyed' isn't right (brought? bought?), and she'll never let that go.

On comes his favourite Pitingo track. Hopefully he can introduce Imogen to Pitingo before the *sevillano* does. But he can't send this one; it's called *'I'm with you, in the distance'*! He plays it again and chuckles to himself; this is ridiculous. It's just that it's odd not to hear from her for... fifteen hours. He gets his phone out.

'You are OK?'

'?? :-s'

'Uffff'

':-('

':-((('

'Grrrrrrrrrr'

He deletes back up to 'Uffff'. He's about to delete further when her message appears with a twang.

'I'm fine, thanks.'

He waits for more. Is that all she can say?

'I'm glad that you are enjoying the book / *Estoy contenta de que estés disfrutando del libro.*'

Well. How very polite and neatly translated.

He sits there with his finger over the keypad. What's the matter with him? She's finally replying, she's there – no, *here*, in his phone – and he can't think what to say. It's that bloody song, putting idiotic ideas in his head.

He looks at his watch. 'I have to go to a meeting now. Kisses.'

'Adios, besos.'

There's still half an hour before he has to leave, they could have talked about the book, Pitingo... Never mind, they can talk tomorrow.

He picks up the guitar and expects to produce something mellow and Cuban. Instead, he finds himself humming something like the melody of Telephone Line over a flamenco *Soleá* – then letting the tune find a natural place in its new foreign home.

※

Fuck, he's never late for Ignacio; chances are he's been allocated a mere thirty minutes, and now it'll be fifteen. But Ignacio is all smiles and not-to-worrys, orders wine, spends some time considering the *tapas*.

'What time's your English class?'

'Half six.'

'Good. Plenty of time. Because I've got two – no, three – bits of news for you. D'you want them bad to good, or good to bad?'

'I don't know. You choose.'

'Ok. They've brought your audition forward. We even have a date: nineteenth of December.'

'Oh!'

Ignacio is smiling broadly, but that doesn't mean anything.

'Is that *good* news?' Santi asks.

'Of course! You've still got plenty of time to prepare. D'you want the next?'

'Go on then.'

'You've got a gig at Sala Berlanga on the tenth of December.'

'Great! Can't wait to tell the guys.' He thumps Ignacio on the back.

'But you'll have to do a lot of promoting for it – including a radio programme the week before, okay? Don't let me down on this.'

'What radio programme?'

'Oh, it's a daytime show, some flamenco fan DJ, it's a doddle, don't worry.'

'Right. And let's have the bad news then.'

'You're not going to like it.'

'Well obviously. Let me guess: they're taking Diego off before the end of the season.'

'Yes.'

'Ah well. I should have a big storyline coming up. '

Ignacio looks straight at him with his mouth in a line. 'Before the end of the *week*, Santi.'

'What? But… I don't understand… And don't they have to—'

'No they don't. I've checked the contract.'

'But *why*? I've got a lot of scenes coming up!'

'That was before you upset the star of the show. Did you bang her, *not* bang her, or what?'

'No! Well, six months ago, just before I met Miri, but we usually get on okay.'

He shakes his head. 'Santi, Santi… some women, you must have noticed – your dick stays in them forever, you know? Bad move.'

'What's she been saying?'

'It's not just her. They say they've put up with your struggle with the lines, but now you've started struggling with the *plot*.'

The Lighthouse Keeper's Daughter

'What? I just made a few suggestions, that's all!'

'They don't want suggestions! Suggestions take time and money. Make sure you learn from this, or we'll have the same trouble in New York.'

'But—'

'You're in with a chance of getting Lorca, Santi. Don't dwell on *Universidad*. Negative energy. Put all your efforts into Lorca. Keep reading up, keep exercising – you're looking better already. Oh – and these English classes with Johnny are good, he says you're doing well, but you now really need to get yourself a one-to-one English teacher for an intensive course.'

CHAPTER 14

TUESDAY 11TH SEPTEMBER, 2012
The South Coast, England

Another envelope. God, every couple of days now. But she's not going to get upset about them anymore – in fact, she won't even sit down to read them. She knows he loved her, in his way, and if he had a secret fantasy affair with a penfriend that wasn't doing anyone any harm, then who is she to criticise.

<u>Mon 5th Oct. '81</u>

'So what's <u>your</u> story?' Len asks me. ''Cause I should really report this, you know.'

'Well, I was in the Birling Gap phone box, making a call,' I say.

'Vince says you were just standing in there, for ages.'

'Ok, I was <u>about to</u> make a call, checking the number, getting my coins ready. Then Vince is there making this stupid face at me through the glass, bloody weirdo making me jump out of my skin. So I come out and ask him if he needs the phone urgently or what. And he starts going on about why would he want to do that, he's got one in his cottage, and I've got one in mine for that matter, so <u>what am I doing</u>.'

'Yeah, so he's a nosey bugger, but that's—'

'And then he starts describing <u>exactly where the phones are in my house</u>, and I thought, what the hell? How would he know that?'

Len's putting a finger up, there's something missing, he knows it, but I carry on. I tell him Vince sorted out the sticky back door and put up shelves in my kitchen. He's been doing DIY in my home, feeling sorry for her that I 'do nothing but read books' when I'm ashore.

Len points out that Vince often mows the lawn for his wife – something she doesn't need to spend her housekeeping on two days before he's coming ashore. But he doesn't <u>hit</u> him for it.

'I didn't hit him, he fell over.'

'You pushed him over.'

'There was a little bit of… shoving, that's all.'

Silence.

'About some <u>woodwork</u>,' he says, eventually.

'No, the way he's accusing me…' I'm floundering, and he can tell. Len's no fool.

'Who were you calling?'

'I didn't,' I say, sounding like a bloody schoolboy. I look out of the window, up at the cliff edge. People always stand too close.

'You didn't what? Oh come on, Hughie, what is this really about?'

He gets up to put more water in the pot, giving me a moment to collect myself. He sits down again. 'It's the penfriend woman, isn't it.'

<u>Woman</u>. May as well tell the whole truth, if I'm going to.

'Girl,' I say.

'Girl?'

'She's twenty-one.'

His eyes widen. 'Blimey. OK, let's start at the beginning.'

Penfriend Sophie was *twenty-one*? Jesus, he really was having a mid-life crisis here – and keen to keep it under wraps. A push and shove with Vince? A bit rough round the edges, but he was always so kind to her and Mum… She lets the first letter drop onto the sofa.

Tues 27th Oct.'81

It's a YES. In fact, <u>more</u> than a yes – she's wondered about it too.

Saturday, Cadogan Hall. The Fauré Requiem again – music SO beautiful that we each had to turn to the stranger next to us to share our feelings about it. The music that—

God! Nearly four o'clock! Can't get used to the clocks going back. Nearly time to get ready to put the light on. Wonder if Dorothy will try out some of her Morse code again. If she does, I'll have to give her a t-h-a-n-k-s. What a star she is.

So. This is the plan. It will look like Dorothy and I are having our annual London theatre trip and B&B for her birthday – but in fact we'll be having tea at the Cadogan Hotel, where Sophie will join us, and then Dorothy will go off to see Cats with an old London friend while Sophie and I go to the concert. Later, Dot and I will have a nightcap back at the hotel, and I'll be telling her how it went…

But meanwhile there's tomorrow. There's supposed to be a very low tide just after my morning shift. I should be able to reach the Birling Gap phone box and – just briefly, she says, just to finalise arrangements, no need to fret – tomorrow we'll talk.

They *met* – or at least planned to. Is that so extraordinary, another concert after two years or so? Perhaps not, if it weren't for the secrecy of it. She should be incensed on Mum's behalf. But… it's the first time she's seen a positive entry in his diary, he's literally come alive here. How can she not be pleased to see him happy and excited, when she knows he only had, what, seven more months to live? If she's going to be really honest with herself, she feels just a little bit envious.

She might now be able to face some breakfast. Or rather, *more* breakfast, because it's been Shreddies for the last three meals. She sits down with a bowl and gazes out at Beachy Head, as it's impossible not to do.

That tri-tone from her phone. 'Teacher! I need English! Lots! Talk talk talk!!!'

Of course he does. And as long as he needs English, their little friendship is going to *desarrollar*. Develop. Well, up to a point. There mustn't be any more of yesterday's bitterly polite responses, she needs to get back to where they were, what they are.

She remembers a TV documentary about penfriends through history. Ewan kept coming in and out of the living room making stupid comments like *Pick up the phone, losers!* Marie Antoinette confided about the French revolution to her pen pal Queen Charlotte. Literary penfriends Emily Dickinson and her bewildered mentor Thomas Wentworth Higginson met only twice during their twenty-five year correspondence. Two women sending letters between England and USA for seventy years experienced uncanny parallels in their lives. Then of course there's '*84 Charing Cross Road*'. She thinks she's seen it among Dorothy's old videos…

※

She pauses the film, makes a tea and takes it back to the sofa. A warm friendship over decades, in time extending to his colleagues and *wife and daughter* – how wonderful.

She re-starts the video. It must have been this pair that made Ewan come out with *Fuck's sake jump on a Pan-Am woman,* because after years of the American delaying her visit to London, the bookseller unexpectedly dies of appendicitis. We all do it: believe we have an endless shelf of tomorrows, next weeks, next months. She wipes her eyes.

A Facebook message, an email and a tweet haven't been heard above the film. Ollie saying he hasn't forgotten about this Saturday's lunch, but won't have long. The magazine asking her for that round-up of Halloween events. And Santi again:

'Imogen, how are you? I need speak english better! Can we make Skype?'

Her heart thuds. Today? *Now*? She sees herself with his eyes – a miserable cow with tangled hair and ancient pyjamas watching old films on a weekday morning – and dashes to the shower room, closes her eyes and lets the warm water stream over her while her heart shakes her body with its strong, rapid beats. She considers putting it off; maybe this is how the American woman felt.

Hairdryer, mascara. The green t-shirt has lost its shape, the black one is too tight. She settles for a turquoise blue pyjama top. The line of view from the computer: Christ! She removes some Boots shopping - including a box of tampons - from the chair behind her. She puts her phone onto WordRef, in case things come to a linguistic standstill. Fetches a glass of water. That's the physical aspects sorted out, other than the state of her cardiorespiratory system.

What to remember – or rather, *forget*. She has *not* seen the photo of the family party. She *doesn't* know the names of the blonde actress, the two or three sweet-faced band members (one of whom may be a cousin) or the smarmy *ok-ciao* Manager chap. She can ask him about his next album, the film and his English classes. As long as he doesn't look too much like the photo on the album cover, it might be all right.

'Okay!'

'You not answering, so I went out!'

'Well come back in again!!'

'Jaja one half hour.'

Good, she could do with going over Skype; it's been a while – in fact her only contacts are Ewan and an abandoned online creative writing course. She soon panics and wonders who she can ask to help her. Ewan of course, but he's the last person she feels like talking to right now. Ollie: he'll be in his lunch hour, so it's just possible…

She goes into Facebook and messages him; she could call or send a message, but their line of communication is so fragile that she doesn't want to diversify. Message sent. Message *seen*. Minutes pass; he's probably thinking, sod that, sod her. But no, he's typing.

'You did it with Dad when he was in LA!'

'Yes but that's ages ago.'

'Hold on.'

Then he's at his computer and they manage to connect.

'Oh *hello!*' How much older he looks, in just a few months: a more prominent jaw line, a narrower face.

He's saying something about her looking like an ancient ghoul. 'Do something about the lighting!'

She opens the curtains wider, puts the desk light on.

'Better. Click Tools, Options, Video Settings and see yourself.'

Up comes a square showing a pale anxious woman with a slight double chin.

'Oh God.'

'The interviewer will maximise.'

'Oh *God!*'

'Mum! *Tranquila!*'

'What?' She looks at him in amazement, her heart pounding hard again.

'Sorry, just been doing Spanish homework. Calm down, just put the laptop on a book or something so you're looking more straight ahead.'

The box folder of her accounts.

'Thanks *so* much Ol, really.' She wanted to add that *they* could start Skyping, but he's saying he has to dash for something.

She's on her own again, with fifteen minutes to go. She sips water with a parched mouth and types *Santiago Montoya*. There are loads of them, but only one in Madrid and holding a guitar.

She can't just sit there waiting for him, so she goes downstairs for some fresh air. Outside, the sun is trying hard against the fog. Dorothy's persisting roses deserve a dead-heading. Later, it might be the only kind of thing she's up to doing; there's going to be fall-out whether it goes badly or – maybe particularly – if it goes well.

Walking back to the front door, there's now seven minutes to go. She picks up a stationery catalogue from the pile of junk mail – another potential bit of occupational therapy for later. Her legs feel too weak for the stairs. '*Hola!*' she practices with a croak. She's crossing the living room when she hears that daft bubbling sound.

Swigging at the water, she sits down and looks at the screen.

Missed call from Santiago Montoya 13:29
Missed call from Santiago Montoya 13:30
Missed call from Santiago Montoya 13:34
Missed call from Santiago Montoya 13:43

He got back early.

The crazy bubbling sound again. Dazed, she clicks to answer.

He's filing his nails, head down, black hair flopping over his unshaven face. Ok, guitarists have to manicure, but *now*?

He looks up, although not really at her. '*Hice las uñas, mira!*'

The Lighthouse Keeper's Daughter

He's telling her that he's done his nails, and holding out a perfectly manicured one to show her. She should tell him that putting one finger up like that is rude in England.

'Ah yes. Hello!'

'I wait. Fiv-teen *minutos*.'

'You said half an hour!'

'¿*Qué? No*. And *half*!'

'Half and... half?'

'¡*Una y media*!'

'Oh! *Half past one*. I thought you said half an hour.'

'I have *past*... much time, waiting!'

'Ok, ok.' *Jesus*.

He puts down the nail file and addresses the ceiling. 'How-are-you today, Imo-gen.'

His voice has a low, clear resonance that makes her pause. Like the bass guitar on Track One. If he could only take an interest in looking at the person who's been helping him with his English. 'I'm fine, how are you?'

'I need English. This is good.'

'Suddenly you need a *lot* of English?'

'Sudden-ly, yes, I need, because... Oh... wait.'

Now he's looking over at something. Or maybe someone.

'Santi?'

'¿*Sí*?'

'Can you see me?'

His eyes fix her briefly, as if to check. '*Claro*, but how-you-say, I... concen-trate. Ok... I need the English be-cause... I have go to...'

'Have *to* go to...'

'Uff *sí*, I have to go to... make *audición* in Nueva York... for a film that... of... Lorca.'

'Oh! You have to audition for a film *about* Lorca.'

'*Sí, sí*, about Lorca. I am trying… to have the *role*!' He chuckles. '*Qué bien, ¿no*? I find the word before!'

'To *get – conseguir…*'

'I am trying to get… the role of Lorca.'

'Good! So Lorca spoke good English?'

'No! It was… *le costó, ¿qué es*?'

'Er… hard for him.'

'Yes. And I have also, a hard.'

Imogen nods and puts a hand to her face.

'*¿No*?'

'Um… yes. You'd say, *it is hard for me.*' She sees the corners of his mouth twitch. 'English is hard for me.'

'Yes…' He rubs his bristly chin. 'I have to speak when I am there, understand more. Before Dic-iember.'

'*December*. Well, we can keep practising.'

'*Kip*?'

'Keep. *Seguimos*.'

'Yes, but I have to find teacher of English for *curso intensivo*.'

'Oh.' A sharp pang of jealousy. Some young TEFL teacher in Madrid will be spending hours and hours with him.

'With which *frecuencia* you can… *can you*… make Skype?'

'How often can I do…'

'Every day?'

He wants to talk to her daily. No, he wants to *practise English* daily. 'I could try!'

'*¡Perfecto*!' He looks at her steadily now, grinning. She smiles back. He looks down. Then up again. 'My teach-err! One day I fond a way… to thank you.'

'I will find. *Encontraré*.'

'Find, *sí*.'

'Found is in the past, *encontré*.'

'And *fond*?'

'Fond is…' She laughs and puts it into WordRef. '*Cariñoso*.' Her cheeks burn.

'Ah *sí*.' He nods and laughs. '*Vale*. O-kay. So… I want to know… tell me… all *about* your writing work.'

⋇

She's sort of done the roses. On the bench beside her are the stationery catalogue and a list of venues with possible Halloween events – but she won't be doing anything with them today.

It's her first time in what Dorothy oddly refers to in the instructions as the *front* garden, perhaps because lighthouses are designed to be seen from the sea. The grass stops at the pale grey sky maybe eight strides in front of her, but she's looking at the horizon, where the sun has broken through the low cloud to light up a small mirage of glistening sea. She's thinking how, if the world were more flat, she would see Le Havre or somewhere. Completely flat, maybe the Pyrenees in the distance. Beyond which she'd just have to imagine the rocky rise up to the city of Madrid.

'I can't remember when I last felt like this,' Jules is saying in the phone against her ear.

Imogen nods slowly.

'Imo?'

'You deserve it.'

'It's a gift,' Jules continues.

'Yes.'

'I'm deliriously happy, but at the same time frankly terrified.'

'I think the answer is to keep busy,' Imogen says, flicking through the catalogue.

'Oh listen to you! We need to get you out of that bloody lighthouse more—'

A tri-tone in her ear. She puts the phone in front of her to have a quick look. Stares at the words in disbelief.

'Sorry Jules, can I call you back?'

She reads it again, her heart tapping away. 'Imogen I talked with my sister, she say you can come stay with her a week! So we can have lessons of talking *intensivo*. Of course I buy the flight for you. You have good time.'

'Really?!! It's very kind of her!!' she replies.

'I am thinking diciember, before the *audición*. And if you are here the 10th you come to my concert!!'

To hear him play the music that first brought them together. To meet him, a kiss on each cheek, a hug. And something's just occurred to her: she heard everything he said on Skype – maybe it's the lowness of his voice, or the fact that he's speaking slowly, looking for words... 'Oh my God!' she says to the sky in front of her, then gets back to her phone.

'I'd love to come!!! :-))))'

The Lighthouse Keeper's Daughter

CHAPTER 15

SATURDAY, 1ST DECEMBER 2012
The South Coast, England

The day it happened, she'd come out of the lighthouse and seen the car – shining in sudden sun – hurtling up the hill towards her. She was filled with a sense of fate, a feeling that her life was about to change.

She puts a wavy line in the margin and bites her pencil. Is that what happened? Maybe. Certainly that's what *should* have happened; nobody wants to think they'd have *no* sense of the moment their life was about to change. She puts the chapters back in the folder, feels the still small weight of it, but it's amazing: she's finally started a novel.

Ollie has texted about a tailback on the A23; they'll be another hour. Ewan hasn't yet texted anything; maybe this time it will be *his* head that's missing when the car drives in. Missing, but not necessarily *missed*. No, that's silly; the whole point was for the three of them to discuss Ollie's plans.

An hour. Just time to keep up with her urgent weight-loss running programme.

It's sunny but with an icy wind. Once out of the gate she turns away from the blustery cliff edge and runs below the garden, the grassy chalk slimy after the melted snow. Beyond the protection of the garden wall, she runs along the windy hill with its multitude of chalk fragments blown up from the cliff – today assembled by walkers into Happy Xmas and LUV U. She's not sure how happy or loved she's going to feel at Dorothy and Anthea's for Christmas. Especially now she's asked Dorothy why she stopped sending excerpts of the diary, and why she sent the ones she did send. The pages showed sides of her father she didn't know, but what was the point of doing that? Maybe Dorothy will give her the diary now, and she can read it all.

She trots downhill between the gorse bushes to her 'running track' beside the road: the only flat grassy path in the area, and, with no view of the sea, one she usually has to herself. She's out of the wind now, but her ears are still ringing and hurting from the cold. She should put her hat by the front door so she can't forget it. And it should go to Madrid – for the run in the Retiro park that Santi was talking about. Although if he meant they would run *together* she'd have to manage without, as it makes her even more bloody deaf. She turns her head and imagines seeing marble lions, but her world tilts, her knee banging into a tree trunk just before she thuds down onto brambly grass. Some scratches, a bruise – she's okay. She's fallen twice before on this run, no big deal, but this time the shock seems to have made her dizzy – how utterly pathetic. She gets up and staggers along the path as if she's on the deck of a boat, wondering if she can still get back and shower in twenty minutes.

※

Ollie's Golf is there – and so is Dylan's van. What? Only yesterday she told him that Ewan and Ollie were coming.

 The Lighthouse Keeper's Daughter

She lets herself in and calls up her apologies. Upstairs, she finds Ewan and Dylan setting up her old keyboard that Ewan has brought with him, while Ollie can be heard shouting excitedly in the lantern room above.

'Oh brilliant! Thanks!'

Ewan puts a hand on her shoulder. 'Wow, have you taken a tumble! Shouldn't you be more careful in this crazy terrain?'

'I run along the bottom of the hill, but it's a bit slippery today… just need a shower.'

'I popped in to see if I've got enough gloss for tomorrow,' Dylan says. 'Remember? I'm starting Dorothy's room.'

'Oh, right.' She doesn't recall him mentioning that.

'I'll just go down and check. See you then.' He waves a hand at Ewan and goes downstairs.

'Dorothy's spy, I'm sure of it!' she whispers to Ewan.

'Too right – you could be up to anything here.'

'Mum!' Ollie has appeared in the doorway to the tower. 'It's great here! *Got* to do a sketch from up there. Oh no, what happened?'

'I'll be fine once I'm cleaned up.'

He looks like he's grown another two inches since they had lunch at half-term; Skype doesn't give you the full person. There's the usual awkward pat of each other's arms. She remembers Pato giving Santi a hug during one of their Skypes.

'I bought that Almodóvar set for you. Oh – but I left it in the car.'

'Let's get it while we remember,' Ewan says, and disappears downstairs.

Ollie lowers his voice. 'This lunch. What did you say to Dad about Parents' Evening?'

'The same as I told you, what else?'

'He's really pissed at me.'

'Disappointed, surprised…'

'But *you're* not.'

'Perhaps I saw it coming. Anyway, we need to talk—'

'Somewhere he can't start shouting.'

Dylan calls up a final unnecessary goodbye from below.

'Hurry up Imo, table's for one-thirty, isn't it?' Ewan is back with the box set.

'Thanks. I'll be as quick as I can.' She goes to her room – and notices immediately. This is what living alone does to you. Her folder with the chapters isn't quite where it was, the pages not quite as aligned. Coming in here to show Ollie the room, Ewan must have picked it up, seen what it was through the transparent folder. Damn – she should never have left it there; from the very first page he'll see that she's heavily lifted from her feelings about his first visit. Why doesn't he look angry? He's quite the reverse, all smiles and consideration. Maybe he won't say anything until after they've talked about Ollie.

She gets into the shower, turns to adjust the control… and it's that dizziness again. Maybe it's a nervous thing? How stupid. More likely she's coming down with Jules' filthy cold.

※

'Well this is good, no trouble hearing us here,' Ewan says as he sits down and shakes out the flower-shaped napkin.

'I know she like upstair table,' the Thai waitress says with a smile, putting her hands together and making a little bow.

Imogen thanks her, and watches her place a couple with a small boy at the opposite side of the room.

'So how's the novel coming on?' Ewan asks.

He's not going to wait at all. 'Well… it seems to be flowing, but it's too soon to say.'

'I know but…' He leans forward, but looking down, choosing his words.

Ollie stops bending the menu card. 'Maybe she doesn't want to talk about it, Dad. Any more than you want to tell me what's coming up in the series.'

'No, I just want to say… I'm so happy you've finally made a start, and let's drink to it!'

'Thanks! We'll see how it goes. At least I'm enjoying it.' She finds she's smiling; maybe she was being paranoid about the folder.

The waitress brings their drinks and she lets Ewan and Ollie decide on the dishes.

'Ollie says you're going to Madrid for some research. Sounds good!'

'Yes. It's going to be fun. Much of it's still at the planning stage really.'

He nods. 'And now we need to start talking about *Ollie's* plans.'

Ollie looks up from the cocktail menu.

'It was great of you to come all the way up to the Parents' Evening.'

'I had a feeling something was up.'

Ollie groans, helps himself to each of the starters that have just arrived and arranges them around his plate.

'Let's just go through this again,' Ewan says, putting a hand through his even madder than usual greying hair. 'Spanish: could-do-better but *might* still get a B…'

He's lowered his voice, as if he doesn't want to share his son's A level predictions with the couple and their perfect five-year-old on the other table. Imogen struggles to hear – but it probably doesn't matter; he's only going to recount what she told him.

'…your accent apparently… well of course it's good… Marbella… But then Art. *Art*, Ollie. What the hell?'

Imogen looks over at the little boy bent over the restaurant's colouring-in sheet. All those years that her handbag was never without a packet of crayons, a couple of Playmobil guys.

'Lacking… resistant… behind with coursework – wasn't that it?' he's saying.

Imogen nods and wonders if she should ask him to speak up.

'D unless something changes fast.'

Ollie shrugs his shoulders.

'Then English. Also behind… own agenda… D. …year off before uni, but… re-taking A levels?'

'Do you *want* to go to uni?' Imogen asks, trying to sound as neutral as possible.

Ollie looks up from picking the petals off his carrot rose. He looks hopeless rather than defiant, something she can identify with from when she was younger than he is now. He mumbles something.

'You're both going to have to speak up. That little guy's getting a bit—'

'Well *obviously* I do,' Ollie repeats.

'Well *not* obviously, it depends on what you want to—'

'Uh… He doesn't *know*,' Ewan says, having no problem with raising his voice. 'It's abso-bloody-lutely amazing: six years in private education and he still has *no* idea.'

Ollie looks over at the bar, catches the waitresses' attention and orders a Mango Daiquiri. 'There *is* something I want to do,' he says. 'I'll probably study English – or maybe English with Spanish – at uni next year. But first…' He looks from one to the other. 'I want to do a Mixology course. It's four weeks –'

'Mix *what*?' Ewan asks.

'I think it's… mixing *cocktails*?' She can imagine him enjoying the art and dexterity of it, but this is a guy who spends most of his time in his bedroom holed up with science fiction and computer games.

Ewan puts his head in his hands. 'Jesus H. Christ, what the fuck?'

Shush, Ewan!'

The waitress puts a creamy drink with mango, cherry and a mint leaf in front of Ollie.

'One for me too please,' Imogen asks.

Ollie smiles at her. 'The course I want to do is in Barcelona.'

'Oh well. Good for your Spanish I suppose,' Ewan says. 'Tell you what – get the hell on with doing some work for your A levels, and we'll pay for you to find yourself in Barcelona, okay?'

Imogen's phone gives out some overlapping waterfalls of harp.

'God that's loud!' says Ewan.

She scowls.

'Sorry.'

It's a WhatsApp from Santi. *'Hello Imoooo, uff this acting course! ☹ And I'm sorry, I forgot say that in the evening I will watch my Aleti team play Real Madrid and Ronaldo!! :-O Skype tomorrow, no?'*

Ewan has started to recount the cultural and laddish highlights of a long weekend in Barcelona in his student days.

Imogen taps out 'OK! Good luck Aletiiiiiii!!!!' ☺

Another day missed. It's not easy getting people together to Skype. Ollie's intended weekly catch-up is more like monthly, and Santi's daily practice is two or three times a week. But this time next week they'll be practising sitting opposite one another.

'I don't know, you two finding yourselves in Madrid and Barcelona...'

'Why don't you take Maddie to Valencia?' she says. He stares at her. She hasn't used Maddie's name for a long time. 'Didn't you always want to go there?'

Imogen expects them to drop her off home on their way back to Surrey, but Ewan suggests coming in and watching one of the Almodóvars. They make coffees and sit like they used to – Ewan and Imogen on the sofa, although at opposite ends, and Ollie sprawled on the armchair. They watch the one about the woman who's a reluctant romance novelist with a failing marriage – but manages to get both her writing and love life back on track.

When they're leaving, Ewan points to the door at the end of the hall, just as he did three months earlier. 'You know why she keeps that door locked?'

'Dylan says it's because she gets fed up with visitors thinking it's the loo. It's just—'

'Ha! Does he? That's interesting!'

'Why?'

'It's a little round *bedroom*, just like yours. Maybe a couple of small boxes in there, but that's it. Dylan was in there when I came down to get the DVDs.'

'Maybe the paint's in there.'

'No. The paint's in the new bathroom – saw it there when he let us in and I was desperate for a slash.'

'Weird. But *he's* a bit weird. Although very kind, and makes my friend Jules happy.'

'Maybe Dorothy doesn't quite trust you with the family jewels!'

'Well, they've invited me for Christmas. She's invited you too Ollie, you could see your cousins again.'

'Hm. Don't know Mum.'

'Christmas… we'll see,' Ewan says. He gives Imo a tight hug and a kiss on her head. 'Thanks. It's been really great. I'll bring Ollie down again soon.'

'I'll be able to bring myself down, if I pass my driving test.'

Ewan looks at his watch. 'Ah, we need to get going. It's all happening in Madrid tonight - it's the *Derbi madrileño*, the two rival Madrid teams playing.'

'It's on telly *here*?' Imogen asks. She could watch it 'with' Santi, on their phones.

'Not unless Dorothy's got Sky Sports! Shame – it'll be exciting stuff. Atletico think they might at last win this time, but they won't have an answer for Ronaldo.'

'Come on Atleti!' says Ollie, punching the air.

Ewan laughs. 'Always supports the underdog.'

CHAPTER 16

SATURDAY, 1ST DECEMBER 2012
Madrid, Spain

Santi lifts the Tangoza photo off the wall and goes through to the living room. Uncle Pedro was right – he doesn't need them. He has other collaborators now he-he; who would have thought that a load of pompous old English soft rock bands could pull him out of his guitar into writing vocals? Miri credits herself with his new interest in songs, because surely it comes from him joining the ensemble of *Los Miserables*, something that would never have happened without her connections at the cinema shop. He hasn't the heart to tell her that it all started with sharing ELO's *Telephone Line* with Imogen.

'What are you doing?' Miri has come up behind him. 'Ah – banishing Tangoza from the bedroom – about time.'

'Except now I've got a blank on the wall.'

'Save it for Lorca?'

The name brings on the usual shiver; almost daily he feels like he's about to get flu. He turns round and hugs her shower-warmed body in the silky bathrobe, presses himself against her. 'Oh for God's sake take a sicky Miri – let's go back to bed.'

'Santi! You should be going over your scenes for the workshop, remember? And haven't you got a haircut this morning?'

The Lighthouse Keeper's Daughter

Can't she see that what he needs right now is to lose himself in her responsive little body and forget about Lorca for a few hours? 'We hardly see each other these days, you putting in all this overtime, me in the French bloody revolution nearly every night... Say you've got migraine and go in later.'

'I can't, I've got a meeting,' she says, wriggling free.

He follows her back to the bedroom and watches her put on those briefest of briefs that leave no visible line – for anyone interested in looking – through her tight black trousers.

'What meeting?' he says, as if he couldn't guess.

'He's dropping off some paperwork for me – and some cash.'

'He can leave that with Leticia.'

'Well, he said lunch.'

'Yeah, well so do *I*. God, you've had more lunches with Ignacio than I have. Come to think of it, he knows I'm not working during the day but never asks me to join you, does he?'

She pulls on her Clapperboard sweatshirt. 'Oh Santi *please*, you can't possibly be jealous – the guy's a lizard! And you *are* working – on your preparation for the audition. He always asks after you. But he wants to talk to me about something.'

Once he can hear the clank of the lift taking her downstairs, he goes back to the dresser in the sitting room and pulls out the shoebox from the bottom drawer. He takes it over to the sofa, as if possibly needing to sit down to cope with its contents. Tangoza days. Which are also Anita days. There she is, laughing with Esme and Fran in a restaurant, painting a bedroom yellow, weary but smiling as she holds a tiny Patricia... Then it's one or other of them with their duck-obsessed daughter at the Retiro pond with the fisherman's cottage, admiring various ducks at the zoo...

Were they really this happy? But then you don't get photos of moments like when he madly admitted that once – just *once* –

he'd had sex with a persistent blonde after he drank too much at a *Guerra* end-of-series party. Nor do you document the moment when she says that she's not sure, but she *might* have fallen in love with an old school friend who's fun, punctual and can talk about more than whether the band break-up is permanent or not.

Ah, here it is. London 2002. The year they separated, but you wouldn't know. A delighted seven-year-old Pato in an open-topped double-decker, pointing out some fancy bridge over a muddy grey Thames with one hand, a '99' ice cream in the other. Nicely blown up to the perfect size for the frame he's just taken down.

Back in the bedroom his mobile buzzes a text message from the hairdresser reminding him of the appointment Miri booked. Fuck that – how can she think he'll want to do the concert with a nineteen-thirties haircut? The concert: another source of jitters. He sits down with his guitar in the living room, reordering the tracks. Surprising how well the songs sit among the instrumentals from the album, but it might be better with Rafa coming on in the second half. *Hopefully* it'll be Rafa. He picks up his phone.

'Rafa! Did you get the—'

'Yes! I was going to call you but Joselito said you've got some acting thing today.'

'Can you do tomorrow? Uncle Pedro's.'

'Sure. But don't you want to sing them yourself? Now you're a—'

'Listen, *Los Mis* is just backing vocals – looking miserable or desperate to fight. I've got the odd line, but they're over before anyone can see I've sung them.'

'Ha! I must come and see it. But this sudden inspiration for songs, where's it come from?'

'Secret ingredient. You wouldn't believe it.'

'The ginger English teacher?'

'No! God! Joselito needs to stop this nonsense.'

The Lighthouse Keeper's Daughter

Rafa laughs.

'And she's not ginger,' he finds himself adding.

'Well I'll be able to check that out for myself, apparently.'

'She'll be at the concert, yes.'

'It better be good then. Actually I could come over now if you're not—'

He looks at his watch. 'Fuck! Got to go – talk to you later! Or come to Esme's and watch the match with us tonight?'

'The biggest telly in Madrid? You're on.'

Jeans, jumper. Can't find the leather jacket, so it has to be the old puffer. Showreel and eight-by-tens – no, he had to send them in with the script when he applied for the course. His script shouldn't be difficult to find; Miri seems to have done a photocopy for every room in the flat.

No time for the nerve-steadying walk to the place – which he still hasn't located on a map. He hails a cab from calle de la Princesa and asks for the drama school.

The driver stares at him in the rear view mirror. 'Didn't you play Diego in *Universidad*?'

'No,' Santi says, turning to look out of the window.

They speed up to get through the lights before they change. 'I'll do what I can, but you *will* be late.'

'What?'

'Well the courses there start at eleven, don't they?' He's checking him in the mirror again. 'You've nothing to be ashamed of – you did the best with what you were given and got out before the series finally lost the plot.'

'How long will—'

'And before Tania Murphy Mendez lost the plot with her interviews. There's no need for all that, it's bad karma. Anyway, best of luck.'

'You're an actor?'

'When things come up. So which course are you doing?'

'Audition for film, intensive.'

'Oh, the selective one... So have you—'

'Are we nearly there?' A lorry unloading life-size Nativity figures is causing chaos at plaza de Santo Domingo. 'Wow.'

'I'll have to go down here and cut across...'

✄

Twenty-five past.

'Down the corridor, on your left,' the receptionist says, as indicated by a board on an easel – which also gives directions for the day's other course...

'Oh! *Acting in English*!' He wants to ask about it, but she's now on the phone.

He makes his way down a hall covered in pictures of stars of stage and screen and opens the door. A studio with a few bits of furniture, a camera, a couple of bored technicians, and a small half-moon of students in front of casting director Katharine García.

'Sorry I'm late...' Santi takes a chair and winces as he scrapes it into position between a girl probably straight from the Royal School for Dramatic Arts and a waving older woman who had a small part in *Guerra*. Across from him is a smartly-trousered guy his age, acknowledging him with a smug smile.

Katharine García observes him with raised eyebrows. 'So let's discuss Santiago's entrance, in the light of what we've been talking about. Ah...'

The receptionist is at the door. 'Sorry, just checking – Santiago, did you say you wanted *Acting in English*?'

Santiago opens his mouth to speak.

'He's in the right place Sara, thank you. At least, he's on my register. He needn't worry, he's going to get plenty here; two of them have audition scenes in English.'

The receptionist and his chance to be elsewhere disappear.

'Right. Imagine Santiago is auditioning for the part of a successful Spanish writer visiting the States. Am I going to say that I knew he was perfect for the part the minute he came into the room? First impressions.' She points to each person in turn.

'Well, he's *late…*' says RESAD Girl One.

'No eye contact,' from RESAD Girl Two.

'Doesn't want to be here?' Smart Guy suggests.

What a *prat*. 'Well of course I—'

'He might be in character,' suggests the *Guerra* woman, who he now thinks might also have had a small part in *Universidad*. 'Maybe the Spanish writer doesn't speak English well and feels awkward.'

'Yes,' Katharine García says. 'And we'll be talking about how to channel your nerves into the anxiety or disorientation of your character in the scene. Good news: your audition scene is usually a pivotal one, so your character often has cause to be nervous.'

An appreciative murmur from all but Smart Guy – who he suddenly recognises as the TV actor taken on by Ignacio a few months ago after Miri's introduction.

'But there was something blatantly missing from Santiago's entrance. Anyone?'

The RESAD girls look at each other, the *Guerra* woman gives Santi a pained smile.

Smart Guy looks at his notes. 'No communication. No emotional connection to the situation or people in the room – by language, gesture or tone of voice.'

There's definitely a gesture Santi would like to show *him*. The whole room in fact, before making a swift exit. But he needs help with that damn script, and this wasn't cheap.

'Exactly, Antonio. We want to see what's going on with him. The camera *will* see what's going on – and what isn't. I'm tempted to ask him to come into the room again. Why *are* you so late, Santiago?'

'Er... they were unloading *massive* wooden camels in plaza Santo Domingo!'

'So you should have told us that. Heavens, look how the camels have drawn more of a response from you than we have! Actors have to learn how to relate to strangers like they would old friends. I'm sorry to focus on you like this – well no, I like to see latecomers get their *comeuppance*, as they say in English – but you're such a perfect example of people, even actors, who're slow to give anything away.'

'I didn't want to—'

'There's no time for holding back at an audition. You have to come in doing something, saying something, *engaging*. Oh, and wearing something that doesn't cover up the gifts God gave you.' She waves a hand at his baggy jumper.

'Right. So this morning we're going to talk about the general on-camera interview for casting directors and agents, and then move on to strategies for on-camera and video-recorded auditions. After lunch we'll look at scene preparation, using your scripts. Then a break before you each audition – among friends of course.'

A nervous chuckle all round.

'I must say, we've never had two people auditioning for the same role before – this will be very instructive. Obviously you'll take different scenes. I suggest Santiago takes the first scene – the depressed, betrayed Lorca on the liner – and Antonio does the New York party scene.'

The Lighthouse Keeper's Daughter

Santi swivels restlessly on the leather chair in Esme's study. Taps Miri's name yet again. Next door, the lads are yelling abuse at the pre-match commentary on the TV.

'Ah – *finally* answering your phone! Why the fuck didn't you tell me about Antonio?'

'He was there? I didn't think he—'

'Why didn't you say he was going for Lorca? You could have told me – *he* knew about *me*!'

'I thought you might not go.'

'What? Oh for fuck's sake.'

He presses End and calls Ignacio. *Busy* flashes up. He calls Miri again. Also *busy*. Of course; she's asking for further guidance on management.

Esme comes in with another beer. 'What did she say?'

'What you said she'd say. Uh, I'm just going to send a text and I'll come through.'

Esme strokes his cheek and leaves him to it.

Santi's fingers thunder out '*Keeping things from me is a betrayal. I expect this from Ignacio, but not from you.*'

'*I was going to tell you this week.*'

'*Yeah right. I wouldn't do this to you.*'

'*You already did. At first you thought it better for me not to know about Imogen.*'

'*What? That's hardly the same. Who else is auditioning?*'

'*I don't know of anybody else.*'

'*There doesn't NEED to be anyone else.*'

'*See? You're giving up already.*'

'*He IS Lorca*', he types, but deletes it.

'*I'm sorry you're taking it like this. I'll see you tomorrow.*'

'No, we're rehearsing tomorrow.'

'We?'

'The BAND, Miri. I'll call you.'

'We saved you the best seat,' Rafa says, patting the middle of the sofa as Santi comes in.

Dani slaps out an aggressive rhythm on the arm of the sofa. 'You need to get her away from Ignacio. I wouldn't stand for my woman hanging around with that Don Juan.'

'Ha! No worries there – Miri *adores* Santi,' Joselito says. 'I think she was just being protective.'

Santi shakes his head. 'You just can't hear anything against her, can you?'

'Well forget about that now, it's starting!' Rafa says. 'Come on Aleti!'

Santi sinks back into the sofa and looks at his friends on the edges of their seats. Had his album been more commercial, it could have taken Joselito away from sitting around waiting for website design work, Dani from his job demonstrating *cajóns* in the music shop, and Rafa from finding a series of young groups – and women – to spend his inheritance on. Maybe the second album – if the company agrees to release one – will do better. He would be back from New York by then, and better known – should the casting director choose him instead of a guy who's a dead ringer for Lorca, a talented actor and a literature graduate...

'Noooo Turan, *coño*!' shouts Dani, thumping the sofa.

'What...?'

'Hand-ball. Pay attention, Santi!'

Ronaldo comes forward to take the free kick. Esme and the Romanian quickly come in from putting the boys to bed and sit on the floor in front of them. Everybody has hands to their faces.

The ball flies up over the wall and down into the Atletico goal.

Groans all round, the loudest coming from the Romanian.

'So you're an Atleti fan, Darius?' Santi asks.

'Oh yes! And also I record this to share with the boys tomorrow.'

'But their father supports *Real*, they'll—'

'No, no, they like Atleti now, they follow their mamá and me.'

The match has turned scrappy. He was looking forward to it, but finds himself checking his phone. He tells Imogen that '*the Merengues scored a goal from a free kick* :-(' then fixes his eyes on the television with his phone in his shirt pocket, expecting the vibration of a reply. He takes it out again and sends '*We need an equaliser soon!*' along with a picture of a row of meringues, in case her memory of the teams' nicknames isn't as brilliant as his memory of the football *vocabulario* she taught him. He puts the phone back. Finishes his beer. Does some shouting at Diego Costa. Where the hell is she?

At half-time he follows Esme into the kitchen to help serve up some of his mother's paella. 'Seems odd watching the Derby without Fran gloating with the enemy.'

She shrugs.

'I'm sorry, you always seem so fine, I forget to ask how you're getting on.'

'Getting on?'

'On your own. Even if it's amicable, it can't be—'

'But I'm *not* on my own,' she says, blowing on a spoonful of paella and putting it in her mouth. 'I told you, Darius is a treasure.' She looks up at him with a cheeky grin.

'Oh my God! Really? Well, if he makes you happy.'

'Why shouldn't he? He's very young and foreign, his only musical instrument is an iPod – but we're a perfect team. How can you explain these things? It just works.'

'But isn't he off back to—'

'He doesn't want to go to back. He's crazy about his Brazilian jiu jitsu here, wants to train to be an instructor.'

'Does Fran know?'

'Of course! He knew even before I did! He's delighted, it sort of… equalises things. Speaking of which, take this tray.'

There's no equaliser. Just a string of stroppy yellow cards alternating with a string of indignant little texts from Miri. Then another Real goal, and too much rioja. When the lads are off to a bar in the centre on their way home, he accepts Esme's suggestion of the spare room and a tankard of water.

He lies in bed, the room spinning. This time next week, Imogen will be lying here; clothes neatly folded on the chair, her iPhone – with all his English efforts and occasional confidences – charging on the bedside table with an adaptor. Peachy hair tied back, a long white nightdress, fluffy bed socks. Of course he could be completely wrong – she might be chaotic and a right slut, for all he knows. One of those pale English girls you see on the beach in Ibiza, desperate for a swarthy Spaniard. He smiles to himself; the rush of blood to elsewhere seems to be relieving his pulsing headache.

His phone makes the broken chord figure of a WhatsApp message. '*I'm sorry about the Mattress-makers* / Colchoneros :-(*I hope they bounce back soon!*'

He types '*I'm on your mattress!*' but deletes it.

'*How are you? How was the course?*' she's now asking.

'*All the day was a battle. I am very tired. And you?*'

'*Oh :-(For me, the opposite – but maybe making peace is also tiring.*'

He looks up 'peace' in WordRef but still wants to ask what she means. Surely she and Ewan aren't getting back together? She's typing again…

The Lighthouse Keeper's Daughter

'*When they left I fell asleep on the sofa for two hours!*'

Blood seems to be returning to his head.

'*Too much beer -> head ache* :-(' he types.

'*Too much cider -> headache :-(We need to go to bed.*'

':-O'

'*Hehe.*'

A minute passes.

'I'm in your bed in Esme's house,' he writes, and means to delete it but finds he's pressed Send.

':-O'

'*Hehe.*'

Another minute.

'Night night,' she writes, and disappears.

CHAPTER 17

MONDAY, 3RD DECEMBER 2012
The South Coast, England

A Jersey letter. It's got a Christmas stamp, but she knows what it's going to be. Dorothy must have found one or two more pages that – for some unfathomable reason – she wants her to see.

She waits for Dylan to go back downstairs, then sits on the sofa and stares at the envelope in front of her. This one's different: it's delayed sending suggests some kind of culmination, a need for her to have had time to assimilate the previous pages, or a protracted decision about sending it at all.

Mon 2nd Nov '81

She wasn't a girl anymore. I wasn't expecting that. In all my imaginings I've been seeing her as she was two years ago – nineteen and a half, not a day older. I suppose at the back of my mind I always hoped we might wait for each other, for some day that would make itself clear to us – but I'm not crazy, I was resigned to being a little deluded. Mostly I was just busy enjoying our little enveloped friendship.

But then there she was in front of me. Oh God.

The same long conker-shine hair with a fringe, sturdy dark-

The Lighthouse Keeper's Daughter

framed glasses. Still in sensible shoes with a simple linen dress. But the eyes. That dark, steady gaze. Maybe you can only <u>be</u> that confident at twenty-one, I don't know, but when I think about it now it's clear that, before she'd even finished her first cup of tea, she knew exactly what was going to happen.

There was that moment when the music started and we both reached for the other's hand. As friends, I was telling myself. But we stayed like that, as if the music was giving us its blessing. I remember little about dinner – other than laughter about the wonder of not having to wait 5 days before getting replies from each other. And neither of us remember me inviting her back to the Cadogan for a coffee, but next thing we knew we were walking back there, arm-in-arm, in a daze.

<u>Sun 20th Dec. '81</u>

Oh God. I was up on the gallery and I saw a woman falling. Falling <u>on purpose</u>. (How can people use the word <u>jump</u> for this most miserable of acts?). I wanted to look away, but it helps the coastguard recover the body more quickly if we can see where it's fallen.

So I put my hands over my ears and waited. It takes a long time to fall off that cliff. Finally she hit a boulder on the beach. For an awful moment I thought she'd been split in two – but it was worse than that. A bundle flew out of her arms at the moment of impact, landing on the sand – and even before I fetched my binoculars, I knew what it was. A baby.

It could still be alive. Maybe it was just the wind lifting the hood of the little jacket, but I'm sure I saw some movement. I shouted down to the others, but Len shouted back that there's nothing we can do in this sea, Bill's been on to the coastguard, for heaven's sake come down, we all need some tea.

I say I'm just gathering up my tools. I can't let them see me crying. She tried to kill her baby, to put a stop to that little life full of possibilities.

I'll write to Sophie and tell her we'll manage. I don't know how yet, but we will. Easy to say, when I still can't quite believe it's happened, but I'm certain of this: however complicated and painful we've made our lives, we can't kill our child.

Child. CHILD. Her heart thuds, there's a roaring in her ears. This dad she thought she had – the practical, responsible person providing for his family, content with his work and interests, quietly loving and humorous – never existed. She fights back the tears; he doesn't deserve them. It was all a lie; inside, he must have been empty, waiting for something or somebody. Then Sophie came along – and a child he would never see.

But… she has a sister or brother. Now… twenty-nine, thirty. Who *she* will never meet either, unless Dorothy knows where—

'You okay?' Dylan's head again at the landing. He's already brought up the post and, saying she looked pale, made her some sugared tea. 'Any better?' He's looking at her half-empty mug.

'Getting there,' she manages.

'Ah — I'll let you answer that.' He looks over at her phone and disappears.

'You're running out of time to get yourself designer-jeaned for your *señor*,' Jules is saying into her ear.

'I know but… I didn't realise Ollie had grown out of cider. I certainly haven't.'

'Let me guess, we're talking two cans here. You're *such* a lightweight. I think I'll go to Brighton anyway… How about I drop by on the way, around twelve. You might be feeling better by then.'

With one thing and another, it didn't seem likely that she'd be feeling better any time soon. 'Okay. But I might have gone back to bed and not hear you, so ask Dylan to let you in.'

Silence the other end.

'Jules?'

'Dylan's there?'

'Yes. Bright and early.'

'How is he?'

'Let's see...' She looks out of the kitchen window. 'He's fussing with repairs to the stone wall. Jeez, he's already taken a load of it down, what the hell? He said he was going to start Dorothy's bedroom today. Other than the usual workaholism, I'd say he's fine. Why?'

'He's been odd the last few days. Yesterday he said he needed to be on his own, something he had to do.'

'Well he came round here in the morning to check he had enough paint.'

'What?'

'So maybe he went to pick up supplies or something.'

'All *day*?'

She puts the pages back in the envelope, but just turning her head to put it in a kitchen drawer makes her giddy and nauseous. 'Oh... Sorry Jules, think I've got to lie down for a bit... Ow! Fuck! Just walked into the table!'

'You okay?'

'*I'm* fine, it's the world that's spinning.'

'That's not cider. Maybe you've got that thing I had – labyrinthitis. Inner ear infection. They give you these pills called Sert or Serc or something, really help. Ring your GP.'

'Well, if there's something...'

'I could take you, buy some stuff in the village and come back and make the three of us some lunch. How does that sound?'

'Well… it *does*… labyrinthitis,' the doctor says in her impossible wispy Scottish accent. She goes into a description of fluids and canals, judging by the pointing of her pen at a laminated diagram, then turns back to the computer and asks it something.

'Sorry?'

She's saying something about a cold, her fingers are hovering over the keys.

'Not for a couple of months. Apparently there's something that really helps, called—'

The doctor starts wittering some kind of agreement. A green prescription form emerges from the printer.

'I see… referred in August to ENT… hearing in…'

Imogen doesn't reply; the computer seems to have all the answers. She's wondering if this brother or sister has reddish hair like her and her father… What sort of person is he or she, with such a tragic start in life? Maybe Sophie couldn't cope, had the baby adopted…

'Imogen? The hospital… turn up… appointment…'

She missed the appointment. It was the morning that she and Santi had a marathon Skype, having a first go at his audition scenes.

'I'm going to re-refer you,' she says, with suddenly unnerving eye contact and volume. 'Unilateral hearing loss needs investigating.'

'Doesn't it say there? It's since I had an ear infection a couple of years ago. And I'm not wearing a hearing aid.'

'Don't you want to know if anything can be done?'

'Of course. OK. Thanks.' Imogen steers her way out of the surgery and over to Jules putting bags in the car.

'Serc?' Jules asks.

'Serc.'

'Give me that, you get in,' she says, taking the prescription form and going off to the chemist.

Once inside, Imogen takes some money out of her purse for Jules. With her head still, she's fine. She feels for her mobile in her bag, takes it out and puts it in her line of sight. Santi is telling her that he's got too much on and won't be able to Skype today. Just as well. He knows her hearing isn't perfect, but she doesn't want to tell him about this; there's something so unglamorous about ears. Hopefully by next weekend this wobbly thing will have gone.

An hour later on the sofa, Italian smells from the kitchen, a Serc tablet and some music on, she's already feeling much better.

'I like this,' Dylan says, jerking his head towards the iPod dock. 'Another recommendation from your English pupil?'

'Yup. Diego El Cigala with an old Cuban pianist. This is called… well something like "*I've forgotten to forget you*".'

'Like… someone realising they still have feelings about someone.'

'S'pose so.'

'Like Ewan yesterday,' he says.

'What?'

'I pick up on these things. You wouldn't give it another go?'

'No. It hadn't been right for ages. And I don't want to be with someone that makes me try so hard, where I always feel I'm not quite good enough. Odd really: I married a man not unlike my father in some ways.'

His face falls in sympathy. 'Oh…' Then there's a closed smile, as if for once he's curbed his nosiness. 'Can I get you anything?'

'You're both making too much fuss.'

He pats her shoulder.

Jules comes over. 'Have you got any pasta? Looks like I left it in the shop.'

'Uh. No, I ran out.'

'I'll go back. Perhaps get some ice cream for pudding – good for damping down the dizzies.'

Imogen closes her eyes and listens to Diego sing about his *Corazón Loco*.

'What's this one about then?' Dylan calls over from the kitchen.

'A man asking his crazy heart how it can love two women at the same time.'

'Ah.'

She sings along, giggling.

'Where's the cheese grater? It's not… where I thought it would be. Can't find it anywhere.'

'Oh…' Feeling bad about lying around doing nothing when she's feeling better, she pushes herself up – but even though she's holding on to the bookcase, she veers to the side and bangs her head on it. She stays on the floor while the pain subsides, her head on her knees.

'Imogen!' Dylan has rushed over. 'This is really bad. Are you sure that doctor's got it right?' She can feel his hands on her head, looking for damage. 'That was quite a thump.'

'Think I'll stay put a bit longer.'

'But get back on here, come on, I'll help you.' He puts his hands under her arms and helps her back onto the sofa. 'I think you should see another doctor.'

She pulls away from him a little. 'It's what Jules had, there's nothing to worry about.'

'I can't *help* worrying,' he says, his arms still round her.

It feels good; it's been a long while since she had a cuddle. But now he's squeezing her tighter and kissing her head. Her *cheek*. 'Um… this isn't right Dylan.'

'But it *is* right. You don't understand.'

Imogen gently lifts his arms off her. 'But how can you…'

'I can explain. I've—'

'Oh please *do*!' Jules, standing at the top of the stairs.

Dylan quickly turns to her, but doesn't come up with anything coherent.

'He doesn't mean what you—' Imogen says.

'Of *course* he does! Round here every day looking after you…' She turns back to Dylan. 'Thought you'd have more time, didn't you. Well bad luck, I just left it in the car… You *bastard*!' The bag of pasta misses him, so she lunges forward and gives his face a loud slap before running down the stairs.

Dylan leaps to his feet. 'Jules! Come back, we need to talk!'

'I don't want to hear it! I can't!' she screams, slamming the front door.

He dashes down after her. Imogen gets herself to the window. In this state, Jules will have forgotten to press the button that opens the gate, he'll catch up with her and bring her back in. But she's not trying to drive away; she's clambering over the dismantled stone wall.

She *wouldn't*, Imogen says to herself, but breathless with the thudding of her heart. Holding onto the rail she gets downstairs as fast as she can. Dylan is now going over the wall. She follows him, and can now see Jules up ahead, striding along by the cliff. Surely she's just frightening Dylan to teach him a lesson. He's almost caught up with her, shouting that he loves her, she *knows* he loves her.

Jules stops and turns to them. Shivering. Wild eyes taking in Dylan, Imogen, a young couple holding on to each other in alarm, two people in chaplaincy team jackets moving quickly up the hill towards them. 'Maybe, Dylan. But you seem to love both of us, and I can't handle it. Too much hurt. Sorry.'

'Let's go back,' Dylan says, 'I've something to tell you, everything's okay, come on…' He tries to put his arm round her shoulder, and for a moment she allows it, but then she shrugs it off, twisting to get herself free. Tripping on a muddy tuft of grass… and disappearing.

There's screaming. Dylan throws himself onto his stomach, his head over the edge. Does she hear *hold on*? She drops down next to him. Yes! Jules is caught in a bulge of the cliff. She's looking up at them, dazed.

The chaplaincy team are with them now – a small grey-haired woman and a giant of a man. They're telling Jules to keep very still, the coastguard chaps will come and can get her off there, she's going to be fine. But she's started crying and shaking her head.

'Keep *still* Jules!' Dylan shouts. 'Listen to me. Imogen's my sister. My *sister*! D'you understand? We have the same father! Now just hang on!'

'You see?' Imogen calls out to her, although wondering if Dylan is making this up. Dorothy must have told him about her father and Sophie, it's given him the idea. It doesn't matter, it's made Jules listen and stop moving. Or is she losing consciousness? A stream of blood is running through her hair. But no, she's turning her head to concentrate on instructions from the burly chaplaincy guy – who Imogen now recognises as Frank's mate Ben who comes into the shop for the collection box.

Then the rain comes down. *Belting* down. A snake of water is coming down the slope to where Jules is, and she's wriggling to try and keep her foot in the slippery crevice. Everyone is reminding her to keep still, reassuring her that the coastguard have turned off the road and are driving up the hill, it'll be just a few minutes more.

Everyone except Ben. His eyes are darting between Jules, the edge, the slope down to the crevice. He leans over to his colleague and says something that makes her shake her head vehemently.

The Lighthouse Keeper's Daughter

They can hear the coastguard vehicle now, but Jules has started to kick her foot to ram it into the crevice, she's moaning and mumbling, moving her bloodied hands from one slimy rock to another…

Ben is suddenly down on the ground on his stomach, easing his body over the edge and shouting for people to hold on to his legs. His colleague and the couple have hold of him while he steadies himself with one hand on the chalk, stretching the other out to Jules. Then he has her hand. Everyone gasps with relief.

The coastguard men are getting some kind of winch together on the cliff edge, while one of them lets down a rope towards Jules. She grabs it with her other hand.

One of them talks to her as he gets ready to be lowered over the edge with the winch. 'Jules – hold the rope with *two* hands… OK, you can let go now Ben, let's get you back.'

The moment Jules and Ben are back on the grass, there's a loud crack as the ground where Ben was breaks off and slides down the slope amid everybody's cries to *get back, get back*… Then they watch it launch into the air and fall down, down, for so long, to the monstrous boulders below.

CHAPTER 18

WEDNESDAY, 5TH DECEMBER 2012
Madrid, Spain

What's happened to Imogen? He pushes his toast to one side and looks at their WhatsApp chat. At the moment it's got four green boxes from him since her white one saying they'd talk tomorrow – which in England means absolutely the next day, as she's reminded him several times. But it's now three tomorrows on.

Perhaps she's busy making further peace with the ex-husband. They've been separated for a year or so now, and he's also a writer – that's all she's told him. Google showed a smug so-and-so at a TV awards show, leggy model-type on his arm; you couldn't imagine Imogen sharing a coffee with him, let alone a bed. But if that's who she wants, good luck to her.

He checks her Twitter page: nothing since Saturday evening – YouTube clips of a Cigala interview and Miguel Poveda singing live – *olé* Imogen, quite the *flamenca* these days.

The phone bleeps in his hand: a text from Ignacio reminding him about the radio show. As if he could forget. He doesn't answer, still annoyed that it was only yesterday that he was told exactly what he was in for. He starts to feel queasy again. Maybe he just needs to eat something. Maybe he just needs to hear from Imogen

– before he can face an hour of *live bilingual* broadcast.

A WhatsApp from Miri saying '*Good Luck!*'

'Thanks,' he replies, but she's already offline.

Only an hour until he has to leave. He needs to get a grip: it's a great chance to promote the concert. He sees Joselito's spotted scarf on a hook by the front door and picks up the phone; talking to someone to get his mouth working might help.

'Lito! You left your scarf at Esme's – I meant to give it to you on Sunday.'

'You at home still? I'll be in your road in about ten minutes!'

'Great! Come up and help steady my nerves. What are you up to then?'

'Going to the Cinema shop. They've asked me to redesign their website – Miri put in a word for me. Apparently one of Ignacio's actors wants one too. Things are looking up!'

'My God, there's nothing she can't fix these days. But that's good, what a break – soon have plenty of work, you'll see.'

'Hope so. But I want plenty of concerts too – don't forget to keep mentioning it on air!'

⁑

'And now we have a very special guest *un invitado muy especial* with us today, does very few interviews – actor, musician and, of course, English student! – better known to many of you as that irresistible scoundrel *canalla* Diego in *Universidad* – Santiago Montoya!' Richi presses a button that produces cheering and applause. 'And knowing you ladies would like a visual, we are filming this to put on YouTube later!' An even louder burst of cheering. 'Welcome to the show, Santiago.'

'Thank you, thank you. I am... please to stay with you here.'

'You're pleased to be here – and speaking English! I have to tell you folks that like many of our guests, he said to me before the show: *cuidado con el inglés* – be careful with the English – but you'll try, won't you? *Lo intentarás, ¿no?*'

'Yes, yes, of course.'

'So Santi, how did you feel *cómo te sentiste* about being killed off *exterminado* in *La Universidad* after three years?'

'I… feel okay.'

'You *felt* okay.' Richi makes a rolling motion with his hand.

'It is time… things new.'

'Well yes – new roles, a concert… But first, a little of your background *tus antecedentes*. On the gitano – gypsy – side of your family, your father and grandfather were flamenco singers *cantaores*, your uncle Pedro is a guitarrista and of course there's your sister, Esmeralda Montoya, *pianista flamenca…*'

'Yes.'

'And you had a taste of musical stardom *estrellato* when you were in Tangoza with her and Francisco Fernandez. Fantastic track, shame there weren't more. And here it is.'

As the song comes on with all its bouncing enthusiasm, Santi recalls that it was Richi that did the show about one-hit wonders and said Tangoza was an unusual example of a band who turned out to be *less* than the sum of its parts.

'So while Esmeralda and Francisco went on to big solo careers, you went into acting. Had you always wanted to be an actor?'

'No. But I liked the The Flamenco Academy film. How you say? Natural for me.'

'And here's your beautiful guitar solo from it.'

The sadness of it fills Santi's headphones and calms him a little. Richi gives him a thumbs-up sign, and Santi hopes they will now be talking about his music.

The Lighthouse Keeper's Daughter

'So now you're in *Los Miserables* at Teatro Victoria. Great stuff.'

'Yes – a little *papel*…role, but the music is beautiful.'

'And preparing for an exciting film audition *audición* in New York, I hear – and improving your English *mejorando tu inglés* for it!'

'Yes. But first a concert with my… *grupo* in Sala Berlanga … *lunes el* ten, music from my *disco Dos Caminos* and new songs.'

'Next Monday. Great. Do I get a ticket *entrada*?'

'Of course!"

'And Santi –' He points a finger at him. 'I've been told *me han dicho* that a very special person will be at the concert.'

Francisco's coming – maybe one of his American musicians is over here, and he's going to bring whoever it is along. 'Er…'

'Santi! Don't say you don't know who I'm talking about *no me digas que no sabes de quién estoy hablando*. Your dedicated English teacher, all the way from England, Imogen Bradfield!'

'Ah… yes!' Miri must have told Ignacio.

'Now come on, we want to hear all about this tw-uition, tw-*enseñanza*… this Tw-omance!'

Santi forces a laugh. '*No, no*, she has listen *Dos Caminos* and sended… *sent* a tweet…. We started talking and help the one to the other with the *idiomas.*'

'Yes but it's now mostly Skype, I've heard. And you've invited her for the concert and an intensive course, ¡*un curso intensivo!*' Richi chuckles and winks at him.

'Yes, for to practise for audi-tion in New York. Also she has work—'

'But it will be very exciting *emocionante* to meet her after hours and hours of talking.'

'Yes.' He gets the rolling motion of the hand. 'Yes it will be very exciting,' he says, unable to come up with anything else.

Santi holds a decaffeinated coffee in a quiet corner of a café in plaza de Santo Domingo. He could do with walking home for a siesta before tonight's *Los Mis*, but what's the point when he's just going to lie there picking over his awful English on the show? To make matters worse, he's just WhatsApped Imogen a cute snap of the giant wooden camels in the square – adding to the stream of unanswered pale green boxes. Like the soft-headed Tw-omancer he's just been made out to be.

The phone rings in his hand. Tania again. That polite drink with her after she came to *Los Mis* seems to have given her the wrong message; every other day there's something from her now. 'Well done on the show!' she says. '*I* could have helped you with your English – why didn't you say?'

'Well, we're both busy, aren't we? Online teaching is the answer for me.'

'But now she's coming over to see you, your *exciting* teacher.'

'Richi was getting carried away.'

'And your concert. I'm still trying to see if I can get back from LA for it.'

'It's not a big deal – I wouldn't change your plans.' His phone vibrates in his hand. 'Sorry Tania, I've got to go…'

It's Miri. 'How was it?'

'My English just *disappeared*… And why did you have to tell Ignacio about Imogen coming over? Richi made a big thing of it.'

'Imogen was important for getting you on to the show – they like an English connection. Never mind, it spices things up a bit. The main thing is to keep you visible… and get people to come to your concert of course.'

The Lighthouse Keeper's Daughter

'Yes and it *will* be visible – he's putting it on YouTube. Aren't you angry about the Imogen Tw-omance talk?'

'Santi. You told me not to worry about Imogen, now you're bothered that I'm not.'

'Okay, okay. See you later.'

A bit of tortilla, a sip of coffee. So where the hell *is* his *special guest*? He picks up the phone again. Feels its negligible weight in his hand. *This* is where she is. Their friendship hangs in the air between their two separate lives, their paths don't cross, there are no mutual friends to remind one of the other's existence; at any time, their connection can disappear without consequence. But there is – there *would be* – a consequence; this intensive English will make a difference to his confidence in New York. And okay, yes – she makes a difference to him *here* too – he's sort of… used to having her around.

The plan was to look for some new jeans on Gran Vía on his way to the theatre, but he can't face bumping into anyone who might have heard him on the show, so he sets off down a road that will quietly take him back towards plaza de España and home, smiling to himself when his iPod selects Supertramp's 'Take the Long Way Home'.

A book with Atleti players drawn as soldiers with a cannon catches his eye in a shop window. He wanders in to have a browse; they said on the course that it was a good idea to read out loud every day, and he's finally finished Imogen's *Time Traveller's Wife*.

'Hello. Can I help you? Or did you want the class?'

A pale man with an English accent. He looks around him. 'Ha! I didn't see… you are English shop!'

'Yes, but we do have some Spanish books… Would you like to join our English conversation group?' He points to a little room through some beads.

'Well…'

'One of them brought homemade mince pies, an essential–'

'Ah, I know about it from a friend. Yes please.'

There's a lot of polite handshaking. The group consists of an English woman and her elderly father, two Spanish women wanting to keep up with their children at an international school, and a taxi driver. They pass him a tangy sweet pastry of fruit and spices, an insipid instant coffee, and an English newspaper that causes a burst of frighteningly good English about a princess and her baby.

An hour later, Santi arrives home with the Atleti book, the newspaper, the last mince pie, and the feeling that Imogen Bradfield isn't the only genial English person on the planet. He lies down on the sofa and reads out a paragraph from the football coverage near the back of the *Daily Telegraph*. Looks at his phone and resists checking it. Goes back to the paper. Checks his phone. Drops the paper. Groans and picks up the mess of enormous pages.

Then he sees it: Imogen's cliff. Beachy Head. His body goes cold. He's trying to read it, but even the words he knows are jumbling and out of order. It seems to be about the number of accidents there, and a woman – to *save… fallen… could have… falling… would have…* What?

He opens his phone. Drops it. Picks it up. Taps at it. He's forgotten to *slide to unlock*. Swipes at it. *Phone. Contacts.* The letter *I.* No, *B. Mobile…*

'Hello?'

She's there. Immediately. She's been there all along, he just had to touch the number.

'Santi?'

'You're okay… Are you okay?'

'There was an accident at the cliff… and it's been… a very difficult time in other ways too.'

The Lighthouse Keeper's Daughter

'*Ay*. I'm sorry, Imo-gen. I was worrying. I read something in English newspaper.'

'My friend Jules was hurt, but she's out of hospital now – and gone away with her boyfriend. And…uh…'

'What happen Imogen?'

'Oh… It's a long story.'

'Is ok *amiga mía*, I'm sitting down. Tell me.'

CHAPTER 19

WEDNESDAY, 5TH DECEMBER 2012
Madrid, Spain

The pilot has just said something about a view of Jersey. Imogen looks down at the yellow curve of St. Aubyn's Bay, as flat and safe as a child's drawing, where Dylan said he was going to take Jules for a stroll. Still horribly shaken, poor thing. They'd begged her to go with them, but she can't just instantly start being a happy big sister – especially when Dylan's holding back about his mother, saying that Imogen will have to wait for Dorothy to explain. It'll be more relaxing for Jules without her there.

Land. France. A happier memory of the cliff: looking out to the horizon after that first Skype with Santi, wishing the earth was flat so she could see as far as Spain. But she's going there now. A couple of days letting the last of the vertigo subside, a little research for the novel, then on Friday – the day before Santi would have been collecting her from the airport – she'll tell him she's already there. Perhaps they'll have an early dinner together before he goes off to do *Los Miserables*.

She can't believe she's actually going to meet him, after spending – she pencils a calculation on the back page of her *Madrid* book – maybe fifty hours with him. Extraordinary really, that they've

The Lighthouse Keeper's Daughter

shared so much, and yet they've never shared a coffee. A car. A pudding. A kiss... Whoops, where did that come from? She carries on with the grammar book until being asked to translate *you should have come to the concert!* makes her start daydreaming about Santi's. It's okay to daydream – in fact, it's an essential part of the research.

The captain is saying Madrid is just over the hills. The plane starts to tip; they are circling, apparently, but what? She can't see anything resembling a capital city yet. Although perhaps there's a density of building over there, a couple of skyscrapers. Santi's Madrid, where he's lived his whole life, three hundred kilometres to the nearest coast.

An hour later, she's hurtling along a dual carriageway with a taxi driver keeping up a rapid commentary over an animated discussion on the radio. The hotel receptionist speaks language-tape Spanish to her, but she can't hear him above a couple of Americans asking for directions to the Prado. She goes upstairs to a cosy little slice of an apartment and flops onto the bed. How is she going to cope with Spanish here? She's either too slow or too deaf to understand a word.

She gets out her phone and does another WhatsApp reply to Dylan saying everything's fine but she just needs time, and Facebooks Ollie with a blurred Colombus standing on top of a fountain. Then she notices that she didn't send yesterday's message to Santi explaining how she didn't have her phone on Monday. She decides to call him later, puts the phone on charge, and goes down to make a start on Madrid.

Four o'clock. At home it would be dark by now, but here the sun has a little warmth and will be shining for another couple of hours – even if it leaves shady places bitterly cold. Places like the top of the tour bus, once it's out of the open space of the *plaza*.

The woman's voice in the headset is painful at full volume and inaudible at less, so she settles for just following the route with her finger on the map.

They arrive at a sort of Spanish Trafalgar Square – and the fountain where the Real Madrid fans celebrate. Not Santi or his fictional counterpart Sami, they support the plucky underdog Atletico Madrid. Now they're going down the Spanish Oxford Street, *Gran Vía* – and she spots the Casa del Libro shop where Santi might have bought the Spanish version of *The Time Traveller's Wife*. Plaza de España now, so they must be near Santi's place. She scans the market stalls and entrance to the metro just in case he's there. There's a park up on a hill, where they might go for an English-practising stroll. Now they're bounding away from Santi's area. A palace. A cathedral. She's getting very cold, tired… and wakes to find that she's missed the art galleries but is driving down the edge of the vast Retiro park where Santi used to take Pato and now goes running.

She feels buzzily nauseous as she goes up in the hotel lift. Otherwise described as being *nervous*. What? She's spoken to him on the phone a couple of times before, and there have been hours of Skype, so what's the matter with her? His voice is low and resonant; it sometimes feels like he's the only person she can hear. Look at this message: how can she be nervous of someone who's sent her a picture of enormous wooden camels?

She doesn't have to call; the phone rings in her hand. He's breathless with concern after somehow having come across that article about Beachy Head in the *Telegraph*, and asks her what's happened. She finds herself telling him about her father's diary. She can't understand why she hasn't told him before; he's a caring, calming listener – even with the odd language stumble between them.

 The Lighthouse Keeper's Daughter

'Imogen… you are tired, *mucho estrés, ¿no?* I understand if you don't come on Saturday.'

'Well,' she says, 'the thing is, I wanted to get as far as possible away from that cliff, so… I'm already here!'

'¿*Aquí*? In Madrid? Imo-gen! Where?'

'An apartment-hotel in the Almagro area. I'm doing a couple of days of research for my novel.'

'Ah yes, your *personaje*, your charac-ter, visits Madrid, I remember. But we must meet soon!'

'Okay!'

'Tomorrow I'm working with my uncle Pedro in his house, but you can come to have coffee, or maybe to eat… I will tell you, *¿vale?* But now I have to go to the theatre – *¡hasta pronto!*'

Tomorrow they'll be doing that kiss on each cheek thing. Dylan said he'll be into 'products' and heavily after-shaved, but Jules disagreed – maybe just a slight hint of ham, she said with a giggle. Touch, scent… he'll be there: a real, warm, breathing human being. One that has nothing – and she must remember this as hard as she can – *nothing* to do with Sami in her novel.

CHAPTER 20

THURSDAY, 6TH DECEMBER 2012
Madrid, Spain

'*Good morning Imogen! Are we meeting really? Are you real??! Jajaja*' he types, then waits for a few minutes.

'*I think so!*'

'*:-o*'

'*:-O*'

'*I have talked with my uncle and aunt, come to lunch, kitchen and vegetalbes.*'

'*HA! CHICKEN and vegetables!! Hahaha :-D*'

'*Uff :-(*'

'*I would love roast kitchen and vestíbulos / halls!!*'

'*We need to practise vocabulario of the house, teacher!*'

'*What time shall I come?*'

'*Wait moment.*'

'What time shall I say?' he asks them.

Aunt Elena shrugs and looks over to Uncle Pedro.

'Well I would want three,' Uncle Pedro says, 'but an English woman will be expecting lunch at one o'clock. Let's meet her in the middle, shall we?'

Joselito gives Santi a mock blow to the stomach. 'And how's

your middle? Is it worse than a concert?'

'Oh for God's sake, it's no big deal,' Santi says.

'So you keep telling us,' Uncle Pedro says, finishing his coffee and standing up. 'Tell her two o'clock and let's get on.'

'I'll see you later, I've got tons of work to do,' Joselito says.

'So how many websites has Miri got you down for now then?'

'Four, including the re-hash of Ignacio's. She's… I'm very grateful.'

'Come on Santi.' Uncle Pedro watches him finish on his phone and move towards the door. 'Your guitar?' He points to the case and shakes his head.

Santi picks it up and follows his uncle down to the studio in the basement. He needs the work, but feels even less enthusiastic than usual about playing on one of the cheesy flamenco-lite production albums or indie film scores that his uncle churns out these days. How can the guy sink to this, after those years of *flamenco puro*? Surely the house is paid off now, he should be taking it easy – but he's busier than ever.

He watches his uncle at the desk; he's pretty deft with the controls and the computer for someone who says arthritis is limiting his playing. 'So what d'you need?'

'Well first, just one more upbeat track on the Spanish Holiday album.'

A pop-*rumba* fills the room. God, if Imogen could hear this. Or maybe she will, in the adverts on her English television. He starts playing along to it.

'Yes, that's the idea. Let's get it down.'

The track comes on again. Luckily Imogen doesn't watch much television; she listens to music, watches films or 'stumbles around' on her electric piano that Ewan so kindly brought down for her…

Pedro stops the track. 'Come on Santi, I've deliberately left you room to give it just a little of your edge.'

'Sorry.'

The track starts again, but Santi misses his entry.

'Sorry.'

'Stop saying sorry and stop thinking... of other things.'

This time Santi imagines himself playing the guitar on a beach to a group of pale-haired English girls.

'Perfect. Right. And next – I'm very excited about this – a drama for Telecinco! About Lorca would you believe! But during the early 1920s when he learnt flamenco guitar from a couple of gypsies and became involved in the Festival of *Cante Jondo*. I'll show you what I've got so far...'

※

'Ten past. Maybe she's lost.' Santi scans the street outside the window.

'She's smart, isn't she? I'm sure she can read a map,' Joselito says, laying the table.

'What does Miri think of her coming over here to see you, this internet friend?' Aunt Elena asks.

'She's keen for Santi to improve his English,' Joselito answers for him. 'She says Imogen's already made a huge difference.'

Santi turns to him. 'Really? She's never said that to *me*.' He looks out again. 'Oh where *is* she?' He taps his phone and puts it to his ear. 'Imogen? Are you losed... lost? Do you have a map?' he says in English. He flaps a hand at his sniggering cousin. 'Ah... Okay, wait, I come to find you... Really? Good! Okay.' He puts his phone away and tells them that she's just found the road.

'Glory be,' Uncle Pedro says.

The doorbell makes them start. The three men look at each other.

The Lighthouse Keeper's Daughter

'Poor girl, it's raining. I better let her in, if you lot aren't going to,' Elena says, and ambles into the hall.

They can hear Elena greeting Imogen like an old friend, and an uncertain response followed by laughter.

Then she's there. Smiling, taller than all of them – except for possibly Santi – but also somehow fragile with her pale glassy eyes, speckled face and strands of pinkish hair falling over the collar of her coat.

'Imo-gen!' Santi moves forward in a daze and hugs her, trying to connect this alien creature with the forthright Imogen in his phone, then introduces her to the others. Uncle Pedro takes her funny coat with wooden toggles. She's wearing a nicely filled navy jumper, a denim skirt with a stitched bunch of English flowers and some mercifully flat-heeled boots. After an awkward exchange, somebody has fetched her an orange juice and set her down in an armchair. Now her mouth is open in concentration as she tries to understand Elena, poor thing.

'A bit louder aunty, her hearing isn't perfect.'

Elena repeats her question.

'From the South of England. I live to the sea,' she answers in her clunky Spanish.

'*By* the sea,' Santi corrects her out of habit, 'and in an old lighthouse!'

Elena asks everyone to sit at the table.

'She's for eating,' Joselito says quickly to Santi with a nudge.

'Sorry?' Imogen asks.

'He says… it's time to eat,' Santi explains in English, giving the smirking Joselito a kick under the table.

Pedro describes visiting London on tour in the nineteen seventies, Joselito asks her about the Olympics, and Elena tells them to let her eat. Santi wonders why she's come to lunch at all; she's barely glancing at him, and doesn't seem to have much appetite. Then Pedro asks her if she'd like to watch them record the music for a film. She nods enthusiastically, makes a big deal of thanking Aunt Elena for her lunch and comes down to the studio with them.

Pedro shows her the notes from the session with the director, explains the numbers of the frames, the difference between background and narrative music. He is clearly delighted with the way she understands how the mood you need for the music is often at odds with what the characters are doing or saying…

Weren't they on some kind of time scale for this? He strums some chords they were going to use. They look over for a moment, but then Pedro carries on talking – now, for God's sake, about how he's recently had to upgrade his software to reduce latency in the recording. Imogen nods and says she needs an upgrade to her brain in order to reduce the latency of her understanding of Spanish.

Santi strums louder, putting an end to their laughter.

His uncle winces. 'Santi! It's not that scene yet anyway.'

They go for a recording of the bit with just a few twanged strings, but there's lots of takes to get it quite right with the dialogue. He glances over at Imogen. She smiles and turns her gaze to the computer screen. When he next looks over, she's gazing at his mobile on the desk, her own just inches away. Has she deliberately put them that close? Those phones that have connected their worlds, now finally in the same room.

They move on to the next scene, the one needing energy and some *rasgueado* – the sort of thing she likes in *Dos Caminos* – but she's getting up and saying she has to go.

'Where?' Santi asks.

'You need to work. I need to buy a thing.'

'What thing?'

'A… string for my mobile to my computer, that I forget,' she says, with her adorable lack of 'r's.

He starts describing how to get to Arturo Soria plaza just down the road, but she's already seen it on the map. She thanks Uncle Pedro and tells them not to come up, they should carry on working. Giving Santi an odd little queenly wave, she turns to the stairs.

It will be different at Esme's, they'll be concentrating on practising his English – that's why she's here. Although of course there'll be Esme and Darius, the twins, Fran visiting, his mother coming round…

'Wait!'

She turns round. A little smile on her face.

'Uncle, I'll come very early tomorrow, okay?' Pedro nods, eyebrows raised. Santi puts down his guitar and turns to Imogen. 'I'll take you to the plaza, and then to the hotel before I drive to the theatre.'

><

Imogen sees that Santi was right about his car being nothing special – just a two-door something or other in the usual Spanish tin-can colour, but plenty of CDs.

'You are driving?' he asks.

'No!'

'*Bueno*, the other side, woman.'

Of course. They get in, and he turns to her.

'Imo-gen.'

'Yes?'

'You are here,' he says in English.

'Yes.'

He gives a little nod and a closed smile. 'Is very good, is all.'

'*It's* very good, *that's* all,' she corrects him.

'Ha!' He throws back his head and thumps the steering wheel with his palms. 'Now here is the Imogen I know!' He starts the car.

Wasn't she herself at his uncle's house? It was *he* who was so quiet, but she's not about to argue with him when he's got that turn-up-at-the-edges smile on his face.

They pull onto the main road. She's only ever been to sunny seaside Spain; these green verges and parades of small shops could be a small town in Surrey. They slow down outside a glass-fronted modern building and drive into the car park. Google described it as a major shopping centre for North-East Madrid, but it turns out to be a little two-storeyed mall suffering from anglophilia.

She points to a bright red pillar-box and an apparently functional English phone box by the escalator. 'What the…?'

'I know, I know. It is everywhere, look,' he says in English, showing her shops called Pretty Ballerina and Moon, then another with a window promoting Oxford University sweat tops – all to the sound of David Bowie's *Let's Dance*.

'Oh but I like *that*!' She's looking over at the enormous Bethlehem model village. They buy a USB cable at a stand and sit in the café next to the display.

'So you bought… *brought* your computer here for writing? But you have said you write in little *cuadernos*.'

'Notebooks. Yes, when I'm out. I always have one with me.'

'Now?'

She opens her bag and holds up a little red elasticated book with a pen hooked into it.

He puts his hand out. 'I can see?'

'No!' She laughs.

'Why?'

'I… never show it to anybody. Anyway, my handwriting's impossible.'

'*Por eso* is no problem to show me.' He grabs it again, this time taking hold of it, but she pulls it away.

'Do you show people a track you have half done?'

'Yes! Well maybe not much…'

'There you go then.'

Now an Elton John track comes on.

'Is funny we are having our first coffee here, two people that hate shopping,' Santi says.

'Yes. Recently I couldn't even face going shopping for just one pair of jeans.'

'Me too! I need good jeans for New York. Or this is what tells me Miri.'

Miri: a timely reminder. She's a bit too enchanted with this exotic creature with the sweetest smile – who is also somehow the guy who's been keeping her company in her phone for the last few months.

'So *what are you up to* tomorrow Imo-gen?' he asks, looking pleased with himself.

She grins and gives him a thumbs-up for his English. 'Well… I might go to the zoo and see the pandas.'

'The zoo? Your English woman who visits Madrid, she would go to the Prado first, no?'

'It depends what's on her mind.'

'What *is* on her mind?'

While she's wondering how to answer to this, Santi's phone rings. Then he's talking about something with a *cariño* – a darling – who is expecting him somewhere. Someone who will easily understand his slurred rapid Spanish. She sits back in her chair and listens to Elton singing about '*two hearts living in two separate worlds.*'

CHAPTER 21

FRIDAY, 7TH DECEMBER 2012
Madrid, Spain

'*Buenos días!*'

'Jules!' Imogen says into her phone. 'How are you doing?'

'I'm doing okay. Really I am. We both are.'

'Oh good, good. Jersey's—'

'So come on, how did it go yesterday? We want to know!' She can hear Dylan saying something and laughing in the background.

'Well… God, I was *so* nervous I got hopelessly bloody lost. And then there he actually was, but with family around and I had to eat this oily stew. But later we went shopping.'

'*Shopping*? You? What's going on here!'

A loud bleeping.

'Oh, it's the hotel phone. I'll call you later okay?'

She picks up the receiver.

'Imo-gen!' Santi's voice. 'Take your things, I collect you in twenty minutes to go to Esme's house.'

'But it's tomorrow I'm—'

'Esme is back from tour and she say you can come now. I take you when I am on way to my uncle.'

'Oh! But—'

'It is the only time I can see... practise English with you today.'

'But I'm still in bed.'

He chuckles. 'O-kay, how you say, horry?'

'Hurry up?'

'Yes!'

Forget breakfast. No, she can't manage this without breakfast. A frenzied shower. Teeth. Mascara. Jeans, jumper. Everything thrown anyhow into the case. Reception telling her there's a gentleman waiting for her downstairs.

The doors open and he's there, pacing the hall. 'Good morning!' He gives her the two kiss thing, then touches her hair. 'A little wet *ratón*! Well done. We go.'

'Sorry, I've still got to check out.'

'¿*Qué*?'

She points to Reception, where two male staff members nod at them with a knowing half-smile.

'No, no, already I have check-outed you.'

She follows him to the car.

'Look you *can't* do this, not as well as the flight.'

'Esme paid, I did the check-outing.'

'*Esme*?'

'She says you will help her English too. You talk with her on Twitter private messages, no?'

'A little. But all in Spanish.'

'Ha! Her English is bad. Good luck!'

'Oh.'

'Imo-gen! Is joke, you no have to—'

'*It's* a joke, you *don't* have to...'

'Uff I'm driving the car! But you are right, I have to stop talk like Manuel in Fawlty Towers.'

'Oh God, I should never have shown you that.'

'Ah, I forgot say, tonight I have some tickets for the show, you can come with Esme, okay?'

'Great!'

'Already Darius and the boys have seen it, so she is happy to go with you. It is only small theatre, remember, don't expect what you saw in London, the stage *rotando*…' He makes a rotating motion with his hand. 'And don't miss my lines – I have only four!'

'I promise.'

'And afterwards we all go for a drink.'

A bar with everyone talking in loud Spanish against a blaring TV…

'Imo-gen!'

'*Afterwards* – good word, well done.'

'Yes, but why so…' He makes a long face.

'I'm not!'

'Don't worry, you will have a good *intérprete* with you,' he says, patting her leg.

They turn onto the Arturo Soria road, passing the little anglophilic mall. She should be saying something, speaking English to him, but she's distracted by the handprint he seems to have left on her thigh. Not counting the universal double-kiss thing, he has already given her two (brief) hugs, several pats on the shoulder, an arm grab when she stepped out in front of a reversing van in the car park and a stroke of her hair – but the thigh… Keeping her face pointed forwards, she steals a look at him. Dylan was wrong; he's not into 'products'. He hasn't used a hairdryer; the damp black hair falling on to his hoody doesn't look like it's even seen a comb. He is shaved but not after-shaved. She breathes in deeply; no, he doesn't smell of anything. She almost wants to catch a bit of morning breath – anything to make him just a bit less damn gorgeous.

The Lighthouse Keeper's Daughter

His eyes turn to her and then ahead again. 'I'm sorry, very busy today. Tomorrow also, rehearsal with the group and two shows again. You will have time for *investigaciones*… re-search. But from Sunday I will concentrate on your English, and take you to something, okay? '

She looks over and smiles, but he's busy turning into a quiet, tree-lined road with heavily gated driveways and glimpses of impressive homes. He stops the car in the entrance to an American colonial style house with what looks like a huge LEGO construction in one of the upstairs windows. The gate starts to draw across.

'Don't worry, she has a *palacio* but she is not a queen.'

They drive in and find a space among a sports car, a people carrier and two smaller vehicles.

'Ha! My mother is here. My aunt has told her of you and now she wants to look.'

Before she can ask what he means, he is out of the car and getting her bag out of the boot.

Then she's saying *hola* and bending down to kiss Santi's mother's cheeks, smiling helplessly as the woman says something in consonant-free Andalusian Spanish. Esmeralda, who is almost her own height and has a wide sculpted face like Santi's, is friendly but formidably striking even in a grey track suit with her wild hair in a ponytail.

Also in a track suit is the young Romanian au pair, Darius – the 'secret partner' Santi has told her about. 'Welcome, Imogen!' he says in English. 'I am one more English student I hope!'

'No, no, *es profesora exclusiva*!' Santi says, and they all laugh. 'I have to go now, I'll see you after the show.'

Esme takes her through to a large sitting room overlooking a covered pool, a lawn with football goals and enough wooden play apparatus for a village playground. Imogen asks after the boys and learns that Eduardo and Emilio are looking forward to trying out their English on her when they return from their bilingual school. Esme asks about Imogen's son, but appears to have difficulty comprehending her description of the Mixology course in Barcelona that he will be going to after his A levels.

A housekeeper brings a tray of coffee and mixed nuts. Esme is saying something about Imogen's teaching, Santi's English or maybe something else being a miracle. Santi's *mamá* – whose name she hasn't caught – smiles but fixes her steadily with deep-set black eyes.

Then the Spanish Inquisition starts. *Mamá* wants to know who is looking after Oliver, whether he likes boarding school, and whether she has a boyfriend. Esme wants to know if the novel will be available in Spanish, and Imogen says she doesn't know, and just manages not to add that she'll be lucky if it's ever available in English. *Mamá* asks if her father is a writer.

'No, he was a lighthouse keeper,' Imogen says, pleased she can remember the word in Spanish.

'A lighthouse keeper!' *Mamá* repeats, her eyes shining. 'And you live in an old lighthouse! So you must love the sea.'

'Yes.'

The old woman seems to be saying something about hating it here.

'I... like other things here.'

They look at her, waiting for her to explain.

'I'm looking forward to Santi's concert and other live flamenco, visiting the pandas, the Retiro Park...'

Esme says something about a local park for jogging, and seems to be inviting her to come to a gym or pool this morning.

'Oh thank you, but I have to do a little work, making notes for the book.'

'So… you make notes about places and… *people*?'

'Well, all sorts of things.'

Darius looks at his watch and points out that they need to go soon to be in time for something.

'Let me quickly show you your room,' Esme says, and takes her up the grand staircase in the hall to a white bedroom whose balcony overlooks the garden.

'This is *lovely*! Thank you so much.'

Once alone, she sets up her laptop on the dressing table and sits down in a comfy armchair with her notebook. Sucks the top of her pen. Looks out of the window. Around the room. Back at the lines she should be filling with notes. The story *isn't* about him. Of course it isn't. Her guy's a musician, not an actor. A singer, not a guitarist. *Tall*, for a Spaniard. He lives in… well, that's still to be decided, but it won't be near plaza de España, and with so many of Santi's relatives round here, it won't be in Arturo Soria either. He's called Sami, not Santi – although later she should change his name, start it with a letter the other end of the alphabet… It's hard, creating a character out of the inverse of someone. Except, in essence, she isn't – she *can't* – because she wants her readers to feel the same as she does about him.

※

The theatre is more school hall than West End; she needn't have bothered with the itchy black dress. Esme is comfortable in a loose glittery top over jeans, her trademark locks hidden in a plaited ponytail – but still gets snapped by a few mobiles.

His sister is looking forward to hearing Santi sing; apparently he was told he had a good voice when he did the drama course a few years ago, but this is the first time he's used it.

'Why doesn't he sing in his group?' Imogen asks.

'Wrong type of voice, he says.'

'Really? Or is he just a bit shy?'

Esme looks at her and says something like, how well she knows him from over the computer, or how could she know that from the computer… but the dramatic first chords of the orchestra are filling the hall and she is soon looking for Santi among a chain gang in nineteenth century France.

Imogen has seen the show in London and used to have the CD, but this small company with their modest theatre and limited run are giving it all they've got. Esme gets a tissue out and hands one to Imogen after Fantine's '*I dreamed a dream*', and they are both so enthralled with the hilarious innkeepers' scene that they almost don't spot Santi in the second row of drunken customers. Then later, just as she feared, there's Santi looking irresistibly idealistic as a student rebel at the barricade, all open white shirt and tight trousers with a red, white and blue scarf round his hips. Esme nudges her and whispers '*qué guapo, ¿no?*'

Imogen smiles awkwardly, not wanting to admit to finding Santi gorgeous.

They've moved on to the bit that always lets it down: the stupid love-at-first-sight between Marius and Cosette. Just a glimpse of her perfect outline and sumptuous tresses, and *ding* – Marius has made up his mind. Now they're singing the '*In my Life*' duet – it's very pretty of course, but then so are they. Meanwhile Marius' spirited and helpful pal Eponine, a slightly ratty little creature, is standing to one side interjecting comments about how these are 'words he'll never say to me'.

※

 The Lighthouse Keeper's Daughter

Santi and fellow 'student' Carlos knock on Eponine's door.

'Come in boys,' she says.

They put their heads round. 'Never mind, *we* love you!' they say in chorus.

'Yeah, yeah.' She goes over and gives each of them a hug. 'Oh God, how would I cope without you two?' She pats Carlos' shoulder. 'How did the Lion King audition go?'

He shrugs. 'Don't know yet.'

'We want you on the tour, gorgeous! And you too Santi – what the hell d'you want to ponce around being Lorca for?'

'Uh, but by the time I *haven't* got it, you'll all be halfway round the country.'

She shakes her head. 'So where are we eating tonight then? Oh no – you've got your English teacher here. What are you doing Santi? Go and see her!'

Santi makes his way to the Stage Door. His sister is full of praise for the show, while Imogen, looking cute in a fluffy grey jacket, seems lost for words or is struggling with her Spanish, the poor thing. There are also two make-up ladies from *Universidad* and a couple from his English class; it's going to have to be the bigger place on the corner. In the middle of the drinks order at the bar, Miri, Ignacio and Joselito walk in. He wants to introduce Miri and Imogen to each other, but he's being taken to a corner.

'You came to the show *again*?'

'Haha no,' Ignacio says, 'but we thought we'd find you here. We've had some news.'

'Oh?' Three earnest faces. 'What?'

Ignacio looks at Miri. It seems that's all it takes these days for her to follow instructions.

'Santi… they're not doing the audition. Not for the first round. They want virtuals.'

'What? When did—'

'They rang this afternoon. Well, *their* afternoon...' Ignacio grabs Santi's shoulder and shakes it. 'Don't worry, I've got you into a great studio for all day Monday. Plenty of time to record the two scenes and update your showreel.'

'But—'

'Just think – four more days and you can relax! Take a break from English lessons!'

CHAPTER 22

SUNDAY, 9TH DECEMBER 2012
Madrid, Spain

Miri's asking about the scenes, the choice of clips in the showreel. A few months ago, she wouldn't have discussed work minutes after gasps of ecstasy.

'I thought you were going to your mother's for the weekend,' Santi says.

'Well, when Ignacio called me with the news about the audition…'

'He said you should keep my spirits up in the way you know best… yeah, I get it.'

She laughs. 'Coffee?'

He nods and watches her spring out of bed. Gone is the Miri who used to want to lie in bed cuddling afterwards.

He reaches for his phone. Texts from Ignacio with details of tomorrow's session. Imogen tweeting a blue *madrileño* sky and retweeting an exclamation-marked reply from her friend Jules; Joselito tweeting much the same and retweeting a similar burst of enthusiastic reply from… @MireyaGonzalez84.

'Since when were you on Twitter?' he asks as she puts a mug down next to him.

'Er… Friday. Didn't you see I 'followed' you? I need it for work now.'

'*Ignacio* work. So has he made your day official yet?'

'Yes, but… *four* days a week.' She sips her coffee.

'*Four*? Miri! Don't you—'

'I'm dropping down to just Saturdays at the shop after Christmas, they've been very good about waiving the notice. Oh and, I've not had a chance to tell you… They're desperate for me to cover tomorrow night's book-signing event, so I won't be able to make the concert.'

'What! There's really nobody else who can hand out plastic cups of wine? Hang on, there's usually a monologue or something, wouldn't happen to be one of your other *clients* would it?'

'Well it's a duo, and Antonio's been asked to step in for—'

'Fuck's sake!'

'Santi please, there'll be other concerts, I'm not happy about it but…'

He's out of bed and into the shower room, slamming the door behind him. Bloody charming; she'd rather schmooze around with a bunch of actors than come to his first concert in ages. Or maybe she wants to be there to hold Antonio's hand – or any other part of him that becomes available to her as the night goes on. Washing himself vigorously, he somehow knocks her special shampoo off the shelf and clattering to the floor, splatting special turquoise gloop all over the place.

'Fuck! Well *I'm* not clearing that up.'

'Calm *down*, Santi!'

'No I won't fucking calm down! You'll just have to call Ignacio for instructions on how best to manage me!'

He comes out in his towel and starts pulling on clothes.

The old Miri would have been upset, but this one's sitting here with the calm half-smile of someone accustomed to dealing with a range of artistic tantrums.

'What d'you want for breakfast?' she asks.

'I'll stop off on the way.'

'Why don't you ask Imogen to come *here*? Sunday: your mother will be round, the boys jumping about, and isn't Fran visiting today? I'm sure she'd *love* to be invited.' She leans back on the pillows and watches him taking far too long to choose a jumper. 'You think I'm bothered about her being alone with you, don't you.' A little chuckle. 'Or that *she'll* be bothered – a Jane Austen woman in need of a chaperone.'

'Jenostin?'

'You know, *Pride and Prejudice*, lots of frustrated, uptight women with convoluted dialogue.'

'She's not like that!'

'I didn't say she was. But you'll get more done here, for sure. Ah, and Pato called – did she text you? She's had a sleep over round the corner with that friend in Pintor Rosales and wants to have lunch with you.'

He looks at his phone; there is indeed a text from Pato. Typical: most weekends he's trying to find a gap for them in her busy social agenda, but the minute she knows he's busy she insists on seeing him.

'So when are you getting the train to your mamá's?' he asks her.

'I'm not – Joselito said he'd drive me over there on the way to see his brother in Aranjuez.' She looks at her watch. 'He'll be here in about an hour.'

A bit out of his way, but then Joselito will do anything for a woman – even someone else's. 'Hey – maybe he could stop by at Esme's on his way and pick up Imo-gen.'

Joselito – the smirking young cousin at Santi's uncle's, but in charming good spirits driving along in his noisy little car. Apparently he's dropping Miri off somewhere too. Now he's asking her if she met Miri, or if she knows Miri, and something about somebody leaving early or quickly. Perhaps it looked like she left as soon as Miri arrived at the bar. She tries to explain that it was Esme who wanted to go, but it's hard without knowing the word for jetlag.

They're now in Santi's road. She was here yesterday, having bought a wallet for Ollie in the plaza de España market. Knowing Santi wasn't around, she walked up past the cinema shop and the cinemas and then on and on, just getting a feel for the quiet street with its modest shops and corner cafes, tempting side roads leading towards the parque del Oeste. Occasionally looking up at the tall apartment buildings either side – ornate with balustrades, sleek-modern, or drably functional – and wondering which was Santi's.

Joselito stops the car outside a minimarket and they get out. She looks up but can only see the underside of a balcony.

'Come, I show you,' he says, taking her arm to cross the street for a better look.

'*Now* you speak English!'

It's a beautifully made but unconsciously shabby building – rather like one of its occupants.

'He has the litt-el one at top, look it,' he says, pointing. 'Nice.'

They go into a dark hallway and deal with a lift in which you have to open the gates and close them after you. Joselito pats her arm. 'Good teacher, ¿no? He need you!'

The door opens. Miri, smiling and looking effortlessly lovely with her hair tumbling over a tight sweater. Imogen fights off a ridiculous punch of hopelessness.

'Hello Imo-chen, how are you?' she says in Spanish. 'Just one day – how lucky you are here!'

Imogen is starting to feel like an anxiously awaited doctor – but the patient is nowhere to be seen. They are in Santi's tidy but cluttered living room: a couple of guitar cases, a *cajón*, several unruly plants and a large bookcase mostly filled with CDs and faded photographs. At the end of the room there are the double doors onto the terrace where they once compared his rooftop view with her clifftop one.

Miri has gone off to find him.

'Your teacher's here – come out you naughty boy!' Joselito calls out in Spanish.

Santi appears in the doorway, looking rather serious or tired. There's talk about coffee but it seems Joselito and Miri need to leave and she soon finds herself alone with this worryingly sullen student.

'Coffee?' he asks, already turning to leave the room.

'No thanks.'

He turns back. 'I don't have some tea.'

'You say, I don't have *any* tea.'

'Yes. Orange juice?'

This would also give her a tummy ache. As will the tension here, if it doesn't stop soon. 'Is there something the matter?'

He looks at her blankly.

She repeats herself in Spanish.

'No, no! I'm sorry, a little tired.'

'Shall I come back later?'

'No! Come, we can work now,' he says, sitting down in an armchair.

Work. A reminder of why she is here, but she was expecting a bit of fun and a palatable beverage with it.

'Look, I'm going to the shop to buy some tea and hopefully soya milk, I can't handle going without them today. Anything you need while I'm there?'

'Hand-el?'

'Cope, er... *aguantar*?'

'Ah.'

'And meanwhile perhaps you can get a handle on whatever it is that's bothering you?' Too bad if he doesn't quite understand this.

He grins at last. '*Llega* Imo-gen!'

'Yes, I've arrived! And I'll be back again in a mo.'

'Ha yes, *see you in a mo.*'

She gets into the lift and sinks down to the ground again. Maybe he's had a row with Miri. No – why is she so quick to think that? Miri seemed fine. More likely he's just anxious about tomorrow; he's been waiting a long time for this.

The shop surprises her with Earl Grey, Darjeeling and a choice of soya milks.

He opens the door, takes the shopping bag from her and disappears. Comes back. 'Imo-gen! Follow to the kitchen!'

'I imagined your apartment would have lots of flamenco red.'

'Ha no, blue helps relax, a bit of sea,' he says. 'Show me how make English tea.'

They return to the living room with drinks and biscuits, sitting down opposite each other.

'This is where you Skype – I recognise the crazy plant!' Imogen says.

He smiles. 'Imo-gen, I'm sorry I have... you know when you have a feeling that something is not al-right but you don't understand? I have this.'

The Lighthouse Keeper's Daughter

'Not all right?'

'Things that happen with work, my manager... there is something that *me pone nervioso, ¿no*? But I try to forget this now.'

'You can forget it, or you can talk about it if you prefer.'

'Is the tea good?'

She takes a sip. 'Yes. Well, not bad. Okay, I'm ready.' She takes copies of the scenes out of her bag.

'*Madre mía*, all the notes you make!' he says, noticing her scribbles. 'And...' He leans over and pulls out a Lorca book. 'I have this in Spanish! Imo-gen, you work too hard by me.'

'*For* you. No I don't. It's interesting, and anyway I also need to know about Lorca, for my novel.'

He nods his head slowly. 'Is...wait...' He holds up a finger. '*Beyond the call of duty.*'

'Brilliant! You're getting too good.'

'No, no.' He shakes his head.

'Of course you are. Soon you won't need me.'

He looks at her with concern. 'Do I have to need you?'

'Of course not!' she says, feeling warmth rush into her cheeks. 'But it will be different when we don't need to do so much English.'

'Yes but listen, you know, your Spanish... it's not good.'

'Thanks a lot!'

'You need to come another time to go to the school where goes Darius...uff no, *where Darius goes.*'

'That's what he and Esme said yesterday!'

'Yes, and they said this to me. But of course I was thinking this too, or...' He grins. 'I *was going* to think it, when I leave off thinking of myself at the moment.'

She laughs. 'It would be great.'

'You need Madrid for the book too. Tonight we can go to a *tablao flamenco* where there is much inspiration for you, you will see.'

'Oh!' It's not over. Of course it isn't. She's coming back. But she needs to forget about that now and concentrate on helping him with the audition that could mean it might be a very long time before she can.

He's taken her copy of the scenes and is putting a lot of lines through them.

'What are you doing?'

'It is almost only the monologues now. How lazy they are, no? And after I kill myself to learn everything.'

He gives the sheets back to Imogen.

'Bloody hell.'

'But okay...' He points out of the double doors to the blue sky. 'Because we will have time to enjoy a little walk before we meet Pato for lunch.'

'Oh – it'll be lovely to meet her!'

'Then later I take you and Pato back to Arturo Soria when I go to Uncle Pedro's... We start, okay?'

He stands up. Paces the room. The deck of the Southampton to New York liner. The depressed Lorca, feeling betrayed by Salvador Dali and that little handsome sculptor friend, is anxious about his trip to New York but composing a happy letter for his parents.

'*Joder* I sound like Manuel,' he says at the end of it.

'No you do *not*!'

'Deli-shus was right? You understand all of the words?'

'I was too involved to notice!'

He goes over and gives her a quick hug.

'Do it again so I can check the pronunciation.'

Before long they move onto the party scene. A Lorca who has confronted his horror of the 'furious rhythm' and 'geometric anguish' of New York, been inspired by the people of Harlem, and – a repressed minority himself – become more accepting of his homosexuality. The poet in his sparkling element, and producing some of his best work.

Maybe it's the shortened script, maybe it's just her, but she isn't seeing an energised Lorca in the living room right now. It's a Santi who she suspects is secretly delighted not to have to confront a panel of New Yorkers, a chap perhaps a bit betrayed by somebody, but widely loved and appreciated – a Lorca who never got off the boat.

'You are not sure,' he says, folding his arms.

'There were just a couple of words, but it's fine.'

He eyes her carefully. 'Fine *significa* very good or just o-kay? I never understand.'

'It's the poem – I find it hard.'

'*You* find it hard!'

'Why don't they ask you to play the guitar?'

'Already they know I can.'

'Yes, but how you *are* when you play… I mean, look here.' She finds a tabbed place in the book. 'This could be the actual party in the scene.'

He sits down next to her and leans over to see where she's pointing. 'It was more the piano at parties, no?'

'Well here it says "he sang *Soleares* and accompanied himself on the guitar". Oh – have you seen that guitar poem? From before the New York period.' She pulls out a stapled sheet of favourite Lorca quotes.

He reads the Spanish version in silence, except for the last bit. "*Oh guitarra! Corazón malherido por cinco espadas.*'

'Oh guitar! Heart mortally wounded by five swords,' Imogen translates. 'Just lovely.'

'I like this, very much. Why didn't I find it?' He looks over the page. 'Ah, but this I have seen: "To burn with de-sire and keep quiet about it is the greatest punish-ment we can bring on ourselves".'

'I… can't remember where that's from,' Imogen says, taking the papers from him and putting them back in her bag.

He gets up and goes over to the coat stand for his jacket, sends a text and receives one. 'Come, we go now.'

'Didn't you want to go over this again?'

'No. It is enough. Thank you Imo-gen. Thank you for *all* your help.'

※

Santi wonders if they could link arms while they walk; they keep bumping into one another anyway. But perhaps better not.

'Where did you go yesterday?' he repeats. She didn't hear him above the bleeping of the pedestrian crossing.

Her serious little face lightens up. 'I had such fun, and a lot of cake and hot chocolate. All the cafes with tiny cakes – cake *tapas*! Plaza Mayor, then the Flamenco Vive shop for some CDs and a practice skirt – did I tell you I've started lessons?'

'No! ¡*Olé*!' He pats her arm.

'And then where… Oh, over to Chamberí and plaza de Olavide—'

'Olavide? Why there?'

'I had to look at the area, find somewhere for my character to live.'

'The English woman comes to live in Madrid?'

'No, a Spanish character. Then I went for a walk in the Retiro, but I didn't realise there's so much to it, I'll have to go back and see more… This is nice here.'

'Parque de la Montaña.' Today seemingly taken over by loving couples. 'So you like Madrid?'

'So far, I love it.'

'Very different from your cliff and the sea.'

'Well sometimes it's good to get away.'

He was going to point out the palace in the distance, but she's looking troubled by the steep dropping away of the ground, so he puts his arm through hers and leads her away.

'Poor thing. I'm sorry, *qué horror*. And to find you have a brother, so sudden! I can't imagine.'

She's looking down at her feet.

'But what luck for this Di-lon, to have a sister Imogen', he says, squeezing her arm. 'And you know, you were needing more relatives!'

'True! And he's already a friend, so…'

'More chocolate? Come.' They make their way to a table in the sun at the park's restaurant. 'I was wanting to take you here for lunch, but Pato is insisting on VIPS, although a few weeks ago she hated it.'

'Ha! I have the same thing with Ollie – nowhere is ever quite right. Maybe they can never quite forgive us—'

'For not being at the table at home, yes. I think you understand these things. *You know the score*,' he adds proudly.

'That's right!' she says, giving a little applause for his English.

Alvaro brings their drinks and stares at Imogen; Santi can see that he will be asked about the red-haired woman next time he comes here.

Imogen points to the path leading off down the hill. 'That must be the parque del Oeste? The one with that ski lift thing to the Casa de Campo parkland, the Tele…?'

'The Teleférico. I will take you next time. Casa de Campo is more fun when the weather is more warm.' Why did he say that? Who knows what season it will be when she comes here again; it *might* be warmer, but it could as easily be this time next year.

She looks at him a moment, as if she's thinking the same thing. 'When will you know about Lorca?'

'I have no idea.' He looks at his watch. 'Have you finished?'

They get up, and he finds himself taking her arm again.

'Papá!' Pato is calling out to him from the road. She's wearing her new boots – and a flimsy little mini-skirt he hasn't seen before. They join her at the pedestrian crossing.

'You must be freezing – no coat?' he asks in Spanish, giving her a hug.

Pato shrugs.

'This is Imo-gen, the English writer who has teached me English.'

'It's "*taught*", Papá,' she says, shaking her head. She says hello in English to Imogen but after they have crossed to the plaza de España she's in speedy Spanish for her description of yesterday's basketball match.

'Talk more slowly and Imogen can understand,' he says in English. 'Or show her that English from the international school!'

They turn off the main road into an unglamorous concrete square with a McDonald's, a pharmacy and the VIPS.

'It's a bookshop?' Imogen asks.

'Books, all types of things, and a restaurant at the back. They are everywhere. If you forget a birthday, is no problem – VIPS are open to one o'clock in the morning.'

'Brilliant!'

Pato folds her arms as Imogen pauses to admire a coffee table book about the Retiro. 'Can we sit down now?'

They find a table and Pato is back in rapid Spanish. 'So you wanted me to rejoin the team, and now you don't come to the match!'

'I would have come too, but I had to rehearse with the group before the two shows of *Los Mis*,' he answers in slow Spanish.

'*Too*? Nobody was there – Miri couldn't come.'

The Lighthouse Keeper's Daughter

'Oh.' Had Miri mentioned that? She'd left on Saturday morning in time for it.

'You and Miri will both come to my match next Saturday, no?' she says in deliberate English now, glancing over at Imogen.

'*I* will, but I think she'll be at work.' He turns to Imogen, sitting next to him. 'Ollie plays backset ball?'

'*Basketball*, Papá.'

'No. Only football, but he prefers to just watch it.'

A waitress comes to take their orders.

'I've heard you're also good at science, Patricia, and planning to study pharmacy at the university.'

Pato answers in Spanish. 'Now that Papá has stopped seducing women and taking drugs across the road, yes.' The corners of her mouth twitch at Imogen's confusion.

'She is talking about my character in *Universidad*. We were making the programme in the building the other side from the *Departamento de Farmacología*.'

'Ah!' Imogen smiles.

'*English*, Pato!'

'Okay. What will your son study at university? The literature, like his mother I think.'

'His only plan at the moment is to go on a course for learning how to mix cocktails.' She looks rather pleased with Pato's open-mouthed surprise. 'In Barcelona.'

'He is still wanting that? Good for him – he is artist!' Santi says with a chuckle. 'Pato used to like art also, and was very good.'

'Papá would prefer I take life of artist, with salary irregular, air condition broken in car and buying presents for birthdays in the middle of the night.'

Santi shakes his head and looks over at Imogen. 'Ollie talks to you like this?'

'Ah, and talking of birthdays, what are we doing for *Miri's* birthday?' Pato continues, and then asks Imogen if she has met her.

'Of course. I saw her this morning,' Imogen says with a smile.

Pato stands up and wanders over to the Ladies.

'*Ay*… Wait a moment, sorry,' Santi says to Imogen, then goes off to catch up with Pato.

'Can you stop being so…'

'What?'

'Unfriendly. Going on about Miri all the time, as if Imogen is some woman I've got on the side. She's a good friend who's helped me a lot, out of the goodness of her heart. She was looking forward to meeting you and doesn't deserve this.'

'What does Miri think of her?'

'She hasn't really had the chance to get to know her, but thinks what she's doing is great. When you come back to the table, ask her about England or something. You never know, you might get an invitation to her lighthouse one day, to polish your English before you set out to dominate the pharmaceutical world.'

'Will you?'

'What?'

'Get an invitation?'

'Well… I don't know, I'm too busy…'

She studies him carefully. 'Okay. I'm sorry. Actually she's quite nice. But there's something weird about this.'

'Oh for—'

'Papi, there just *is*. And if you can't see it, you need to look harder.'

The Lighthouse Keeper's Daughter

CHAPTER 23

'How it go?' Esme asks, letting her in.

'Good. He seems confident, *tiene confianza.*'

'And he say me you go to *Los Tarantos* tonight, for *celebrar.* But Imo-chen, you have…?' She makes a key-turning movement with her hand. 'Because, you know, tonight Darius and I we go to Toledo for concert and… hotel, *¿no?*'

'Oh yes, I remember.' Imogen picks the keys up from the kitchen table and puts them by the photo of Esme and Santi on the hall table next to where she hangs her coat. 'Done!' she says, coming back.

'Good. Maybe siesta – you are white, like milk. Are you *enferma?*'

She must have been asked this every day since she arrived. 'No, just a bit tired. But yes, maybe I will. I hope the concert goes well.'

She ascends the carpet-muted grand staircase, takes off her boots and lies on the bed. There's not a sound. The boys are out with their father and then off to their grandmother for the night, Esme and Darius are a whole house-width away. She could be anywhere: an English country house, a colonial mansion in

Barbados. They've been very kind, but when she comes back for her Spanish course and more research for the novel, she needs to be *madrileña* – rent a tiny apartment, shop in the local Día supermarket, go to sleep with the sounds of people going for *copas* in the early hours. In Chamberí or Argüelles. Not far from Santi.

She shifts position. Turns over. Santi. '*Show me how make English tea… Imo-gen, you work too hard by me… Do I have to need you?… To burn with desire and keep quiet about it…*' She opens her eyes. She's too weary to write the notes she should be taking about the morning, but too full of it to go to sleep. Then there's this evening, more of his hand on her arm… She can't get used to him taking up physical space. It's not just him; her own physical presence is alive and alarming in a way she hasn't known for years. If ever. She gets up and runs a bath of bubbles. Slowly takes off her clothes. She must enjoy this feeling – even if just on her own like the hapless Eponine.

※

'Listen, I have recorded a *soleá* with guitar, for the showreel tomorrow, for between the scenes.' He puts the CD in the car stereo.

Soleá: the slow flamenco song form with the serious lyrics, you're supposed to count twelve with the emphasis on beat 3,6,8,10 and 12 but it's difficult to work that out, and the whole thing often feels long and inaccessible. But this is different. The same descending chords, the mesmerizing rhythm spelt out by the *cajón*, but the voice – after the usual *ay-ay-ay* that always sounds like the singer's easing himself into the mood – has a melody less modulated and guttural, a folk singer perhaps, not fully flamenco but with the same flights of emotion.

'That's… really lovely. You must translate the words for me. And it's Lorca!'

'I think this. He also is not brilliant singer,' he says, chuckling.

She looks at him. '*You* sung that?'

He gives a little nod.

'Santi! It's wonderful! And something the other Lorcas won't be able to come up with.'

'It was *your* idea,' he says, patting her knee. 'I tell you, if I get the role, is… everything for you.'

'Er… I don't think that's what you mean.'

He glances over at her and then back at the confusing crossroads of several narrow streets. 'What do I mean? I mean… you tell me.'

'So now I have to tell you what you're thinking as well as how to say it?'

The car behind them blasts its horn. Santi grins and moves forward. 'You can try.'

'I think you wanted to say "if I get the role, it will be all because of you". Although obviously that's ridiculous.'

'No, you encouraged me read, speak English, put the *soleá*…'

They leave the car at Santi's and get into a taxi.

'It's a *tablao* with always a very good show, very *auténtico*. Of course there are lots of tourists – they have the money for it, but they do not know how good it is! Then after the show it is a place where meet the *flamencos*.'

'Where the *flamencos meet*.'

'Uff, yes. But Imo-gen, you will have to speak Spanish here!'

There's just a single door, with the name on a board above it. In the street outside, a small group of men with caps or scarves on their heads hug themselves to keep warm as they draw on roll-ups. They stare at Imogen with animal interest or possibly disgust, until they recognise Santi and break into smiles. There are hugs which include her, and blurred Spanish, nudges and laughter that don't. One of them, a ponytailed chap who comes up to her shoulder, manages 'are you from Lon-don? I am there makes two years,' but Santi answers him for her in Spanish.

A woman at the door has a word with Santi and lets them in. They go through a narrow dark-wood bar area with framed photographs of flamencos past and present covering the walls, and then she sees that, like many places in Madrid, it's bigger than it seems, opening out into an area with flamenco-spot covered tables around a small stage.

He takes her to a reserved table at the front and explains how there is a dinner before the show. Surrounding them are loud Americans and a group of excited Spaniards who don't seem to have seen each other for a while. Santi cups his hand to speak into her better ear, shows her how it's more Spanish to share a bowl of *salmorejo* soup than have separate ones, and gets her *tortilla española* from the lunch menu instead of the bulls' tail stew.

The lights dim for a spotlit solitary guitarist on stage. He begins a long *soleá* raw with loss and impossibility, then he's joined by two other guitars, *cajón* players, singers and musicians who clap out rhythms. She should be entranced – and initially she is – but somehow it's bothering her, the way it draws her in but keeps her at arm's length with its strange complexity.

Then there's her favourite: a *seguiriya*. Very difficult, according to Santi, but they did choreography to one in her class and she loved its intense chugging rhythm, *One-and-Two-and-Three-and-er-Four-and-er-Five-and…* A trousered female dancer stalks out from behind the curtain, all tightly held passion, her hands and fingers sensitive to every nuance, but her footwork emphatic and irascible.

The Lighthouse Keeper's Daughter

A male dancer now. Perhaps Pato and Ollie's age. Another intense performance, a young virtuoso, but a sensitive soul without the usual machismo.

A couple more female dancers, this time in traditional spots and frills and dancing sassy *bulerías*, all loose-hipped, skirt-flapping flirtation, eloquent arms and bursts of irrepressible stamping. Some of the audience are clapping along and shouting out *olés*. She wonders at the joy of being able to communicate such a lust for life, but then maybe that comes more easily to people here.

They wait for the crowd to leave before they make their way to the bar.

'I loved it, thank you *so* much!' she says to Santi.

The small but fiery-looking owner seems to like her reactions and insists on buying them more *sangría*. One glass and she's already walking unsteadily – but the woman can't or won't understand her, so Imogen soon has another one in her hand.

Now Santi's telling her about someone who's going to arrive, or has arrived; it's becoming impossible for her to understand Spanish. He introduces her to the sister of one of the dancers then goes over to join some guys at the bar.

The girl wants to know about English courses in Brighton – as does her friend. They are joined by one of the *cajón* players – the tiny chap who's been to London – who tells them he's been doing a course online, but it's not the same... She's suddenly tired of being the benevolent advisor on all matters English. If she can't be with Santi, she'd rather be back at Esme's. Relaxing with a hot chocolate, perhaps taking the opportunity to have a lengthier look at that family photo album Esme had shown her...

Then it comes to her: the photograph of Esme and Santi where she put the keys. And where – distracted at the last moment by an irritating text from Ewan asking if she was looking after herself in

Madrid – she left them. Damn, damn, damn. Now she's going to have to wake up frightening *Mamá* and borrow keys from her to get into the house. She looks at her watch: half eleven. The sooner she calls, the better. No – the sooner *Santi* calls; she has neither the phone number nor the Spanish to deal with this.

The bar has filled up again, and Santi was right about the *flamencos*: she edges her way past Tomatito, looking rather older than on her CD at home, and possibly one of the members of that band La Barbería del Sur.

Santi, rather smiley and dazed, beckons her over and introduces her as his English teacher again – prompting questions about vocabulary and technique and more bursts of laughter.

'Santi I've forgotten my keys. Can you call your mother so I can go round and borrow hers on my way back?'

He takes a moment to understand. 'You no have keys?'

One of the friends sniggers and comments.

She explains again in slow Spanish, loudly enough for them all to understand.

'Santi pulls her nearer, his Sangria breath on her cheek. 'I have keys at home.'

'Oh. OK.'

'We go soon.'

'Soon' could mean anything, so she decides to avoid any more Spanish male jokes or English coaching and go upstairs to the loos.

When she comes down, she finds Santi pacing at the bottom of the stairs.

'Sorry,' she says.

He doesn't do goodbyes, so they are soon in a taxi.

'Sorry about this,' she says again.

He says something about not being silly.

'Thank you *so* much, I loved the show.'

The Lighthouse Keeper's Daughter

Another mumbled Spanish reply. He's looking ahead wearily, watching to see that they're taken the quickest way, or thinking about tomorrow's audition recording, or maybe the concert in the evening. Well what did she expect? This was a little treat, not a date. He'll give her the key, and she'll get straight back into the cab.

When they arrive she starts trying to ask the taxi driver to wait, but Santi takes over and pays. They go up in the lift.

'You are cross,' he says.

'No! Why would I be cross?'

Then he says something that sends a shiver through her.

'Um… What did you say?'

He shuts the door. 'I say, *said*, why you so want to make clear to taxi driver that you don't stay with me?'

Stay with him. She walks into the kitchen and puts water into the pan to boil. The Spanish need to discover kettles. 'I don't know what you mean.'

'The same this evening – is why my friends are laughing.'

'Your friends think all English girls are *putas*, that's why.'

'Imo-gen! Listen you! One of them name you The *Virgen* Queen Eliza-bet, you not hear?'

She taps the electric ring to zero. 'I think I need to go.' She spots a taxi card on his pin board and gets out her phone.

'What you are doing?' He laughs and puts one hand over the card, the other tapping the electric ring back up to nine. 'You can't leave me with all this English tea and milk *soja*. Take a *trono… how-you-say?*'

'Throne?'

'Take a throne in the other room and I bring it.'

'Well, I—'

'You told me Queen Eliza-bet with the red hair was very good and clever, so is so bad, this joke?'

'They were *laughing* at me,' she finds herself saying. 'It's not very—'

'No! They laugh at *me*, you don't understand!'

They go next door and sit on the sofa.

'You could go over the scenes once more, I don't mind.' She picks up the script.

He takes it off her and puts it back on the table. 'How strange is this 'don't mind'. I don't mind if I do, I don't mind if I don't. Don't mind me... It's all in the mind... Mind you remember your keys. Ha! The mind is everything to the English.'

Did she really teach him all that? He'll be throwing something at her next, like a male Eliza to her Professor Higgins. She picks up her tea; once it's finished, she'll go. There's the concert tomorrow, which she'll love, and then it's off home to reality.

'Imo-gen? What-is-the-matter? Come, have hug from your favourite student,' he says, pulling her over to him awkwardly, his arm trapping her hair.

A cuddle, but not as she's been imagining. One arm's going instantly dead and her neck feels snapped; it's as if even their bodies speak a different language. She sits up. 'Uh... too much *sangría*. Better get back.'

She goes over to her coat, but he follows and comes up behind her. She's suddenly warm in his arms, his chin on her shoulder as they steady themselves against the wall.

'I'll see you tomorrow, okay?' she says, turning her head and feeling his rough cheek against hers. 'I don't need to call, there were still lots of taxis down in the Princesa street.'

Then he says something about staying there. He must mean in Pato's room, but she doesn't hear him say that. English seems to have left him. There's another thing, said into her hair. Then, as if impatient that she hasn't understood, he says *he wants her*.

She can't have heard that right.

Now he's saying something else, and kisses her cheek.

This can't be real, but for a moment pretending it is, and just because she can, she turns and gives him a little kiss on the lips.

He might want her, but he doesn't seem to expect to *have* her; he's pulled away, trying to explain something. Asking if she understands. Why can't he say it in English? She concentrates. Then it comes to her that he can only be meaning one thing.

'In English we call that *friends with benefits*, Santi.'

His brows furrow. 'I no understand Imogen. You—'

'Well *I* understand perfectly, and it's *not* going to happen.'

Now he's talking in earnest but slurred Spanish, and she has no idea what he's saying.

'Oh for heaven's sake, we'll talk tomorrow okay?' She presses a kiss on his protesting face, opens the door and calls the lift. Descends, shaky and reeling.

While she tries to recall how to open the front door to the building, she hears the lift shaft clanking behind her. The lift opens and Santi is there with raised eyebrows, holding out keys. Saying he'll help her get a taxi. How chivalrous. But outside, their earlier taxi driver is still there, listening to some music, looking at his phone. Santi opens the car door for her.

'I wait for you, is no problem,' the taxi driver says. 'I'm sorry my English, I need practice, you know.'

'Fine. Perhaps if you take me to the airport on Tuesday. But not now, okay?'

CHAPTER 24

TUESDAY, 11TH DECEMBER 2012
Madrid, Spain

'Papi your concert was awesome – I love those new songs.'

'I'm glad, thank you sweetheart. But shouldn't you be in your first lesson? Better get off your phone.'

'Five minutes. Are you coming to the basketball on Saturday? If so, could you drop four of us at Nerea's afterwards?'

'I'll have to see if Miri's coming, or there won't be room in the car.'

'She's not.'

'Oh?'

'She told me she wouldn't be coming for a while.'

He takes this in for a moment. 'I thought you said she just didn't turn up last week?'

'No, I knew she wasn't coming. Papá! What does it matter? Can you give us a lift or not? It's Nerea's birthday and we're going to start off with the pancake place then…'

He can't follow the description of their carefree teenage plans. He remembers Miri getting out of bed on Saturday morning, saying something about the match – how this one was important or something – and getting into the shower. Shouldn't she have added that it was a shame neither of them were going?

'Papá?'

'Okay, I'll see you there. We'll do something together on Sunday. Now off you go.'

He calls Miri. 'Just making plans with Pato… Any chance of you coming to the match with me on Saturday?'

'Oh… no, I'll be working.'

'She missed you last week.'

'Well I couldn't help it, the shop called.'

'So… when did you tell her you weren't going?'

'What? I don't know… from the car? Does it matter?'

Yes it does. It matters a lot. She's lying. He can't think why, but she is. She might well have something better to do than watch his daughter in her basketball 'B' team, but for some reason she wants it to look like a last minute change of plan. He spoke to her that day, called her from the rehearsal at Uncle Pedro's while they were waiting for Joselito, whose car had broken down. Then there was the lingering wonder about why she happened to be with Ignacio on Friday night when the news about the audition arrived from New York.

He goes out onto the terrace - his Madrid cliff, as Imogen called it once, comparing views. He would like to compare views with her now – views on deception and how to handle it. Something she probably knew far too much about.

Imogen. Hundreds of miles away now. Perhaps already back in her lighthouse. Glad to be home. By the sea. Speaking English. No friend suddenly trying it on. Except, he *wasn't* trying it on. He was trying to say, 'you could stay the night in Pato's room, don't worry, I love you but I'm not going to try anything', but sangria made it all come out wrong. *Very* wrong. He has explained and she's accepted his apology, so why does he still feel, as the English would say, 'in the doghouse'?

His phone again. 'Ep!'

'Nina. Oh never mind, let's face it, I *am* Eponine. Look, I'm still in shock after your concert last night. So beautiful! I was bracing myself for a Tangoza re-run.'

'Oh thanks. And you looked after my English teacher!'

'No – she looked after *me*. I arrived in a strop but she cheered me up.'

'Did she say anything about me?'

'Nothing at all. And everything.'

'What does that mean? I need to know, we had a bit of a… misunderstanding the night before.'

'Uh-oh, did you try it on with her?'

'No! I wouldn't do that to Miri. Mind you…' He finds himself recounting his doubts about Miri.

'Hm. I think you need to sort out what all these little pieces of puzzle add up to. Look, sorry gorgeous, I've got to dash – hairdresser. Good luck with the auditions today.'

※

Ignacio said it was for a series of adverts for a bank, although looking at the script he's basically Diego again, tamed into respectability by the bank's start-up loan for his music shop. Actually not bad, quite funny. He might even get it.

He arrives in a stark waiting room like the inside of a fridge and exchanges a nod with the row of seated chaps similar to himself. He's the last to arrive, but there's no logic to these things: he's immediately called in to the studio. He's about to do his usual presentation to the camera when the casting director interrupts.

'Your guitar. Didn't you bring it? We said we wanted to see you playing.'

The Lighthouse Keeper's Daughter

'I could go back and get it.'

'From where?'

'Plaza de España.'

'Oh no. Ah well. Present yourself please.'

※

Ignacio doesn't reply, so he randomly selects Facebook messenger and thumbs out a message. '*Why didn't you tell me about the guitar? Almost certainly lost that.*'

He copies the message and sends it to Miri, imagining their phones donging just slightly out of sync as they sit in some bloody restaurant somewhere.

He changes metro lines and loses signal. His eyes want to close but he needs to look at the next script, which only arrived this morning. He's not a gypsy, and it's a comedy. But the guy is out of work – how funny can that be? An unemployed actor with all the usual delusions, by the look of it. Capable, long-suffering girlfriend? He turns a few pages. Check.

He breathes out heavily and goes back to the beginning. Then notices from the attached email that the casting director is Katharine García. He's doomed; she couldn't have been less impressed with him, right from the moment he arrived at that workshop. On the other hand, her view of him as a laughable excuse for an actor might actually help her see him in the role; nothing would surprise him in this ludicrous business.

The train's taking forever. Why can't all roles be auditioned for with a showreel? Each actor could do an example of each of the three kinds of parts he usually gets asked to try for – in his case, gypsy / troubled minority / handsome cannon-fodder – and the casting directors could use their fucking imaginations.

He finds the road, but… this can't be right.

He presses Ignacio's name. 'Can you check the address? Number 23 is a *clinic*.'

'I sent this to you. Come out of La Granja, and calle de la Granja is—'

'What?'

'La Granja metro. You are *there*, aren't you?'

'I'm in calle de la Granja near Metropolitano! You never said—'

'God's sake, get a taxi! What's the matter with you?'

'*Me*? It's *you* who's—'

'Go! We'll talk later.'

The taxi driver picks up on Santi's mood and hurtles off, but then there's a diversion sign, and Santi decides to take a diversion of his own.

'*Two* auditions completely fucked by your incompetence!' he yells, bursting into Ignacio's office.

'*Your* incompetence, Santi. But I really haven't got time for this right now.'

'I'm surprised you have time for anything – you spend half the week dating my girlfriend!'

Ignacio closes his eyes and shakes his head. 'Okay,' he says, his thick ringed fingers splayed on the table. 'Listen. Are you going to listen?'

Santi stands still, his heart racing.

'Haven't I always told you not to mix women and work? Yes? Yes. And the thing about being an arrogant bastard is that I do tend to take my own advice.'

'All that time you're with her – don't tell me it's just work!'

'I like her, of course. *Everyone* does, and that's one of the reasons she's going to do well. Yes, she's for eating. But she's much too valuable for me to go taking a bite out of her.'

The Lighthouse Keeper's Daughter

'How do I—'

'If there's something wrong in your relationship, you need to talk to *her*, not go around accusing people of taking what you see as yours. And do this soon, because you are *seriously* losing the plot. I told you about the guitar, and gave you all the directions – check your emails. Now go home and get a grip – or you'll mess up at that little theatre and find yourself completely out of work.'

✄

Uncle Pedro looks at him carefully. 'Don't worry. She's coming back. Nothing's impossible.'

'Has Joselito told you something?'

'Only that she forgot her key and had to go back to your place after Los Tarantos.'

'What? No! It's *Miri* – we seem to be drifting apart.'

He raises his eyebrows. 'Perhaps that's not surprising.'

'*No* Uncle, she knows there's nothing going on between me and Imogen.'

'Yes, but are *you* sure about that?'

'Uh… Where's Joselito?'

'Here!' his cousin says, coming into kitchen. They go through and sit down on opposite sofas, surrounded by pictures of their fathers and grandfathers singing or playing the guitar. 'I've been getting so many comments on Facebook. People loved it!'

'Shame Ignacio couldn't come and see the reaction – all he'll see is that a third of the seats were empty.'

'So the New York tape's gone, and meanwhile you've got *Los Mis* until…'

'Christmas. But I'm waiting to hear if I can do the tour.'

'That sounds fun. Anyway, what did you want to talk to me about?'

Santi puts down his coffee. 'Miri and I... well, she's changed. I just wondered if you'd noticed anything different about her?'

Joselito's face falls. 'I'm sorry to hear that. She just seems very busy. I mean, she's got *two* jobs until—'

'Yes, but what I'm trying to ask is... Do you think she could also have two *boyfriends*?'

Joselito's mouth opens in surprise. 'Miri wouldn't do that.'

'This Antonio guy, for instance. She's putting a lot of time into him.'

'Antonio? Oh no. No way.'

Santi shakes his head. 'You have such confidence in her.'

Joselito picks up the English book Santi has brought with him. '*Advanced* these days! You've got a class now?'

'In about an hour.'

He hands it back to him. 'Amazing what you've done with your English. You really deserve that role.'

'I'm probably not right for it,' Santi says.

'Well at least it made you learn English – and make a lovely new friend.'

'Yes, Imo-gen's great.'

'It was obviously special for you to have her at the concert.'

'Ha! Don't believe everything you hear on the radio.'

'Well, I'm going on the fact you went over and hugged her when you came off stage.'

⚞

'You need to talk to *Miri*,' Ep says, hanging up her costume.

'She rang just before the show. We're having lunch tomorrow.'

'Well that's something. Sort it out Santi, this isn't good for you.'

'Was it that noticeable?'

The Lighthouse Keeper's Daughter

'Late by two notes? I think the production can bear it. Who was that guy watching you tonight?'

'The chap who's going to do my role on tour.'

'Oh no.' She squeezes his arm. 'You should have asked earlier darling. But maybe he'll be crap, or someone else'll drop out. There's still a few weeks.'

'Here, let me have a go at that – I used to brush Esme's hair when we were kids.'

She hands him the brush. 'Well if you can get through her luscious locks, you can certainly manage my few strands.'

'It's lovely. Very shiny. Especially with the new highlights. Are you still going to dinner with Dear Marius?'

'He's saying hello to some relatives first. I'm meeting him at the restaurant.'

'There you go', he says, putting down the brush. He watches her get a red sweater and a pair of trousers out of her bag.

'I'll let you get changed,' he says, moving towards the door.

'Don't be daft. You and Carlos have caught me half-dressed loads of times. Turn away if you have to.'

'Okay.' He does, but accidentally glimpses in the mirror that she's selected a rather modest pair of baby blue knickers for the possible seduction.

His phone rings. Joselito. 'I'm in the area and wondered if you'd like to go for a bite.'

'Hm. I'm a bit knackered actually, it's been quite a day.'

'We can go to that smart place right by the theatre.'

'La Clavel. Ok. See you there in about ten minutes?'

He closes the phone.

'That's where I'm going!' Ep says.

Ep sees the choice as a refined start to what she hopes will be a marvellous evening, while Santi assumes Joselito must be going to tell him about some marvellous finance-changing opportunity with Ignacio's clients.

Until they arrive. 'Marius' – wholesome and handsome Jose Manuel del Rio – is rather too polite for tonight's romantic protagonist, and Joselito has the wide-eyed look of someone who's just been whacked with bad news.

'How are you doing?' Santi asks his cousin, steering him towards a table the opposite side of the room from Ep's.

'Fine, fine. A cousinly paella together?'

A waiter comes to take their orders.

'So what did you need to talk to me about?' Santi asks.

'Ah. Yes…' Joselito is looking over at the bar, as if he can't start without a drink in his hand.

'It's still okay with Ignacio and the clients?'

'Oh yes.'

'Right. So…'

The waiter arrives with wine for them to try. Joselito tastes it rather enthusiastically and nods at the water. Then he interlocks his fingers on the table, as if in prayer. 'I heard about the row with Ignacio.'

Santi leans his head in his hand. 'Not my finest hour. But really, can you blame me?'

'Not at all. I can understand how you feel.'

'God, you're not going to tell me it is Ignacio after all, are you?'

'No, no.'

'But… you think it could be someone else.'

'I don't think Miri would ever cheat on anyone,' Joselito says, looking at him steadily. 'Even when you were keeping her at arms' length all those months, and she didn't know whether you were seeing other women while you had your "space", she was faithful.'

'Wait. What's all this? I always made it clear that I wasn't going

The Lighthouse Keeper's Daughter

to shag other girls. Is that what all this is about? In which case you can tell her that I've not had the need – nor the energy – to have anyone else.'

Joselito winces and takes another mouthful of wine. 'Look, this row with Ignacio…'

'I know, I'll call him tomorrow. It's not him.'

'So you're still sure there is *someone*. What are you going to do at the party, sound out one actor after the other?'

'What party?'

'Ignacio's Christmas do for his clients, you know.'

'No, I don't know.'

Their paella arrives. Joselito squeezes lemon over it, while Santiago gets out his phone to look at the calendar. The family Christmas party. The *Los Mis* end of run party. The *Universidad* Christmas thing.

'Not in my diary. Oh well, I'll just have to find some other way of getting them all in one place for questioning,' Santi says with a grin.

Joselito doesn't smile back.

A WhatsApp from Ep flashes up: '*Had enough.*' He looks over and sees her returning from the Ladies.

'*Possibly ditto,*' he sends back.

'Don't worry, I'm seeing Miri tomorrow – as you say, she's very busy, and that's affected our confidence in each other.'

'Right.'

'Right. So is that what you wanted to talk to me about, my disruptive witch-hunt among Ignacio's clients? Sounds like Ignacio has taken you on as company counsellor too. Job done. I promise to behave.'

Joselito puts down his fork, bites his lip, his hands in prayer mode again. 'I don't want you to behave. I just hope you'll understand. Nothing's happened. Miri isn't cheating on you. She loves you. But… not how she used to. She's changed, as people do. And… she's in love with someone else.'

Santi's heart thuds. *His Miri*. But really, he's known this for a while, hasn't he?

'Who?' he asks quietly.

The waiter asks if they've finished. They say they have. They want the bill. Santi's phone buzzes a text, and he glances down and reads '*Let's go*' from Ep. Joselito is taking much too long to answer. He looks up at him, ready to hear it.

'Me.'

The Lighthouse Keeper's Daughter

CHAPTER 25

THURSDAY, 13TH DECEMBER 2012
The South Coast, England

She closes her phone and leans against the drinks machine. An old man doesn't seem to hear that it's stopped blasting brown liquid into his cup. Next to her, there's a poster of a woman 'smiling inside' despite the droopiness to one side of her face. While she's been looking at it, a grubby old crone with hideous hearing aids has descended purposefully upon the machine. What's she doing here among these people? The audiogram clearly didn't go well for the left ear, but that's no surprise after that awful infection a few years ago. This is just one hugely annoying waste of time.

She eventually sits down with a hot chocolate that's come out so thick you could use it for *churros*. Her phone buzzes the arrival of a WhatsApp.

'*What says the doctor of ears?*' Santi is asking.

'*I'm still waiting :-(*'

'*Bloody NSH!*'

'*NHS*,' she corrects him. '*Any news?*'

'*Yes! They asked for more of I playing the guitar! Thank you Imogen, your idea!*'

'*Great!*' It is great. It sounds like they're interested in him, he might get the role. Her returning to Madrid for the Spanish course will just have to wait; he'll probably go on the *Los Mis* tour, and then it'll be time for him to go off to New York. She has no idea when she'll next see him, and he's got so much on, he hasn't even mentioned it. But how lovely that he's remembered where she is today.

The nurse is calling her name.

How do doctors choose their specialty? Mr Haddon – or was it Hatton – has a bulbous nose and a pair of tactlessly prominent ears either side of his bald head. He's pointing to graphs of what she can hear.

'So as you can see,' he bellows, 'hearing is slightly reduced in the right, and more markedly in the left – especially in the higher frequencies.'

'Well that's just—'

'It says here you felt like you were on a boat?'

'When I had the labyrinthitis, yes.'

'Have you noticed any problems with balance before?'

'No. Ah… well I've fallen over a few times when I've been running. Got to remember not to turn my head too quickly when looking around.'

The consultant quickly scratches a few words with an ink pen in her notes.

'Any *ringing* or other sounds in your ears?'

'No. Although the one that had the infection sometimes has a sort of high "pinging".'

He writes something else, underlines it and puts the pen down. 'I think we need to take a good look at what's going on behind your ear. I'm going to book a scan. We have to inject a little dye, but it's all quite painless.'

He says something to the nurse that makes her smile briefly at

 The Lighthouse Keeper's Daughter

Imogen and leave the room.

'But surely… I mean, is it so unusual to lose hearing after an infection? I think my eardrum burst or something.'

He looks down at her notes and up again. 'Hearing in the right is on the low side but within normal limits.'

'No, I mean the *left* ear.'

'Ah, well hopefully the scan will soon explain that.'

'Explain… what the infection did?'

He checks a letter and what looks like a print out from her GP back in Weybridge. Turns back to the audiogram. 'Imogen… the infection was in the *right* ear. There's no history of an infection in the left.'

'No, no. I'm sure it was the left.'

He looks at the letters again. For some minutes. 'It's very unlikely that two GPs and an A and E doctor would have all got that wrong.'

What's going on *behind* her ear. She's suddenly got a ringing in her ears *now*, as it happens.

'We'll get an answer as soon as possible and make a plan. Try not to worry.'

The nurse returns looking pleased and saying something about a cancellation. The consultant is also smiling now. Everything's okay for them, because they can have a look at her brain *today*. It looks like she's supposed to be going somewhere with the nurse, but she can't seem to stand up.

'Is anyone with you?' the nurse asks.

Imogen shakes her head.

The nurse takes her arm. 'The good news is, we're going right past the café. We'll get you tea and one of Florrie's chocolate brownies while we're passing, okay?'

She closes the laptop. It's obviously what they think she's got. Could be worse. But oh God, why *now*.

Framed by the little window above her desk, her father's lighthouse winks into the early evening. *A lighthouse doesn't do anything*, he used to say, *it's just there if you need it*.

She puts on her coat. Picks up her phone. Puts it down again; the minute she tells anyone about this thing she'll be letting it into her life. But there's just a small chance that the hospital might call about the results, so she pushes it down into her duffle pocket.

Outside, the monstrous frayed-edged hills lie calmly under an almost full moon. She follows the drive down to the layby car park. It's empty. She hesitates. Then starts along the path of flattened grass that gently rises up towards Beachy Head.

She's nowhere near the edge, and the moon gives all the light she needs, but she occasionally points her torch onto that impossible earth-sky interface, to keep it at bay. On and on, not a sound. The grass is longer here, perhaps it should be rustling against her boots. You typically lose the sound of birds singing, the website said; she'll test that tomorrow. Soundless car lights are coming down the road up ahead. Now she's read that article, she's looking for what she can't hear.

The hill becomes steeper; it's good to feel the strength in her legs, her body warming up. Then she can see it: that scary summit of grass-sky. She points the torch to her right: the other summit, the cliff edge. Up ahead, she knows what happens after the summit: a steep but harmless grassy slope swoops down, only to immediately rise up again towards the highest point of Beachy Head. But up until almost the last moment you can't see this trough, just a summit indistinguishable from the cliff edge; it

The Lighthouse Keeper's Daughter

always makes her heart race. It's worth it, because just as you reach the top, her father's old lighthouse comes into view.

Tonight, it's in a flat, low tide of moon-glittered water. The sea that her father must have admired so often from the lantern room, and whose every mood and trick he thought he knew – but finally took him in a moment of weakness.

Wink, wink, wink. What is it about this stupid old pile of striped stone that soothes her? It helped her father betray her and her mother, and then killed him. Maybe it's that childhood love of a nightlight – a hundred times stronger in a child of a lighthouse keeper.

Her phone rumbles in her pocket. She takes it out. A message rather than a WhatsApp from Santi.

'*You don't answer. Internet problem? Are you OK?*'

She puts the phone away. Considers this a moment. No dizziness, nausea, sounds in her ear. Hearing not great, but nothing new there. She takes the phone out again.

'*I'm fine, thanks. You?*'

'*Good :-)*'

She's getting cold, standing still, so starts walking back down the hill. Her phone buzzes again.

'*Fine? But Imogen, already I have told you I don't like this word FINE. I don't trust in it. Tell me what is the matter. Imogen!*'

She stares at the message, lets its warmth spread through her. How incredible: there isn't usually any signal in this area, but somehow he's got through.

CHAPTER 26

THURSDAY 13TH DECEMBER 2012
San Pedro de Alcántara (near Marbella), Spain

Another list of missed calls and messages. Hasn't Esme passed on that he's just having a break and wants some peace? He should have gone somewhere with reliably dodgy mobile coverage. The phone rings again, but this time it's Ep.

'Another sunny day?' she asks.

'Hold on.' He takes the phone from his ear, sends a snap of his table against the deep blue sky and the sea lapping on the pebbles. 'Twenty-five degrees. *San Pedro* now, nice and quiet.'

'Looks lovely.'

'Didn't you jump on a Malaga AVE when you broke up with that set designer guy?'

'No – I went on the Barcelona one. Bad idea. Well done for considering the weather before you took your tantrum train.'

Santi chuckles.

'Has she called yet?' Ep asks.

'No, she's got...' How strange; he thought for a moment she was talking about Imogen. 'I mean, *yes*, she has. It was okay. Honestly, more people should take tantrum trains; it really helps to see things from a distance. We've been growing apart for *months*. But

The Lighthouse Keeper's Daughter

she could have told me herself. Of course she said she was *about* to, blah blah blah.'

'And Joselito?'

'I'm not quite ready to talk to fucking Romeo.'

'Oh the male ego! But better him than cocky Antonio, surely? After a while you'll be happy for Joselito, you'll see. And hey, you now don't have to worry about being caught messaging Imogen every two minutes. You can message her all you like. *See* her all you like.'

'What? She's back in England. And—'

'No she's *not* just a friend, Santi! Why can't you see that? Everybody else can!'

'But—'

'Got to go, sweetheart. Think about it.'

Ridiculous. Why would Imogen ever want to leave her son, writing career, friends and beautiful coast in England just to be with him? Ha - her a writer and him a closet dyslexic - what a match! No. Visiting Madrid, however often she does it, is just a wonderful escape and research opportunity for her. They're good friends, the very *best* of friends. Yes, he caught her looking at him and blushing, and he was amazed to find himself struggling to keeps his hands off this speckled creature – but that's it.

He takes out his phone. No reply to the jolly '*Good Morning*' he sent earlier. Ah, but Thursday – she's got an appointment at the hospital about her hearing. Apparently a complete waste of time; her ear was damaged by an infection some years ago.

He pays the bill and sets off along the beach. The wind's getting up a bit, the sun lower in the sky and losing its warmth. The beach is a narrow stretch with bushes bordering the pebble and sand, just the occasional apartment block. If he keeps on walking, he'll eventually come to the Marbella lighthouse – but it's a town-based thing, Imogen wouldn't be impressed with it at all.

He reaches a river and should turn away from the beach now, the path taking him up to the bridge just outside the town, but it's hard to leave the sea. He watches the waves tumbling more insistently onto the sucking pebbles, lets the bitterness of the salty air fill his lungs. There's something energising about it, as if reaching the edge of the land forces you to face up to things.

He makes his way to a bench facing the river, the waves out of view but still in his ears. He takes out his phone and goes into WhatsApp; he needs to know Imogen's okay. He asks how she's doing and waits to see the *last seen today at* change to *online*. It doesn't. He walks on to the next bench. She's still not there. He goes up the steps to the bridge, along the main road, through to the plaza, climbs the two flights to his bare little room, sits on the balcony. She still hasn't replied.

He sends a text instead… and apparently she's fine. But what if she isn't? That friend of Uncle Pedro's wasn't seeing well out of one eye and turned out to have cancer.

'*Fine? But Imogen, already I have told you I don't like this word FINE. I don't trust in it. Tell me what is the matter. Imogen!*'

'*I had a scan (escáner) today. It's almost certainly a little harmless blob that they'll leave and watch.*'

'*Oh… When you will know?*'

'*In a few days. But look… I want to do the Spanish course soon!*'

'*Of course! If the doctor says it's okay to travel.*'

'*I'll see if they have a place in early January.*'

'*I can help your homework! I have a job on one day and some work with Uncle Pedro, but I'm free in the evenings at that time.*'

'*At last! I'm sure Miri will be pleased.*'

'*Ah… no. Miri and I are not together now. We are broken.*'

He waits. The message has been *read*. Maybe she's lost signal. Ah but no: three little bobbles showing that she's writing.

The Lighthouse Keeper's Daughter

'*Oh. I'm so sorry Santi. Are you okay?*'

'*Yes. It's for best, it was going to happen. Look, I'll ask Esme if you can stay again.*'

'*Oh no. Thanks, but I need to be in Chamberí, where my character lives. I'll look for a little apartment.*'

'*Okay. Tell me it and I will check it for you.*'

He stares at the phone. If he wanted to go somewhere with dodgy phone connection, Imogen's hills would have been perfect.

She's online again. '*Sorry. Now on higher ground again! Maybe we could Skype about it tomorrow?*'

'After the show?'

'Perfect.'

':-)'

':-))'

';-)))))) jaja'

He puts the phone down. Gets a beer from the minibar. Even if he does the tour, they could have a week, maybe ten days. It'll be fun.

His phone buzzes a message. Joselito again.

'*Cousin, please answer. Are you all right? You will never know how hard I tried to persuade myself that Miri was just a wonderful friend, that she'd never feel the same about me.*'

Santi calls him.

'Santi—'

'It's okay.'

'Okay?'

'I'm sorry, I just needed some time on my own. Can't really talk now, but I'll come and see you when I get back, okay?'

'Of course, I understand.' There's a voice in the background. 'Papá wants a quick word.'

Pedro with more work for him, probably.

'Santi. I'm so glad you two are talking again. It can't be easy, but you've got to ask yourself… Look, I've been trying to reach you. You know these extra songs they want? I think we should throw in a few instrumentals too, perhaps one with a sort of American 1920s jazz flamenco fusion… See what I'm thinking? We could pitch for the sound track. Why not? Nothing to lose. I know part of you thinks that preparing for the Lorca role was a big waste of time, but now we can use that research. Things have a way of happening for a reason, you know?'

CHAPTER 27

SATURDAY 22ND DECEMBER 2012
Jersey, Channel Islands

'There's no reason for it. Just bad luck. But hey, I'm one in eighty thousand!'

A semi-circle of uncertain smiles. Dorothy sips her tea. Anthea refills Imogen's cup, and Jules still has her hand over her mouth.

'What's it called again?' Dylan asks.

'An acoustic neuroma.'

'And it's definitely benign?'

'Yes. And as I say, mine's only little so they're just going to watch it.'

'And if it gets bigger?'

'They say I've probably had it for *years*, that's not going to happen,' Imogen says, as if the way the tumour's story is going to play out is up to her.

'It's appalling that you've had to wait so long for the results,' Dorothy says. 'I insist on you letting me pay for you to be seen privately in future.'

'That's very kind, but there's no need. I've got a repeat scan in March, and they'll probably be six monthly after that. Going privately wouldn't make any difference.'

They can hear Ollie and Anthea's two boys laughing and slamming doors as they come back into the house.

'How's Ollie about all this?' Jules asks, lowering her voice.

'It's really nothing to worry about, Jules. He's fine, but he promises to work really hard now, as if he thinks my stressing over his exams might make the tumour grow. Should have got a diagnosis earlier!' She turns to Dorothy. 'Anyway, enough of this. When are you going to tell me about Dylan's mother?'

Dorothy raises her eyebrows. 'Imogen. One thing at a time! The boys are back. Later.'

'And we need to get ready for the restaurant. You're going to love it,' Anthea says.

⁑

Too many people, too much clatter – but she can't keep avoiding restaurants other than ones with so few clients that they're about to close. The Lighthouse Restaurant is not such a place; it's on the headland with a panoramic view over the rocky shoreline and Jersey's most photographed landmark, Corbière lighthouse – the Saturday before Christmas. Poor Jules and Dylan are repeating bits of conversation for her, while Dorothy alternates between being too quiet and laughably too loud. Anthea's husband's flutey voice is completely inaudible, and their two university boys and Ollie are mumbling but intermittently bursting into nerve-jarring guffaws.

Now she's waiting with Jules, Dylan and Ollie at a meeting point lower down the hill, from where a guide will take them down across the causeway to the white-painted lighthouse on the tidal island.

Jules points to a plaque on the wall next to the old keepers' cottages. 'Oh my God: *in nineteen forty-six an assistant keeper*

The Lighthouse Keeper's Daughter

drowned while trying to save a woman cut off by the incoming tides... He was only thirty-four.'

A year younger than her father when he drowned. 'Yes. Apparently his family was told there was little chance of his body being found, but the father studied the tides and the currents and found it himself,' Imogen says.

'Did someone do that for your dad, Mum?' Ollie asks.

'I'm sure they tried,' Dylan says.

'You weren't quite born yet, were you Uncle Dylan?'

Dylan wraps his scarf around his neck. He seems to be frowning, but it might just be the cold.

'Why's Dorothy got to be the one to tell Mum about your mother? Was she much younger than him or something? Cos it doesn't matter, she doesn't mind, do you, Mum?'

'It'll be easier for her to explain how it all happened,' Dylan says.

A smiling woman with a blue Jersey Tourism badge comes towards them. 'Mr Beaumont and family? For the lighthouse? I'm Rosemary. Beautiful day for this!' Rosemary starts describing the lighthouse's history; for Imogen, much of it blows away in the wind, but she's already read up about it.

They walk down the hill and along the concrete path through the rocky beach. Rosemary is telling them about the causeway being under water for most of the day, and that there's a dangerous rush of tide round the rocks. Imogen looks either side; like at Beachy Head, it's hard to imagine the playground-yellow sand and rocky paddling pools being transformed into a deadly swirl. Then, in the largest pool, near the end of the causeway, there's the reflection of the lighthouse shimmering white in the water before her.

She looks up. Not her father's lighthouse, but that same intake of breath, that anxious attraction.

They climb the stone steps to the door; no treacherous little metal dog-steps here. Rosemary has reached it and is dealing with the locks. They're about to go in. She's going to be inside a real lighthouse for the first time – or the first time that she can remember.

Inside, there are notices and leaflet displays, a collection box for the RNLI. Of course, this is a tourist attraction; the lighthouse has been automated since 1974. They go up the wrought-iron spiral staircase to an equipment room with explanations and old photos on the walls, once the living area for the two keepers on their two-day duty of six hour shifts…

It's cosy rather than claustrophobic, but there's something dizzying about the constant winding of the stairs, and the views through the tiny windows of increasingly vertiginous drops to the crashing sea below. You can't forget the sea, not for a moment. Neither its beauty, nor its resentment of the impervious concrete.

She's now in the lantern room, shielding her eyes from all the reflections from the lens. Perhaps her father confided in his fellow keepers and grew weary of their advice. So he went down, picked up his fishing stuff and spent time with another old friend: the sea. The barrier should have been across the open door, but at some point it must have been left open, or broken, or he opened it himself to go out onto the set-off to let the sea wind clear his mind, tell him what to do. And for the sea to—

'Imo? Come down and look at this. It's what it's all about!' Jules was calling from the level below. 'Careful there, Ollie!'

Imogen steps down, steadying herself with both hands on the rail. Ollie, wearing surgeon-like white gloves, holds out an electric bulb the size of a newborn baby.

CHAPTER 28

SATURDAY 22ND DECEMBER 2012
Jersey, Channel Islands

Dorothy knocks and comes in with a glass of something. 'Are you okay, dear?'

Imogen props herself up. 'Just a headache. Should have worn my sunglasses. It was such a lovely meal, and thank you so much for booking the lighthouse tour.'

Dorothy smiles briefly and sits down on the chair. She notices the notebook on the duvet. 'You're writing?'

'Just making a few notes.'

Dorothy tilts her chin up to look down through her glasses at Imogen's labelled sketches. 'So it's a book with a lighthouse?'

'It's about… communication. Difficulty with it. Unexpected connections. But lighthouses do come into it, yes.'

Dorothy nods her head slowly. 'It's not about your father,' she says, her face neutral.

'No.' Imogen sips the apple juice and puts it back on the bedside table. 'I wouldn't be able to get inside his head.'

Dorothy looks hurt. 'Not at all?'

His feelings about the lighthouse. His unexpected distant friendship that became… 'Well, a bit. But the trouble is, I can't help being *angry* with him – such a stupid accident.'

'It's only natural to feel like he *left* you, Imogen. Gracious, sometimes I feel like that about my husband, even though he died right next to me in his sleep. But your father didn't *want* to leave you.'

Imogen feels her throat tightening. 'I don't know... there are times when I just can't accept it at all.'

Dorothy's mouth falls open. '*Accept*?'

'Even after talking to Bill, I can't help wondering if... I mean, why did he say that he would "already be gone" by the time the lighthouse was unmanned? That sounds more like he was planning to... put an end to everything.'

Dorothy has stood up and gone over to the window to draw the curtains.

'I'm sorry, I know you must have been through all this before,' Imogen continues. 'I should have got over the denial stage a long time ago.'

'But you're right,' she says, turning round. 'It is indeed very hard to believe. He was such a sensible man.' She sits back in the chair. 'Aren't you going to ask me about Dylan's mother?'

'I'd certainly like to ask why you won't let Dylan tell me about her himself.'

'I can give you a better picture.'

'Do I need a picture?'

Dorothy hesitates a moment. 'Well yes, I think you do.'

'So... they met at a concert.'

'London's Cadogan Hall. They didn't go for a drink or anything, but agreed that the next time one of them had to go to a concert on their own, they'd write to the other and see if they wanted to come. You can imagine that Sophie's first letter was probably written for the novelty of writing to a lighthouse, and maybe

The Lighthouse Keeper's Daughter

his reply had a question about her music collection... I don't think either of them thought for a moment that their friendship would become... all-consuming. Eventually, they did arrange another concert. Autumn 1981. Hugh had just been told the lighthouse would be fully automated by the following summer, and your mother was pressurising him to apply for a Principal Keeper job on another lighthouse, even though they were all going to be automated sooner or later. Then there was Sophie – undemanding, sharing his passion for self-improvement and the arts. When they met again – well, Sophie had grown into a woman...'

'Yes, yes, I know. And I've got a half-brother. It takes some getting used to, but Dylan and I are already friends, so it'll be fine. What happened to Sophie?'

'She fell out with her parents and went to live with her French grandparents on a farm in Normandy. Dylan was born and lived there until he was twelve – when Sophie died in an accident.'

'Oh.'

'His grandparents were no longer alive, so he came over to England to live with me in the lighthouse.'

'Oh! So that room downstairs—'

'Is his old bedroom, yes.'

Imogen drinks the rest of her juice, taking this in. She's finally hearing Dylan's story, but it doesn't feel quite right, or something's missing. Maybe it's the still unexplained delay in its telling. 'What kind of accident?'

'Sailing. A boat collision.'

'So they both drowned. How strange.'

'Yes.'

'But... coming back to my father... He must have been gutted when pregnant Sophie went off to France, on top of having to find himself a new job, a different life. Maybe that's why it happened, he was depressed, distracted...'

Dorothy's face breaks into a sad smile. 'Even the most sensible people can make terrible mistakes under pressure. I think you're beginning to understand him, my dear. I always hoped you would. It's why I invited you to stay in the lighthouse, with Dylan keeping an eye on you and the Visitor's Centre teaching you about the area. It's why I've been sending you these diary pages. I can now see that you're ready for more.'

Imogen watches her leave the room. There's no longer any difficulty in her walk, the stick is still propped up against the chair.

Her phone peals in her coat pocket. It's Santi with a WhatsApp: '*uff already enough of Christmas familyyyyy! Only 16 days now!*'

She'll tell him about this. They'll have another chat about *fathers*. She'll read this next lot of entries – how much more can there be to say? – and then answer him.

Dorothy comes back with a hardback notebook, pulls the chair next to the bed and sits down. Taking a handkerchief from her pocket, she lets the diary fall open at a page bookmarked with an old envelope.

Sat 9th Jan. '82
What a day.

A lovely start, with Sophie arriving at Dorothy's, pulling her out of the car into a hug, her little hard tummy against me. Putting her bag in the old keeper's room, hers for a couple of nights, then tucking into shepherd's pie with Dorothy and an embarrassed Clive.

But poor Sophie: now that the posh London girls' school suddenly doesn't need her secretarial skills anymore, she can't pay the rent but can't face going back to her furious parents. She's going to try and find some work locally on Monday, but she's so tired and nauseous...

The Lighthouse Keeper's Daughter

I assured her we'll be together by the time the baby comes in July, but I need time to work out how to do the best for Beryl and Imogen.

Back home, Beryl returns from an afternoon with Bill's wife, and of course starts up again about why I didn't go for the North Foreland land light job. When she finally stops ranting on and on, spent and tearful, I ask her what she wants. Overall. In <u>life</u>. She stands there with her mouth open. Does she really want to move again, disrupting Imogen's studies? Wouldn't she rather make some changes <u>here</u>? Do something that my work patterns have made difficult for her? Voluntary work? Classes? What does she really <u>want</u>?

She looks around her, back at me, and shrugs. 'This,' she says. 'Not having to worry about anything. My home.'

'Trinity House looking after you... us.'

'I suppose so, yes. I don't want to change. Is there anything wrong with that?'

I kissed her cheek with a heavy heart. Then I wrapped up and went for a stroll around the village before supper.

A couple of people say hello and ask when I'm due back at the lighthouse. Why do they always ask that? As if I don't belong on land. Then the DLF guy who fixed the boiler on the light and borrowed one of my Orwells spotted me through the window of the Tiger Inn and dragged me in for a beer. But who's he with? Only bloody <u>Vince</u>. As soon as I can, I get away, but the bugger catches up with me on the footpath cut-through to the road.

'Had a good day, Hugh?'

'Yes thanks. You?'

'Beryl preparing a nice supper so you can... restore your energies?'

I stop and look at him. It's a cold evening but his heavy features are sweaty. 'What? Look I'm sorry, I've got to—'

Then he says something about punctuality being important for double-living.

'I suppose all keepers feel like they're living two lives, yes. But I've really—'

He chuckles. 'But _you_,' he says, patting my shoulder, 'you are the double-life _expert!_ Hell, do _you_ know how to have it all! Practical lighthouse keeper who could turn his hand to anything, but also self-made intellectual. Respectable professional, but also meeting up with that shady old Greek yacht owner who's wriggling out of a smuggling charge. Dependable family man, but also romantic secret lover.'

Felt like I'd been struck in the chest.

'Oh Hughie, your face! But you never notice me, do you? It's amazing what you can see from out in a boat. People don't think, they forget a boat has a person, a man with eyes, a man with a _sense of right and wrong_.'

'Look—'

'And runs in the family, doesn't it? Your sister has it all too: snooty wife of an important doctor, but also "treating" that Yankee—'

I grabbed him and pushed him against the wall. Told him to stop bloody making up things about people, just because he can't get a girl of his own. But that makes him laugh even more.

'God, I really am invisible to you, aren't I! I've got a girl all right. About a year now. But not all of us have it so easy. Seems so wrong, that some should have so much, while others have a cottage that'll fall onto the beach, a boat that needs expensive repairs, and no way of affording a little dirty weekend.'

So I'm sitting here now just gazing at the black square of the window. Trying to think what to do. Supporting two families might just be possible, if I get that job at the hotel. But also paying Vince to keep his gob shut... and for how long? In six months' time, I'll be with Sophie, nothing to hide. But if Clive ever found out about Dorothy...

I've got to deal with this.

'So he was going to leave us.'

'But he wanted to do the best for you and Beryl; it wouldn't have been—'

'And what's all this about smuggling?'

'I don't know. He never goes into it.'

'Why can't he just *tell* my mother? Tell Vince to get lost? I don't think he would have said anything to Uncle Clive – or if he had, he wouldn't have been believed.'

She sighs. 'Well, as you'll see, he had his reasons… He had a plan, and didn't want Vince to scupper it.'

Dorothy turns the page. 'Read on.'

Mon 8th Mar. '82

Vince. I thought it would just be the boat repairs. But then he wanted the deposit on his holiday in Benidorm with the girlfriend. Presumably I'll be expected to pay the balance when it becomes due. Then today when he brought the post and had a tea with us, he mentions seeing a private dentist about the alignment of his teeth, looking over at me for a reaction. He's an orthodontist's dream; God knows how much that could run to.

And all this after a weekend persuading Beryl that we don't need to replace the Marina yet. But suppose this week's service turns up horrendous faults with it, she gets talked into trading it in, and then tries to draw from our now nearly empty building society account to pay for a new car?

Sophie thinks it's time to stop this; we should just tell Beryl about us, and let Dorothy make her own decision about how she wants to deal with him. If he tells Trinity House that I'm involved with Thanos, it's just his word against mine. Besides, she's decided to take up her grandparents' offer to have her to stay, so she'll be off to Normandy soon, and suggests I could even tell Vince that she's left me.

But she doesn't know what I'm planning. Nor does Dorothy. Not yet. When they do, they'll see why I mustn't be linked with Thanos. Why I can't risk Vince telling Clive about Dorothy's affair and making life impossible for her at the old lighthouse; I need her there for a few more months. I'm still considering the options, but both involve Vince being out of my life, for good.

'Oh my God, he wasn't thinking of…'

'You have to remember it's his *diary*. Maybe it just felt good to put that down on paper.' She reaches forward and turns the page.

Sun 2nd April '82

There's just a weak shaft of sunlight coming through the window over Len's bunk, my own now in darkness. So perhaps I'll sleep now, four hours before I've got the Middle. But it's hard. Now the plan's coming together. Now I've decided. Now I'm on a countdown.

I got the chance to speak to Len. I can almost hear his thoughts as he creeps around in the lantern room upstairs, stunned. Downstairs, I think Bill heard our raised voices and senses there's a problem, so we'll have to invent something. I wish I could tell him too, but we're both sure he couldn't cope with it. He's turned off the Falklands programme on the telly, probably already making the cheese spread sandwiches to take up and share with Len before taking over the shift. I hope to God Len's calmed down.

I've written to Beryl. It's over. Even without my plan, this was going to happen as soon as I came ashore for good. I loved Beryl once, in many ways she was a wonderful wife, but she stifles me. God, I feel more claustrophobic during an evening at home than I do sitting here with two chunky guys in a twelve-foot diameter pole stuck in the sea. It's awful, but mainly I just feel relieved. I've got to be careful, I'm aware these last letters will be looked at for clues – and for Beryl,

The Lighthouse Keeper's Daughter

who'll never understand, I'm fighting the temptation to leave some. I was brought up to be straight with people, look them in the eye. But then, is that how you want to hear that someone has left you? Better to be told some other way, surrounded by friends who can support you. Not by the person who's physically there but already gone. Heavens, it must be about thirteen years since it happened to me with that actress on Thanos' boat, but I still remember it. No. Beryl will have Len, Bill, their wives – and most importantly, her beloved Corporation of Trinity House, looking after her as one of the family. She'll be okay.

I've written to Imogen. Wanting to give more than the congratulations and commiserations on her school grades, a joke about Bill's alphabetical ordering of the food tins, how we coped with the seagull that came in the window. But now is not the time to hope for anything more from her, or give more of myself only to take myself away. I just hope that one day she understands. One day not too far away. I'm starting to wonder about Dorothy's suggestion of Imogen having this diary, if and when she's ready for it.

'Hope I understand what?' She turns to her Aunt. 'What, Dorothy? Tell me what happened for God's sake, *now*!'

'I am. But I think you've had—'

'Give me the diary!' Imogen says, as her aunt moves it out of her reach. 'Give it to me *now! Right now!*'

'Imogen, calm down! We can't do this like—'

Imogen lunges forward to grab it. Dorothy shrieks.

'What's going on in here?' shouts Anthea, coming in and rushing to her mother. 'Imogen, control yourself!'

'It says in there that you *wanted* me to have the diary, so why can't you just hand it over?'

They fix each other with wide, tearful eyes. Everybody downstairs has stopped talking.

Then Dorothy takes the book from under her arm. 'You're right. I did. I just hope…' She opens the diary at the second to last page, and puts the letter behind it.

<u>Sun 21st May '82</u>

Off. For the very last time. I need to be fit and alert, physically and mentally, but how, when I'm broken in half? Imogen. Imogen, Imogen, Imogen. Hello Imogen, if you're reading this! <u>When</u> you read this, because I've told Dorothy to give you my diary, when you're ready. She'll know when that is. But that's only if I can't give it to you myself.

You'll hear it was an accident, maybe suicide. In your fantasising little head, there will be times when you don't believe either. I can just see you, staring at the lighthouse, inventing an outrageous alternative ending. It worries me, the way you see everything as a story, moulding the grey muddle of life into something linear, extraordinary, elevated. But just this once, your story will be the reality. I hope.

In a few days' time, there'll be a mid-morning high spring tide and quite a swell. Len will be watching the Falklands news after sleeping off the middle watch, and Bill fussing with his lunch duty. I'll go to the lantern room for a brief confirming Morse code with Dorothy, put a half wetsuit on under my clothes, and go down to fish.

Len – if I forget – will query the supplies, sending Bill into a sufficient fluster of counting and rearranging, as well as dealing with the stove, that when Len makes tea after half an hour or so, there's no way Bill will leave his precious kitchen to bring me my cup. Len will come down with it, but I'll already have had my last tea on the lighthouse. Having used the cup I drank from earlier (in case forensics bother with it), he'll pour it away and leave it by the door. He may be tempted to peer out and see how far I've managed to

swim, but he won't because he could be spotted doing so by someone walking on the cliff. He'll go back to Bill until lunch is ready and he's sent down to fetch me. Then he'll run back up, laughing and telling Bill that I'm playing silly buggers, going up to the top shouting out how he knows I'm up there. Then he has to come down and scream at Bill that he can't find me. I hate to think of Bill's distress, but it will be less than the burden of being involved in this. Finally, Len – hoping he's given me enough time – will call the Coastguard.

Meanwhile, I'll have either drowned or reached Falling Sands, where I'll hide in that cliff crevice until Thanos' men come in their rib. One of us will crouch at the bottom once I'm on board, so that anyone watching the boat from above will see it disappear from view when under the cliff and then coming out again still with two men in dark jackets. Then we'll head out to sea to board Thanos' new Hatteras, hoist the rib onto the flydeck, and do the 6-8 hour crossing to Le Havre.

D'you remember Thanos and his wife? They visited us once when you were eight or nine, he taught you how to tie a bowline. Anyone could have saved her when she went overboard – it's just that I happened to be awake, sleepless with heartache. Now he'll save me. Strange how things work out.

From Le Havre it's less than an hour's drive to Sophie's grandparents' farm near Étretat. A place with a lighthouse on chalk cliffs that will always remind me of that picture you drew with your wax crayons.

So there you are. That, I hope, is the story. No more diary until I get to France – I must give this to Len to pass to Dorothy, before I forget.

So goodbye for now, my beautiful, talented, sweet daughter. You're going to be fine – just remember to take that noddle out of the clouds and look around you sometimes, okay? Goodbye for now. Just for now

'Goodbye?' Imogen says quietly. 'He didn't mind sending a goodbye that... I'd only get after thirty years?' They both start reassuring her that that was never the plan, but she can't hear them and the writing blurs, hot tears stinging her cheeks. Anthea passes her some tissues and puts a hand on her shoulder. 'And what's this letter...'

1, Birling Cottages
Birling Gap
Sunday 27th June 1982

Dear Dorothy

I am truely sorry for your loss. And for not writing you earlier, but I'm hoping that after a month your ready to hear what I have to tell you about the day Hugh died.

It was a Sunday, and I don't go to the lighthouse on Sundays but an American couple booked me to pick them up from Brighton and take them back to Eastbourne. So I put out from Birling Gap and I wasn't thinking, habit I suppose, but I started off in the direction of the lighthouse before I realised and turned the boat round. But just as I did I saw him. Well I didnt know it was him of course, the water was right choppy, it could have been some idiot traped by the tide or even a body in the water come off of the cliff. I went back again full speed to reach him. When I was nearer I saw the person was swimming, such a relief but it didn't matter how I shouted he didn't answer. Like I wasnt there. Should of known then that it was Hugh, he never saw me, I was invisible, didnt count for nothing. But he's swimming that far out in that water. Over at the lighthouse I thought I could see a fishing rod, it looked like he'd fallen and was being dragged out on the current so maybe like was in shock or something and why he wasn't answering. So I bring the boat alongside him, HUGH HUGH I'm shouting. When I'm almost on him he looks up

at me, a face like I never seen of fear, but not taking the oar I put out for him to grab, looks like he even pushed it away. There's me screaming I'm trying to HELP but I can't catch what he says. It goes on and on like this and then I think oh god he's not with it I'm going to have to jump in and get him, and I tell him that. Then he does answer me, he goes GO PLEASE VINCE LEAVE ME I'M OK ITS WHAT I WANT. Then I starts shouting out about Beryl and his little girl and you and Sophie and the guys on the lighthouse, how can he do this to them. He shouts GO again but he's breathless now so that's it I have to go in. I turn the engine off and get the anchor and lob it over. We're running out of time see, I need to be quick, but the boat has turned while I was getting the anchor and Hugh... I don't know, still I dont understand, but he must of got some last energy to swim away from me and that's why it happened. The anchor caught him. I could see the blood on his head and he's just floating now. I'M COMING IN DON'T WORRY I'm shouting even though really he looks dead, but then he says it again. GO ITS OK. I definitely heard that, but then nothing more just still.

How could it be ok to leave him there, how could I do that, but I was scared you see. There was a boat much further on, and if I left now they might not see me. I couldn't be near Hugh, nobody would beleive it when everybody knows things are bad between us. So I pulled up the anchor and went off to Brighton at full speed, I don't look back, telling myself its what he wanted. And I tell myself that every day since.

But really I'd killed him before, I'd been killing him as soon as I started to make him pay for what he was doing, for what you both was doing. Maybe he never told you. Blackmail it was, although I didn't call it that. I never thought it would get so bad, but it was too easy. I started it just to make him and you think about the wrong and right, how you can't have everything and hurt people like that. It kills people too, my mother she slowly died from hurt from my father's affairs. I don't know your husband, but Beryl is a good woman, she don't deserve it. Nor does the girl, all reddish and clever and superior like her Daddy, but when I did the shelves she made me tea and said thankyou so much, then saw me in the village much later and said how happy her books were on it. I decided I was going to stop getting money out of her dad, once me and Karen have had the holiday where I pesuade her to come live down south.

But then Hugh has to go and jump in the sea and throw his life away, like if he can't have it all he don't want none of it. Anyone else could of helped him but theres been too many years not listening to each other. But now – now I think of him a lot, like he's the only one who will understand what I'm going to do, can almost feel him pat me on the back and offring to buy me a pint later, wherever we end up. But first I've got to end up... well it's a nice day for it today. I'm going to do some weeding on the cliff side of the garden near where that crack has appeared and well you will have heard by now what happened to me.

So I'm saying again I'm so sorry for your loss and I mean it. Do what you like with this letter, it won't make any difference to me now. But this money, its not nearly all I took off of him, but please one day give it to his little girl and tell her I'm sorry.

Yours sincerly
Vince Harris

'We put it in savings for you, it's now quite—'

'I don't want it! The bribe money. God, how could I? Is that what you've been giving me this story for? Because there's no other point in it. He left us, for a girl just ten years older than me, an improved version of his daughter, and—'

'No, Imogen! It looks like he really thought he'd be able to contact you.'

The Lighthouse Keeper's Daughter

'Oh come on. How can you say that? He had a plan, but he chose to *drown* rather than be saved and brought back to us!'

Dorothy and Anthea start protesting.

'Look, enough! You can defend him all you like, but I don't want to spend one more minute trying to figure out my father and whatever the hell he did.' She gets up, steadying herself with the bedhead. 'In fact, I'm sorry, but this just isn't going to work. I want to go home. There's a flight at eight something and Ollie and I are going to be on it.' She looks at her watch and lifts her suitcase onto the bed.

'Home?' Dorothy asks.

'The lighthouse, if you don't mind me staying there until I—'

'You can stay there as long as you like, dear. But three days before Christmas, there's not a prayer of you getting two seats on tonight's flight. And *flight* isn't the answer, Imogen. How is it going to help you, holing up alone for Christmas? This is what you always do: run away. Dashing off to the coast away from your family, diving into a fantasy romance on your phone, pretending your serious health problem is just a joke. And probably putting the many parts of your life that you can't deal with into this novel you're writing, fictionalising them to protect yourself from… having to actually *feel* anything.'

'What! How the hell d'you—'

'Hugh was right; it would be much better for you, and others, if you could get your head out of the clouds sometimes.'

Imogen opens her mouth to shout at her, but then has a sickening sense that the old woman might have a point. She slumps back down on the bed, closes her eyes for a moment, her temples throbbing. 'It's just been so hard…' She wipes her nose. 'Staying at the lighthouse and reading the diary, I've remembered so many things I'd forgotten – or made myself forget. When I was a child – even if I didn't always show it – everything I did... it was for him. And he loved me too, but it now seems... not enough.'

'*No*, dear', Dorothy says, taking her hand. 'As I said, I think he really thought he could make it all work. In fact...' Anthea and Dorothy exchange a look.

'In fact, what?' Imogen takes back her hand. 'We don't *have* any facts, other than that he planned to leave us, and then died. You're right, it's time I faced this head on. I wasn't enough. Somehow I always knew he deserted me. But I'm not going to let this drag me down anymore. And you trying to console me with guesses at his plans to see me again is just annoying, okay? It doesn't help, so please stop.'

Dorothy and Anthea are glaring at each other again. It looks like Anthea sees Imogen's point, and will try and stop Dorothy going on like this. But Dorothy hasn't finished.

'We *do* have—'

'Mother!'

'It's time, Anthea, she—'

Anthea grabs Imogen's arm. 'Imogen, you've got to swear that you'll never tell anyone about this.'

'About what?' Imogen looks from one to the other. '*What*?'

Dorothy takes a big breathe. 'It's not conjecture. We know for a fact that his life was not enough without you. Imogen... he survived. He made it to France.'

'Oh! Is he...?'

'He drowned, but twelve years later in France, with Sophie, when a speedboat crashed into their dinghy. Shortly after he'd asked me to help him plan how to get you and baby Oliver over there for a visit. He was about to write to you...'

'No. I don't believe you.'

 The Lighthouse Keeper's Daughter

'He kept diaries in France, and the last entry is… oh…' Dorothy starts to heave with tears.

'The last entry is a letter to you,' Anthea says. 'The diaries are in a safe at the bank. You understand that nobody outside the family must ever know?'

'Yes, yes, of course… Is that why you've been telling me everything so gradually, watching me – you thought I might go to the police or something?'

'We had to be sure,' Anthea says. 'There are still people around who'd like to see my mother jailed for her part in it, if they found out – Sophie's parents for example. We have to be very careful. And the publicity would be dreadful for all of us. We'll get them out for you to look at next time you come. But we'll send you a copy of that last page.' Imogen is staring over towards the dressing table as if in a trance. Anthea sits down on the bed and puts her arm round her. 'Are you okay?'

'That lamp.'

Dorothy smiles tearfully. 'We wondered if you'd recognise it.'

'What's it doing here?'

'When you moved to Surrey with your mother and her new husband, a lot of the furniture was left behind – they probably wanted a completely new start. Beryl asked Len if he'd deal with the things for her. He invited me over to see if I wanted anything… and when I saw it – all blue and white striped – I knew it had to be the one Hugh told me about. The one you flicked on and off, thinking you could send messages to him in his lighthouse. I think it was the only thing I took.'

Imogen smiles through tears. 'I think you might have to lend me a slightly larger suitcase when I go back.'

CHAPTER 29

MONDAY 7TH JANUARY 2013
Madrid, Spain

Brave as well as kind, funny, beautiful. Well, maybe not beautiful, but if he can't stop wanting to look at her, she might just as well be. And she has no idea; he's never met a woman so unaware of how lovely she is. On her Facebook page, Ollie has posted a series of photos from the lighthouse visit in Jersey, thanking his great Aunt Dorothy. A rather tactless outing, surely? And just an hour or so before they would finally give her the full story about her father... good God. But she looks happy holding what looks like a giant light bulb, the reflections casting an angelic glow over her face. Then there's a picture of her looking back and grinning as she climbs the spiral staircase, unaware of the pleasing curve of her little jeaned backside.

He puts the phone down, checks the time. A few more minutes before he needs to leave; he doesn't want to be late for Ignacio this time.

Scenic photos from the top of the thing; a shot of Imogen's half-brother, judging by the freckled narrow face; and one of the blonde friend who nearly died at the cliff but thankfully now looks full of the joys of life. He catches Imogen in the background and pulls the photo larger. She's looking stunned, or hurt, shielding her eyes as she looks out of a small window. Maybe they noticed her face, because in the last photo she's in the centre of an arm-in-arm group shot, Ollie towering slightly awkwardly above them. Perhaps he'll meet these people one day because... although she was appalled when she thought he suggested being 'friends with benefits', there's just a tiny chance she might want to become lovers with the benefit of also being friends.

※

Ignacio opens the door himself. 'On time, for once! Happy New Year, Santi. And I'm sure it will be. Come in, come in. Your startling punctuality is rewarded; the chap from the café's just brought up coffee and some warm pastries.'

'Perfect!' Santi follows him into his office full of baking smells and helps himself to *pain aux raisins*.

'All for us – Miri and the receptionist are still sitting around eating too much with their families, bless them.'

'Ah yes, you said. Good Christmas?'

'Marvellous. And you? I hear the Three Kings have brought you a little English lady.'

'She arrives tonight for the Spanish course starting tomorrow. My turn to help. So you needed to speak to me about...?'

'A number of things, and there's some paperwork.' They sit down, Ignacio handing him a coffee in a polystyrene cup. There's a fuss about sugar. Ignacio bites into an enormous croissant, wipes his mouth, leans back in his chair with a sigh; the giving of news is his only chance to perform these days. 'What d'you want first: the bad news, the not-so-bad, the good or the brilliant?'

'Ooh - the brilliant!'

'Ah, but if I give you that, you'll realise what the bad news is.'

'Ah. The Not-So-Good then.'

'Right. Concerts in Madrid. Can't get you one at Arganda del Rey. But Café de Berlín can fit you in next Tuesday, and that little place on calle Mancebos is getting back to me with some dates – but that'll have to be after the *Los Mis* tour.'

Tuesday – just a day after Imogen goes back. Maybe they can change her flight. 'Well thanks for getting those, great. Now I'll go for the bad, please.'

Ignacio puts down his coffee and leans forward, both hands on the table. 'Santi. I'm sorry, but you haven't got Lorca. Nor has Antonio, if it's any consolation. They suddenly found some money for a B-lister. That Mexican who played—'

'That's actually... a relief. I don't think I ever for a moment believed I would. Or *should*, for that matter.'

'Don't do yourself down. It *could* have been you. But here's the brilliant news: they want you to play a flamenco guitarist in a flash back scene, singing and playing – you've even got a couple of lines.'

'Oh wow!' He thumps the table with both hands. 'So I get the fun of being involved, a bit of money, and using my English!'

'Well actually, you'll be in subtitled Spanish – and you need to start practising a Granada accent! Your English lady will be appalled, but at least you'll now be able to communicate while you're there. It's great news – who knows what it could lead to. And there's a bit of story there for the media, you having some of the music in the film.'

'My uncle and I are putting in for the whole soundtrack, he's done quite a lot of that kind of thing. We're waiting to hear.'

Ignacio nods his head slowly. 'So I gather. Sounds like things are coming together for you, Santi. In fact, you seem more... settled in yourself. I'm glad. Although I think it might mean that you won't like the last bit of news. The bank ad – they'd like you for just a one-off photo shoot on Wednesday.'

'Oh no. I've already got that naff modelling thing tomorrow, and several projects to do with my uncle. Some of it's cheesy too, but musical cheese is… easier to swallow.'

Ignacio chuckles. 'Okay, I'm hearing you.' He takes the last pastry. 'I'll have that,' he says. 'You're looking good, don't want that weight going on again. And keep the English going. What am I saying? Doesn't look like that's going to be a problem.'

><

'Papi! That's wonderful!' She even leaves her quesadilla to get up and give her dad a hug. 'So now you're *bound* to get the soundtrack too!'

'Oh no, we'll just have to see.'

'Must be annoying having done all that work preparing for the Lorca role though.'

'Well, at least it got me learning English and reading.'

'No, *Imogen* got you learning English and reading. While Miri *pushed* you to go for Lorca – a role you never felt right about. Maybe that came between you.'

'I'm sorry Pato, you two got on so well. You can still be friends, you know.'

'Naa, she's too busy.' She looks at him a moment. 'Aren't you still upset about her dumping you?'

'Must you put it that way? I've moved on.'

'Of course. When does Imogen get here?'

'Tonight. Here for a Spanish course and some more research for her book. We're *friends*, Pato.'

'Right,' she says, with a grin. 'Hey, wasn't it in a VIPS that I met her?'

'Yes, and you were vile.'

'I won't be this time, I promise. Will I see her next weekend?'

'Maybe, I don't know her plans. Have you got everything you need for college tomorrow?'

'Just a few bits we can pick up on our way out,' she says, tilting her head to the stationery shelves not far from the restaurant section.

'And you're sure it's going to be Pharmacology at Complutense?'

'Yes, Papá. Or wherever I can get into. I'm not an artist. You know how you told me once that acting freaks you out?'

'Did I?'

'At Esme's party, you'd had a bit to drink… Well that's how I feel about Art. I'd rather just do some now and again, rather than have that pressure and end up hating it. I know you can't believe it, but I'm really interested in Pharmacology – and I can *do* it.'

'You certainly can. How in hell did you turn out so smart?'

'While Imogen's son – who surely must have inherited a good brain – just wants to mix cocktails. Isn't she fed up about that?'

'Probably, but she knows he's not had a good time of it this year, with his parents splitting up, so for now she just wants him to be happy.'

'And is *she* happy? All alone in that lighthouse? I mean, has she had a boyfriend since her marriage broke up?'

'Pato, *please*. How would I know?'

'Because *friends* talk about these things, Papá.'

⁂

He drives into the airport car park, finds a space and turns off the engine. Pato has a point; how come Imogen has never told him anything at all about her love life? She moved out ten months ago;

                    The Lighthouse Keeper's Daughter

surely she's met somebody during that time. But then she probably takes these things very seriously, so perhaps not. In which case, in that English way of laughing about yourself all the time, shouldn't she by now have made a comment on her solitary lighthouse life or the tedium of cooking for one? But no, she always seems so… complete. As if she *wants* to be alone. *Or isn't.*

He looks at the car clock. Not long until she lands. Perhaps she's right now turning her phone back on and reassuring a chap back home that she's arrived. He gets out of the car and slams the door. Oh for God's sake, of course she doesn't have a boyfriend; he'd know.

Nothing yet on his phone. He crosses the road; may as well get a coffee and watch the Arrivals board. He's surprised to find that he's feeling… not *nervous*, exactly, but—

'Hello!' It's her.

'How did you—'

'My phone's out of—'

'The plane was…?'

'Shall I go back inside?' She's laughing, her pale blue eyes searching his face. He should be kissing each of her cheeks, but he finds he's giving her a tight hug, her silky hair against his neck. She smells of minty English flowers. He let's go, but holds her shoulders, grinning uncontrollably.

'I… hope is okay, I have something I need finish with Uncle Pedro, and… my aunt say there is *roscón de Reyes* cake of yesterday that you can try.' God, what's happened to his English?

'Okay!'

'And then later come my mother and Esme, for to have dinner. If it is too much, I will say you are tired and I take you to—'

'No, no, that's fine… I'm sorry, are you still doing Christmas?'

'Ah, well the thing is…' He takes her across the road and puts her case in the boot. 'It's a little celebration. I tell you in the car.'

She's biting her lip.

'Don't worry, I don't have Lorca – that would be aw-ful. But I do have a little role.' He tells her about the guitarist.

'Maybe the one who inspired the poem!'

'Is what I have been thinking! And it is good that you celebrate too, because you are part of this, to happen.'

He starts the car, and the radio jumps into life with the catchy *Vente pá Madrid* song. Imogen laughs and starts singing along.

'You see?' Santi says. 'Madrid wants you!'

CHAPTER 30

TUESDAY 8TH JANUARY 2013
Madrid, Spain

Mayte the teacher has a wonderfully low, well-projected voice, but two of her fellow students – a softly spoken Chinese woman and a London girl with a Communications degree – are mostly inaudible. Since she can only connect with the handsome and gloriously loud New Yorker, she's probably coming over a little too interested in him, something that's drawing sulky looks from Miss Communications.

'Imogen?'

'Er...' They are being asked to practise superlatives by making up sentences about possible ways of meeting a partner, but they're running out of ideas. With great reluctance, she comments that it would be *divertidísimo* to meet someone through Twitter.

It certainly has been very amusing. Although it's recently, maybe for a while, been getting... No, it's probably just her imagination. Luckily she'll have a few hours to calm down between the end of this class and meeting him later – after he's been photographed with an electric shaver, poor chap.

Now they're doing something on the subjunctive mood. Imogen likes the subjunctive. Not the awkward flipping around of word endings needed for formal or negative commands. Nor the subjunctive used for 'uncertainty'; when Santi kept using it during their chat about when she could come over and do the Spanish course, she eventually perplexed him by writing *'stop using the subjunctive, I'm definitely coming!'* No, it's the *imperfect* subjunctive she likes, with its yearning 'era' and 'iera' sound: *si quisiera, si pudiera, si fuera…* If I *wanted*, if I *could*, if I *were…*

'Imogen?'

'Si no fuera tan… nerviosa…' If I weren't so nervous…

A smile of encouragement from the New Yorker.

'Lo pasaría bien.' I would have a good time.

⚝

Having lunch with the two girls in the bar across the road, she realises they are even harder to understand in English. The effort of trying to do so, after a morning of Spanish, is reducing her to a grinning witlessness – in which she seems to have agreed to go with them to the Prado that afternoon. Now they are discussing the artists. Velazquez, Goya. Goya: wasn't he the one whose paintings took a very dark turn after he went deaf?

Then she sees a WhatsApp from Santi across her buzzing phone. *'So what are you up to doing?'*

She feels a heat in her cheeks, and can't help smiling to herself. There's no way she's in a fit state for an art gallery. 'Sorry, something's come up. I'll have to do it another time.'

⚝

The carriage clanks through the tunnel, silencing everyone. Imogen leans back in her seat and relaxes; she's had enough of the aural world today. The zoo will be perfect; lots of written information, and if the Spanish gets her down she'll just watch the animals.

She gets out her phone and looks again at the '*so what are you up to doing*'. She's going to have to correct that – even though it's pretty much exactly what she's been asking herself ever since he hugged her at the airport.

Coming out of the station, she finds herself on the edge of parkland with a sign pointing along a sandy path to the zoo. She breathes in the pine-scented air, the sun warm on her hair. Santi must have taken an excited little duck-obsessed Pato along here, while she was doing the same with sheep-mad Ollie along Regent's Park's Outer Circle to London Zoo.

Inside, the paths meander through streams and ponds with lots of ducks – '*patos*'. A signpost: she's going to be learning her animals in Spanish. But what's this – *panda gigante* immediately ahead? She was going to save them for last, or at least hold out until she couldn't wait any longer. She goes inside the building.

The mother panda is slumped like a carelessly placed teddy, munching her bamboo, while the baby is surrounded by staff members weighing, photographing, and picking him out of his plastic crib into an unscientific cuddle. Two older women next to her are chatting excitedly about him, but when the baby is returned to his mother and she gathers him up, they are stunned into silence. Perhaps they too are recalling the deep satisfaction of holding a baby in your arms, something you remember as yesterday after eighteen years or fifty… If she ever had another child, if she could, *si tuviera, si pudiera*…

Back outside, there's an enclosure round a tree with a small group of red pandas.

Her phone buzzes. '*Where are you?*'

She sends him a photo of one of the little bears, its luxurious fur turning copper and gold in the sun. '*I love them!*'

'*Of course, they are your colour!*'

'*What?*'

'*No, you are more like melocotón seco.*'

Dried peach. Well that's a new one. She wonders if he and his friends have made the usual wonder-if-the-carpet-matches-the-curtains jokes.

'*Imogen!*' He follows her name with a line of fruit emojis. Mostly orange or red ones.

'☹'

She walks on. Folds her arms and remembers the hug again. It could well be that, however fond of her he may be, he just can't find her attractive. She frowns at her reflection in the glass of the kiosk: she could still lose half a stone, but there's nothing she can do about her colouring.

A rhino slowly thuds up and down its paddock. She reads that it – *she* – is mostly a solitary animal. How can any creature want to be that? *She's* been solitary for nearly a year now, but it still takes delicate planning to maintain a sense of well-being. Apparently rhinos have awful eyesight, but their exceptional sense of *hearing* helps their search for a breeding partner.

Her phone rings. 'Now what are you doing?'

She's thinking what an awful rhinoceros she'd make, but tells him to hang on and sends a photo of the doleful creature's face.

'Imogen? I was saying I have finished, and soon I will be at the zoo!'

'Oh! Great!' Her heart pounds. His meeting her here wasn't in the plot – although of course nothing's in the plot today, the page totally blank. She makes her way to the toilets, brushes her dried peach hair, pulls at the sweat top that keeps riding up under her coat, slings her heavy language school bag back over her shoulder. If only she'd gone back to the apartment to change before coming here. Ha! As if that's going to make a difference.

A large brown bear sitting on the edge of his concrete hill views her with sympathy. Lemurs next. She likes lemurs. But two of them are unenthusiastically having sex. Ignoring a gentle group of orangutans, she makes her way to a kiosk and orders a tea she doesn't want.

Sitting herself down at a wooden table, she realises she's feeling buzzily sick, lightheaded and impossibly in need of another pee. Otherwise called being nervous. What? She needs to remember the facts. Okay, Santi's not in a relationship now, and there are the hugs, but he's never given her any reason to believe that he thinks of her as more than a friend. No. Wait. That's *exactly* what he seems to have done, even though she has no idea how or when this started.

She takes another path; she should probably be making for the entrance to meet him, but she's lost her sense of direction and, unfolding the paper map for the first time, can't make any sense of it at all.

Her phone. 'I'm here! Where are you?'

'Er… I've got a rhinoceros here. *Rino-cer-onte blanco.*'

'Again? What goes with you and *los rinocerontes?*'

'But this chap's African. She was Indian.'

'I'm looking at the *mapa*… ah, I see it. Why not they put together, the *rinocerontes*, the poor things?'

'I don't know, they're… different I suppose.'

'Maybe they like the one to the other. *How* different?'

'Um, well one's got one horn, and the other's got two.'

'H-orn? What is?'

'Oh, you know, the hard thing at the front.'

'Ah…' he chuckles. 'Wait there. Oh – you have seen the *orangutanes? Qué preciosos…* Ah – and now I see you!'

They walk towards each other. It's that daft unstoppable smiling thing again, but then he just kisses each cheek and pats her on the back, leaving a tingling imprint on her spine.

'To where we go?'

'*Where shall* we go. What's happened to your English today?'

'*Ay…*' He looks down, puts his hand to his chin. Looks up again. 'Teacher, you make me miss… lose *confianza.*'

'What? I *gave* you confidence!'

'Yes but…' He sighs and puts his arms round her.

'But what?' she asks, leaning her head against his, imagining his thoughts passing straight into her head.

For a moment she fears she's about to hear how if he could, he would, but he can't… Then he comes closer, and, hesitantly at first, as if trying out a new language, puts his lips on hers.

><

This close, he can see the transparent ends of the eyelashes she's missed with the mascara, the way there are even freckles on her eyelids. Strands of hair between his two fingers are so soft he can barely feel them. He wants to kiss the lips of that clever little mouth. How can a woman be so fragile and so strong, all at once? She'll be different now, needing reassurance, things that are obvious will have to be spelt out. But she mustn't be allowed to control him, bamboozle him with all those words of hers – although just a little of that is probably good for him.

He pulls the dressing gown covering her lower half up towards her t-shirted shoulders. Shame it's not summer; he'd be lying here looking at her naked. As things are, he hasn't really seen much

The Lighthouse Keeper's Daughter

of her yet. Good God, what was he doing, fucking her like a teenager? One minute they were in the taxi kissing and cuddling, the next minute he had her up here, jeans down and he was on her. Although there again she's a puzzle: so endearingly awkward, but so easily and quickly pleased.

Remembering, he presses up against her and kisses a freckled eyelid. Then it's just as he thought it would be: she opens her eyes and smiles, runs her fingers through his hair, but can't hide a cloud of worry passing over her face.

'Imo-gen, *no te preocupes*. Everything will be good. We are *expertos* with to be friends of the *bolsillo*…er… pocket, when there is a distance still we are together.'

'But maybe I could come to Madrid.'

'*Sería maravilloso*. But step by step, no?'

The cloud again.

'I say this that you don't feel you have to decide so fast, that you relax.'

She nods uncertainly.

'Would you like some tea, madam?'

She smiles. 'Yes please.'

'You can take it with your homework.'

He goes to the kitchen to put the water on, then looks for her rucksack in the hall. The big textbook falls out, and while trying to put it back in again, he sees the elasticated writing notebook that she never shows to anyone.

'So were the Spanish lessons useful for your book?' he shouts out.

'They *were* actually,' she calls back. 'But I'd still like to sit in on one of your English classes, if the teacher doesn't mind.'

'I'm sure it is okay, but I will ask him.' He comes through with the rucksack. 'And the zoo. Was that useful for it?'

'Maybe.'

He sits down next to her on the bed. 'And *after* the zoo?' he asks with a grin.

'No!' she says, with a little laugh. She opens the textbook and finds a pencil.

'So there is no sex in the story?'

She's busy filling in gaps with verbs, but she's smiling.

'Imo-gen?'

She shakes her head, either to mean there isn't any, or she isn't going to say.

He leans over to see what she's writing. 'No, no, what is this 'si sabiera'? It is *si yo supiera*. If I knew.'

'Uh.' She rubs it out and replaces it.

'And here it is *si hubiera sabido*.'

'If I had known. Yes. *Joder*.' She corrects it.

'And what happens here on the spots?'

'Dots. Dotted line. We have to make something up.'

He makes a coffee and a tea, and comes back to find her biting her lip while forming something in his language. Then he sees that she's written '*Si quisieras, podrías vistarme en Inglaterra*.'

'Of course I *quisiera* visit you in England!'

CHAPTER 31

SATURDAY 12TH JANUARY 2013
Madrid, Spain

She can't write about it. She's been thrown into a scintillating present tense. Somewhere she hasn't been since… when she was a tiny child at that beach lighthouse her father worked on. When she met Ewan? No, too much tipping forwards and backwards with his enthusiasm and commitment phobia. When Ollie was born? Maybe when he was about three, when there was a briefly successful balance between motherhood and work. She seems to have lived most of her life *out* of the moment, except when having a small child or being one herself. Until now.

Here she is, wrapped up warm on Santi's cliff-balcony with her laptop and a coffee. Enjoying a few hours on her own, getting on with things, but occasionally stepping back in amazement at what's happening. She's happily got down to editing a couple of pesky articles for the magazine, and even the thought of tonight's scary celebrity reception for Esme's new album isn't going to spoil her afternoon. Of course, she *would* be considering using this evening's event in the novel, but…

She goes back in and sits down at the small table Santi has put in the bedroom for her laptop. Under it, in a locked folder, are the printed chapters of the novel so far. She takes them out again, feeling the forty-three thousand word weight of them in her hand, and breathes out heavily. It's not just that she's fed up with the moaning English teacher, Lizzie. There's Sami: he seems to have paled with envy, no longer able to compete with Santi's physicality – and the effect this is having on his creator. Then there's Santi himself. Even if she made the protagonist an Inuit trapeze-artist living in Venice, the way the guy meets Lizzie on Twitter would still make Santi feel he'd been studied and played with. Laughed at. As indeed he has been a little, at times. How did she ever think she could *do* this to him? No. Maybe one day there'll be a way to take the essence of this story into a new novel, but this one has to stop.

She's tempted to flick through – find a favourite Madrid setting, an amusing bit of language confusion – but she opens the drawer Santi emptied for her clothes and puts it underneath a jumper. They say every successful author has an unpublished novel in a bottom drawer; well, she's now made her sacrifice to the God of Literature.

Oddly, the notebook is harder. The silk-soft red leather, the paper-clipped pages, the twang of the elastic as she pulls the pen from it for what she realises will be the last time. The new novel – whatever it turns out to be – will have a new notebook, a different colour.

She opens it at the last – un-transferred – pages: the chapter at the zoo. The rhinos didn't make it into the scene, while the fluffy inactive pandas have taken undeserved cameo roles. Then there's the kissing in the taxi, pretty much as was. Back at the apartment, however, it's not the same at all; the abruptness of what really happened, the lack of dialogue – this would never be believed or tolerated. Even though she and Santi later laughed about never having communicated better.

She closes her eyes. Santi, Santi, Santi. It aches to love him so much. She picks up the pen and writes: *This has to stop! Time to get back to real life!* She was about to add: *…which is for once so exciting and real that I can't compete with it here!* – but she hears him opening the door and calling out to her, so she throws it in with the novel and closes the drawer.

'*¡Hola!* How did it go?' she asks.

'Uh, the *catarata* hasn't changed and she doesn't want an operation on the eye. I didn't need to be there, but sometimes my mother just likes to have a little *atención*.' He comes in and puts her arms round her.

'Aw, fair enough. So is she coming tonight?'

'Yes, with Pedro and Elena. Joselito and Miri are coming separate-ly. And there are other aunts and uncles, Joselito's brother from Aranjuez…' He lets go and opens the wardrobe.

'Of course, and I suppose there'll be lots of musicians you know.'

'Some… Uh, what-in-fuck am I going to wear?' He clacks through the hangers.

'It's what-*the*-fuck – get it right, *hombre*. And what the fuck am *I* going to wear?'

'I think maybe we have to go to Gran Vía.'

'But look, seriously, if it's going to be awkward – me turning up with you in front of all these people – I understand and don't mind staying here and watching a film.'

'Imo-gen! Already we have talked about this.'

'I know but… I really mean it. We've only been a couple for five days! You could tell your family I've got a migraine or something.'

He turns round and looks at her. 'I don't know why you think is so difficult. You not going to hear or understand some of the talk at the reception, is true, but the most part is… *chisme*-chat, you don't need it. Anyway, is more than the five days, other people were knowing about us long time before we knew it!'

She smiles and shrugs. 'That's true.'

'You don't *want* to go?'

'Of course I do!'

He's smiling again. 'O-kay take the coat,' he says, putting his jacket back on. 'We go to the shops now, come.'

※

He comes out of the fitting room wearing a black shirt with pale grey spots.

'Well *olé*!' exclaims Imogen, rather loudly. A couple of women coming out of the ladies' changing room look at him and then her.

'It's good, no? And at last I am smaller *talla*.'

'Size.'

'Yes, *size*.'

More women staring at them. You'd think he'd taken up with an alien.

'*Vale, ahora te toca a ti,*' he says.

'*¿Qué?* Oh, my turn, *sí.*' They pay for his shirt and then go over to the women's section. 'Just a top really.'

'Tob?'

'Top. *Camisa*. Something to go with my black trousers.' They find the evening wear rail and pick through slithery shirts, sparkling tank tops and off-the-shoulder things that Imogen can't even work out. 'God I hate shopping. Even the feel of these things gives me the creeps.'

He studies her face and then takes her arm to guide her out of the shop and back in the direction of the apartment.

'Where are we going? Sorry, I'll try harder,' she says with a giggle.

He takes her into an incense-scented accessories shop round the corner in a side-street.

'You have that black *top* that I like, no?'

'Yes.'

'*Vale*. Wait-a-moment.'

He disappears among the rails of cloth. She wonders if any of the hand-made necklaces would perform a sufficient transformation – until there are hands on her back and shoulders, along with a silky embroidered shawl of sea-turquoise and embroidered black flowers coming round her...

'Oh!' She feels the soft material between her fingers, the tickle of the tassels on her hand. 'I *love* it!'

※

Amazing the difference a triangle of material can make. Something to fiddle with when the Spanish gets hard, something she can talk about with Santi's smiling but rather suspicious *mamá*. She pulls it tighter around her as Santi leaves her with Uncle Pedro to go and take his turn being photographed with Esme in front of the giant poster of her new CD.

'So Imogen,' Uncle Pedro says in Spanish near her good ear, 'do you recognise any of these people?'

'Er... let me see.' She scans the room of beautiful or confidently extraordinary people. She proudly identifies a couple of famous guitarists, and a female singer whose album she's just ordered from a flamenco website.

'Very good, very good! But you know, there are too many television people here. I wonder how many of them even listen to Esme's music! Ah well, they're in for a treat. Oh - this blonde with the very handsome friend – who sadly for her, is well known to be homosexual – is the star of *La Universidad*.'

Imogen looks over at the cheerleader-cute woman who stared at her when they arrived, the one with perfect curves in a long, crimson dress and uncannily matching lipstick.

'A bit difficult, apparently. She's very pretty,' Imogen says.

Uncle Pedro laughs and pats her arm, while Santi's mother is shaking her head in some kind of disapproval.

'But isn't she a bit old to play a university student?'

Aunt Elena is saying something about make-up and illustrating her point with claw-like scratching movements that make Imogen laugh. Then Elena waves at Joselito and Miri, who are making their way across to them. Miri is elegant in a pair of skinny trousers and a pale silk shirt, and Joselito, who she's only ever seen in ancient jeans, is all in black with a new haircut, transformed by his new love. There are kisses all round, and an extra little hug from Miri.

'How-are-you Imo-chen?' Miri asks. 'Very nice, the *mantón* flamenco on your *color* English!'

'Thank you!'

Is it her imagination, or is Santi's mother looking a little sad on seeing the lovely Miri with her nephew rather than her son?

There are soon introductions to more aunts, uncles and cousins. It's going well, given the inevitable gaps in understanding, but nerves are having an effect.

There's a queue in the Ladies'– or there would be, but the Spanish don't seem to like putting themselves into a line. She memorises the women in front of her: an actress-type in an Abba jumpsuit, a black-haired woman in a white dress, a white-haired woman in a black dress, and a self-conscious, overweight eleven-year-old. She gets out her phone. It's 20:49. She thinks the concert was supposed to start at half eight, but nobody looks in the slightest bit worried.

The door opens behind her. 'Jeez… Oh hello, you're Santiago's

The Lighthouse Keeper's Daughter

English teacher, aren't you? Tania. From *La Universidad.*' Imogen is grabbed for the double kiss.

'Hi.'

'Didn't expect to hear English here, did you? I'm half-Californian.'

'Ah.'

'Although I'm sure Santi's getting damn good at English now!'

'Yes. But my Spanish isn't, so we've sort of swapped over.'

'So I've heard! I think you met my friend in a shop on Gran Vía today? She told me how easily the two of you jump between languages – and you've got him shopping!'

'No, we both hate—'

And of course there's been *lots of swapping* hasn't there? Miri has swapped cousins, and Santi has swapped blondes – *yet again...*'

'Blondes?'

'Oh, he sure likes his blondes. Let one break up his marriage when he was in *Guerra,* and then there was Nina and now you.'

'Nina?'

'Eponine in *Los Miserables.* Surely you know about *her.*'

'Oh yes, she's great. I've always called her Ep, like Santi does. But she's not been a girlfriend.'

Tania's mouth opens and closes again, a shine of sweat appearing above her crimson lips. 'Oh, I nearly forgot – we have to slip me in there, between the *Guerra* blonde and Miri. Although there are probably plenty of others.'

There are now only two in the non-queue in front of her: the older woman, who has just winked at her, and the eleven-year-old, who has started humming to herself.

Imogen turns back to Tania and checks her hairline. 'Well frankly I don't see what this has to do with us.'

'Oh?'

'I'm not a blonde.' A pointed glance at Tania's parting. 'And nor are you.'

Imogen is quickly out of the door, for a crazy moment fearing that Tania might pursue her. She dashes into a disabled loo further along the corridor, then makes her way back to Uncle Pedro. He would no doubt find Tania's behaviour highly amusing, but for Santi's mother it would just be confirmation that blondes – which in Spanish clearly means anyone with anything less than dark brown hair – are nothing but trouble.

Then there's an arm round her shoulder and Santi asking how it's been.

'It was fine. Except for Tania in the Ladies.'

His smile disappears. 'Why? What did she say?'

People are beginning to move out of the room towards the concert hall.

'I'll tell you later. It's nothing.'

'No, what happened?'

'Well, let's put it this way,' she says as they walk arm in arm, 'if I didn't already know about your previous relationships, I would now be fully informed.'

'What *is* her problem?'

They take their seats in the third row of the ancient lecture hall, saying hello to Darius, who wisely opted out of the gossipy reception.

'But she… I will not permit that she talk with you like this.' Santi continues in rather rattled Spanish, something about respect and privacy of his private life, the importance of it.

'Santi, please. I wish I hadn't told you now. Don't let her spoil our evening. Wow – look at the ceiling in here. Amazing.'

'Sorry. You are right.'

The lights dim. Musicians open with a sombre song, then Esme

The Lighthouse Keeper's Daughter

enters to much applause, draped in white, her wild hair clipped by a flower and falling around her shoulders. It's the track she played Imogen earlier in the week: a modulated, haunting verse, with a more melodic and uplifting chorus. Imogen doesn't understand the words, but gets that intense shiver that only flamenco gives her. The audience are passionately approving and vocal. Esme says a few words into the microphone. The crowd sigh and laugh, and a few call out responses that cause further applause. Then she puts her hand on her heart and is saying something about friends and family. There's more clapping and crying out of '¡*Olé*!'

Santi smiles at Darius and then takes Imogen's hand.

'What did she say?' she asks in his ear.

He leans over to her. 'She thanks God for her happiness this year past, and for the happiness that *all* her family seem to have at the moment.'

CHAPTER 32

SUNDAY 10TH FEBRUARY 2013
Madrid, Spain

'I've had such a great time,' she says, leaning against him. 'Never realised Malaga could be so warm in winter. But brr… this train is f-freezing!' She stands up to put on her jacket, a little shower of grey sand trickling from the pocket. She sits down again and rests her head back on his shoulder.

'Always like this in the AVE train. So how-about Gran Canaria?'

'I've got that meeting with the magazine.'

Can't she move it? He takes out his phone and scrolls through the itinerary. 'Or Valencia! We have shows there the first to the three of March.'

'Uh… I've got my scan on the fourth.'

Couldn't she fly back on the afternoon of the third? When are they next going to see each other? He wasn't used to this; or rather, he wasn't used to being on this side of the question. He's got the last couple of weeks free in March and that gig on the twenty-sixth, a perfect time for her to come over – but nothing's fixed. Then there was the course for learning how to teach English to foreigners; back in January she mentioned a place just the other side of Gran Vía that did it, and seemed keen – but she hasn't actually booked it.

Her head is heavy on his arm. He shifts a little, careful not to wake her. Kisses the soft peachy hair. He has to be patient; she's been through a lot recently, and it's very early days. Anyway, there's a whole forty-eight hours before her flight, the same amount of time as they had in Malaga. His lids close. He's back on the beach with her, but this time it's summer and they're in the sea…

His phone vibrates in his pocket. Twice. A third time, and immediately a fourth. Actually, it might have been doing this quite a bit, but he thought it was just vibrations from the train. Ep has sent two more WhatsApp messages. There are also – what? – thirty-nine posts on Facebook. Seventy-two on Twitter. What the hell is going on?

'*Santi! Have you seen this?*' Ep has written. There's a link to Tania's serialised biography in that stupid paper.

'*Yes, yes,*' he types.

'*But have you seen TODAY'S?*'

He clicks on the link. It's in chunks separated by quotes in large handwriting fonts: 'I was a straight-A student, no time for dating', 'it was a dream come true', 'Spanish men are so much more charming'… What a load of pap. Tania can do better than this. Then he scrolls down further and sees his name in one of the quotes. 'Santiago Montoya was a ruthless heartbreaker; he *was* Diego.'

'Oh for fuck's *sake,*' he says through his teeth, trying to read the section, the words jumbling and doubling as he tries to follow the tiny lines on the screen. Friends… once he had what he wanted…

The phone rings. Ep. 'Santi?'

'Why's she doing this?' he asks quietly, hoping Imogen won't wake up. 'It wasn't like that, you've got to believe me.'

'Course I do. I just tweeted her and told her it's slander. Although I meant libel. It's gone crazy on Twitter.'

'Uh… let me have a look.'

She's right. It looks like every expat who has ever had an unsuccessful relationship with a Spaniard is on there, using hashtag '#DamnThoseDiegos'.

Ep again. 'Santi, you've got to say something. Just short and to the point, don't get into a stupid argument like I did.'

'Okay. I'll think of something. Thanks Ep. Bye for now.'

He opens Twitter again. Apart from the endless stream of women saying they hate him, love him, can well believe it or really can't, over in Direct Messages there's conflicting advice from cousins, a guy from *Universidad* telling him he's a wanker, and a chap he was at school with congratulating him on shagging the hottest girl on TV.

Now it's Ignacio on the phone. 'You've got to sort this out with Tania – and quickly. Reason with her, or threaten to expose something about her – whatever it takes. She needs to stop this, and preferably retract it. She's on telly tonight in that new chat show on Telecinco, so now Santi.'

He promises him he'll sort it out.

Imogen sits up blearily and looks at him. 'Something wrong?'

'It's Tania. Look what's she been doing now. It's all lies, lies, lies.' He goes back to Twitter and hands his phone to Imogen, watches her eyes widen as she scrolls down.

'Jesus. Aren't you going to say something here?'

'I think I need to *talk* to her.'

※

Tania has collapsed onto the white sofa – possibly the same one on which the wretched act took place – shoulders shaking with sobs. Oddly, he finds himself wanting to put his arm round her, but glances around instead: awards and photos of her with various celebrities on the walls, a huge mantelpiece of invitations and a white baby grand piano. Life is good for Tania Murphy Mendez. Or would be, if she could give up her stupid obsession with him.

'Oh come on Tania.'

'I tell you... it's the *editor*,' she says again. There's a strange catching of her breath – she should use this next time she has to cry on screen. 'She exaggerated it to spice up the article.'

'But you really *believe* I tricked you, don't you? Somehow you've re-written the script, or got it confused with the one in *Universidad*. We were friends. But whenever you had a few drinks... It was an accident waiting to happen. You *knew* I didn't want a relationship, I always made it clear.'

'You just assumed I was a loose American girl, up for anything. But I'd only had one boyfriend before—'

'I didn't assume anything! It was just something we both wanted at the time. For you, it was a mistake, but I just don't understand why you've let this resentment *increase*.'

'Well... my *feelings* for you have increased.'

He leans forward. 'Listen, the Santi you think you want doesn't really exist,' he says gently. 'Honestly, I'd drive you nuts.'

Tania pulls out a tissue and blows her nose. 'Can't you at least sit down?'

Santi chooses an armchair opposite her. While he's wondering how he's going to bring all this to a peaceful close, she taps into her phone for a minute and holds it out for him to read. It's an apology mentioning communication breakdown, Santi's good character and forgiving nature. It makes him sound a bit soft, but he can live with it.

'I'm sorry. I'm really sorry, Santi. And about Imogen too. I don't know if you'll ever forgive me, but I'll do my best to put things right.'

'That'll be good for all of us.'

She looks up. 'Was Imogen upset by what I said to her then?'

'She's English, they make themselves laugh things off, but I'm sure she could have done without it.'

'So… is she going to come and live here?'

'It's early days.'

'Well, she seems to come over quite often anyway.'

'Half her new novel is set here. She's doing research.'

Tania bites her lip for a moment. 'Coffee?'

'Haven't you got to get to the studio for the show?'

'I've still got a bit of time.'

Tania disappears to the kitchen and comes back with a tray of two mugs and a plate of home-made 'cookies' – as if she's been expecting a guest.

Santi bites into a *magdalena* and wonders if he can take one back for Imogen.

'What's Imogen's story about then?'

'Apparently authors don't discuss "work in progress".'

'Must have given you *some* idea.' Tania's forehead furrows. 'When did she start it?'

'Couple of months ago, I think. Not sure.'

'Doesn't that worry you?'

'Why?'

'Well… How d'you know she's not writing about *you*? Or about the *two* of you? I mean, what kind of *research* is she doing?'

⁂

Actually, he *does* have some idea about the book. There's an Englishwoman who comes to Madrid to teach English. There are various Spaniards, and one of them – she once let drop – lives

266

The Lighthouse Keeper's Daughter

around here, as it happens. He goes down to the *Canal* metro, pulling his cap down further onto his head; some of those Tweeters earlier had illustrated their comments with a close-up from *Universidad*, so he stands in the carriage as it rattles through the stations, keeping his gaze down.

Imogen loves the metro; she says it's like a full colour child's version of London's grisly 'tube', and is happy to whizz about all over the place in it. What sort of research is she doing? Well, visits to some of the famous squares and parks of course, the *Teleférico*, the zoo – but mostly just wandering around and looking for 'things that resonate with the story'. When something does, out comes that little red notebook and she's scribbling away. She noted the times of the puppet show in the Retiro Park, but walked straight past the Prado. She took photos of a pedestrian crossing near the entry to the parque del Oeste, but ignored the famous Templo de Debod right behind her. He's seen her do funny things like jotting down a stranger's words in a café, snapping the VIPS menu with her phone, timing journeys on the metro, and sketching the layout of a shopping mall.

Odd that the AVE train didn't get the book open, and he doesn't remember seeing it in Malaga. In fact, it's been a while since he saw her take anything down; as far as he knows, even Esme's album presentation evening, which you'd think would be a writer's people-watching goldmine, didn't get that pen out of the elastic.

He's out of the metro, nearly home. There's an hour or so before they head off to Esme's for a family dinner. So lovely the way Imogen and Uncle Pedro get on so well.

Of course, maybe she's still putting things down in the notebook, but *when he's not around*. What? Tania is speaking in his head, with her assumptions that all women are as scheming as she is.

He's in the lift. He'll ask Imogen about the notebook. Maybe she has all she needs. The novel could be nearly finished – maybe she's ready to start telling him more about it, just needs some encouragement.

He opens the door – and can immediately sense that she's not there. He checks the rooms all the same, just in case she's fallen asleep, curling up like a cat as she did in the train. In the bedroom, both suitcases are almost empty, and – bless her – he can hear the washing machine whining away. Her phone is charging on the bedside table; she's probably just in the road, buying paracetamol for her headache from the freezing AVE.

He hangs up his jacket in the hall, puts his keys in the tray – and wonders how he missed it: a note. '*Hope it went OK*', followed by a face with a wiggly mouth. '*I'll be back by 6.30*' and a row of English 'x' kisses.

Back to the bedroom – and the mini-study she's set up on the table. Her laptop, a mug of pens, a memory stick, a map book, some leaflets – but no little red book. His foot meets something under the table that falls over with a light pat onto the floor. It's the folder for her novel – but she must have taken the chapters out of it and moved them elsewhere, like a cat hiding her kittens. He'll tease her about that.

Or will he? Maybe she's moved the novel *away from him* – although the folder's lockable, so why do that? He hesitates a moment, then pulls open the shallow drawer in the table: a couple of funny notes he's left her, passport, a plastic wallet of euros. He closes it. He's not being nosy, he's not going to *read* it, just wants to know if she's *using* it. She may have taken the novel home last time, but she wouldn't want to be parted from her notebook. He opens the wardrobe: just a Spanish grammar book and a pair of slippers at the bottom. She must have it with her; there's nowhere else it could be. Other than the drawers for her clothes.

He stares at the bottom drawer. It's probably not in there, but

The Lighthouse Keeper's Daughter

if it is, what does it mean that she's put it there? Why would she suddenly start hiding it now? Well, not *now*, but… *since they became lovers*?

He listens for the sound of the lift. Goes out onto the balcony and looks down in the street. Comes back in. Stares at the drawer. If it's in there, is he really not going to try and read it? *Any* of it? Of course he will. It's her fault for keeping him so in the dark; she should realise that he might be concerned that the novel could be about him.

He opens the drawer. A jumper and a scarf. But a red corner visible. It's here. And underneath it, the sight a blow in the chest, what looks like a whole novel.

※

She opens the door – and can immediately sense that he's not there. She checks the rooms all the same, just in case he's got headphones on, nodding and smiling to himself like he was on the train.

She checks her phone; it's now fully charged, but hasn't received anything from Santi. Back at the hall table, there's no reply to the message she left.

Surely, *surely* he can't still be at Tania's. For a moment she has an awful, hollowed-out feeling in her stomach. No, he's probably just gone to the shops for something. She goes out onto the balcony, hoping to spot him on the street below. He's not there. Never mind, he'll be back soon.

Back inside, she sits on the sofa with the shop's bag and lifts out a shiny orange spiral notepad like the ones he uses for his songs, followed by a matching pen that he'll probably forget to use with it. From then on, everything is blue. Royal blue. Or marine.

Ultramarine? A delicious colour; more deep Mediterranean than muddy British Channel. Four elasticated notebooks (she'll have to go back for more later), a couple of pads, three matching biros, a pen pot, and a folder. New colour, new start – even though she's not sure what that might be yet.

She can leave some of it here. She goes through to the bedroom and re-arranges her mini-study. The folder is a bit big; maybe she should put it in the jumper drawer for now. She looks round the room for the full effect. Ha – the blue even matches the bed throw. But something's different. Santi's suitcase, that's it. He must have been home and gone out again. He's put the case away in the hall cupboard, and finally tidied away the lump of clothes on his chair and the trainers under it. His favourite guitar isn't on the wall, so perhaps that's what he's doing, he's dropping it off for more tweaking at the guitar place.

She looks back at her now rather busy little table; the folder can definitely just come out when needed. She pulls open the drawer.

Even before she looks inside, she can tell by the lack of resistance. She stares in disbelief. Grabs at the folder under the table. Empty, as she knows it is. Back to the drawer. Kneeling in front of it, as if in prayer. Taking out jumpers, a pair of jeans. Then she opens the next drawer up, and does the same with underwear, running clothes, the turquoise scarf. She sits back on the cold floor, steadying herself against the wall, rummaging hopelessly for the notebook among the folds of the clothes, her head spinning...

Why? Why now? If he'd asked her, she could have explained. Told him not to worry, it's going to be transferred from the bottom drawer here to the bottom drawer in her room in the lighthouse; he is far more important to her than the novel. Ah! Her notebook will fall open at the last entry; when he reads that, he'll understand. It will be okay.

But it isn't okay yet; he's not answering his phone. She manages a breathless voicemail asking him to call her, please, they need to talk. Minutes drag past, her heart thudding in her chest as she tries to work out what she'll say. Six-thirty. The time that he wanted her to be back. Surely he'll come home soon.

Maybe he's come across them, just had a brief look and put them down somewhere to talk to her about later. She jumps up, holds on to the wall as her body catches up with her head, and goes through to the living room. Nothing on the table or the shelves. Then something occurs to her. No laptop. And… his suitcase isn't in the hall cupboard.

She sinks down onto the sofa. Tries him again. Straight to Voicemail. Twitter. @Santi_Montoya. She presses on the cog. But then her thumb hovers over the options… What? *She can't send a message, because he no longer follows her.* Quickly back to WhatsApp – and her message that was never delivered. She sits there cold, shivering, dazed. He has severed all communication, at the moment when they need it most.

She picks up the phone again. Esme. No reply. Despite her kindness, his sister always shared a bit of her mother's suspiciousness about her; there won't be any help from her.

Ep isn't answering either. Imogen sends her a WhatsApp message begging her to ask Santi to call. She holds her breath as Ep comes online for a minute before disappearing. Perhaps she's calling Santi now.

She takes the phone with her to the kitchen and finds herself taking out the washing, pulling his clothes into shape, hanging them up. Then the apartment turns into a watery blur. More tears, on and on. Her throat aching. Holding the shirt she remembers him wearing at Uncle Pedro's when they first met. Uncle Pedro. Family are different here, or different to anything she's known.

Fiercely protective and connected. But Pedro has always been so supportive of their relationship – even from before they themselves knew it existed.

She hangs up the shirt, wipes her eyes, swallows some water. Sits down with the phone. Tries to get the Spanish together in her head, takes a deep breath and lets it out slowly. But it's no good, her Spanish will leave her and she might not hear him; she'll blow her only chance. Better to write.

'*Pedro, I hope you can help,*' she taps out in Spanish. '*Santi is angry and isn't answering me. I don't know where he is. Please tell me that he is safe. If he reads the last line of the red notebook, he will see that I have stopped the novel, and that I love him so much. I am sorry to ask you, but there is nothing else I can do. Imogen.*'

Delivered. *Read.* But she can't expect him to reply until he's spoken to Santi.

She goes back to the washing machine. Their clothes mixed together. English and Spanish instructions. Her phone tings; it's a miracle that she's heard it. She sits down again, her knees weak. The Spanish seems harder than ever, but she thinks it says:

'*Dear Imogen, Santi is safe but very discontent (upset?). He is staying with a relative near Madrid. He needs time to read the novel, and to think. I told him about the last line in the red book, but he answered that it only says that you have enough, that you don't need any more information from him.*

He will talk to you when he is ready. I have told him he should. I hope that you can find a resolution (solution?) together. But you must prepare yourself to accept that sometimes when trust is lost, it cannot be found again.

With all my heart I wish you well, Imogen. Take care of yourself. Pedro.'

The Lighthouse Keeper's Daughter

CHAPTER 33

MONDAY, 18TH MARCH 2013
The South Coast, England

Imogen spots Ewan's Lexus in a line of cars making their respectful way along the Beachy Head cliff road, and turns back to last night's washing up. 'God. Only six, seven months ago he drove down with the Jeep and I was all jitters about what to say to him.'

'And now he's part of the family,' Jules says. 'Well... in a way. It's funny, I always imagined him to be a complete bastard, but come to think of it, you never really said he was one.' She shifts position on the sofa, sips her glass of water. 'Although he does lose points for driving all the way to Eastbourne for croissants, rather than trusting the village shop.'

Imogen looks at her. 'Here, have a banana and quick. At this stage with Ollie I had to have three digestive biscuits the minute I opened my eyes in the morning.'

'Uh, thanks, I must try that. So... he stayed on the sofa and didn't try to come and join you in your keeper's bunk then?'

'Of course.'

'He *did*?'

'Of course he *didn't*, you idiot. He stayed because he's hoping I'll change my mind and let him come to the hospital with me.'

'Well I think *someone* should.'

Imogen groans. 'I've told you, I'd honestly rather go on my own. It's going to be fine, nothing's changed.'

'But you've been feeling dizzy.'

'No! That just comes and goes.'

'And there are the headaches.'

'Oh come on, we know what *they're* about.'

'*Who* they're about. How long can it take to read half a novel?'

'It's not him, it's me. I have a self-loathing headache... still can't believe what I was doing.'

'Imo! Another guy might have been delighted to be written about. But *still* no answer at all... I really think you've just got to... let it go. The uncle's obviously a lovely man, but you can't expect....'

Let it go: what a strange – what a very *English* – expression. As if you can just decide what to feel. Or can just set a feeling adrift, with no care as to whom, how or where that energy transfers.

'I wrote to him this morning, actually.'

Jules slowly nods her head.

It seems there's a point at which sympathy starts to madden. It's lovely having Jules and Dylan living here with her, but sometimes she thinks their concern for both her physical and emotional states makes her feel even worse.

Ewan comes bustling in with bags. 'Gorgeous out there today! Spring has definitely sprung. How about we go for a walk after breakfast?'

'Definitely,' Jules says, getting up. 'If you don't mind I'll leave you to it and have a quick shower. I think Dylan's out of it now.'

'Fine, we'll give you a shout.' He waits for her to go down the stairs, then beams at Imogen. 'We haven't really said good morning, have we?'

She smiles back.

'You're looking great today. Yesterday, a little pale, but today…' he kisses her on each cheek. Like a Spaniard. 'What time is your appointment?'

'Thanks for the offer, but I really—'

'I know, I know. But I could at least stick around until you come back so you can tell me how it went. I've got stuff to do, but nothing I can't do from your lantern room. Got to re-write a bust-up scene; all I fucking need.'

'Is there really no chance…?'

'Oh no. She can't let it go, and anyway she's thinking of moving in with that actor now. Even more hopeless than your situation.'

'Ewan, I really don't want to talk about Santi, okay? Anyway, we better get this breakfast on; Dylan's got to get to work.'

He scrambles eggs, the two of them wordlessly recalling that he's better at it, while she prepares everything else. Then he leans over and kisses her cheek.

'What's that for?'

'Just because.'

Then he gives her another hug, her head on his shoulder. It feels good. She couldn't stand it if they were still awkward with each other, and it's been great for Ollie. Then he kisses her on the lips.

She pulls away. 'Um… I'm sorry, but two broken hearts don't make a whole one.'

'I know. We need time. It's complicated and weird.'

'Yes. But I can't go back to how we were.'

'We would be going *forward*.'

'I don't think I can do forward either. I'm… I've sort of become a day-to-day person.'

He turns back to serving up the plates. 'How very *flamenco*.'

'*Don't*.'

He puts a hand on her arm. 'Sorry. Bad choice of dialogue.

But… you're still coming up for Easter, aren't you?'

'Course. I promised Ollie. And I've already bought your egg.'

'It better be—'

'Lindt, dark, no innards.'

'Ha! Perfect.'

※

Imogen stares at Mr Hatton and, despite his volume, can't believe what she's just heard.

'We've booked you in for next Tuesday,' he continues. 'Tuesday for the op, coming in Monday evening… I'm sorry; this is why we were trying to reach you to bring this appointment forward.'

'I… don't tend to notice voicemails.'

'Is Tuesday okay for you then? Should get you home for Easter.'

But it's not just Tuesday, it's the month or more of dopey recovery afterwards… 'And I can't just have the gamma knife treatment?'

'Well as I say, it's grown so unusually fast, and with its position… it's not the best option. It's a lot to take in, I know. Can you come back tomorrow morning at nine, bringing one of your friends with you?'

Tuesday. Tuesday the twenty-sixth, the day of Santi's concert; she hasn't let go of the crazy hope that this still just might happen. 'Next month would be better.'

The nurse says something about tea and leaves the room.

Mr Hatton nods slowly. 'There's never a good time for this. But as I say, we want to do it sooner rather than later. You're doing well at the moment, but we want things to stay that way, don't we. And…' He looks at the scan again. 'You really haven't noticed any tingling or numbness in your face?' He puts a chubby hand to his cheek to encourage her to do the same. 'The other side, dear.'

The Lighthouse Keeper's Daughter

'Ah…' she rubs her face harder, touches her other cheek. 'Well…
maybe very *slightly*…'

He nods and scribbles something down.

The nurse comes back with a polystyrene tea. It has a
morphinous dose of sugar in it. Mr Hatton pulls at his large ear
and starts telling her again about the other specialists involved.
Can't he just write all this down? They should include impaired
difficulty with verbal instructions as a symptom of this stupid
disease. Then he hands her a rather smart folder with everything
she needs to know and asks more about Jules and Dylan.

There's a vibration from her bag. She takes out her phone; it's a
bit rude of her, but could be relevant to the planning.

*'Imogen, Santi has finished the book. The problem is not so much
the content, but the way you never told him, and see (is that him, or
her?) no future. He is very…* (distressed?) *that you…* (betrayed?)
him with this. He asks that you don't publish it in Spain.

*I'm sorry. There is no more I can do. You made a mistake, but you
are a good person and I wish you all the best. Pedro.'*

'So is nine tomorrow okay? Bring your friends and we'll talk
more. Then we can get some of the pre-op stuff done.'

She puts her phone away and gets up. They are waiting for her
to say something. 'Okay.'

※

She pulls the car into the Beachy Head car park. Reads the message
again. There's nothing more Uncle Pedro can do; he also wants her
to let it go. Oh, she's going to *let it go* all right.

A last quick flick through some of the messages to and from
Santi. Twitter. WhatsApp. Facebook. Texts. Emails. Hundreds of
them. Hundreds and hundreds. Her phone is so thick with them;

their deletion would be its demise.

She gets out of the car. This morning's spring day is now cold and damp. The parking machine wants money: 80p for 30 minutes, £1.40 for 2 hours. How long is this going to take? But a parking ticket, in the scale of things, isn't going to make much difference to anything. Next to it, the Samaritans have a poster reminding her they are available day and night.

She starts walking up the grassy slope to the sky. Perhaps this is how most people do it, they just keep walking. She's heard that some run at it, like a PE exercise in the school gym. Then there are those that make for the seat-like ledges near the drop, to ponder for a while first.

Her mobile gives a feeble tri-tone trill in her pocket. Twitter. What? In an effort to appease her, it's picking up some 3G here – if only to inform her that the Eastbourne Car Centre is now following her. She could now reply to Pedro, tell him again to pass on that she had no intention of publishing that book anywhere, but her Spanish isn't up to that right now. Anyway, they'll soon figure it out for themselves.

Halfway there. She looks to the right: her borrowed lighthouse, sitting far away on its cliff, the lights on already; Jules, Dylan and Ewan waiting for her. A couple walking slowly down the dip that will rise up again to where she is. To the left she can make out somebody with the red jacket of the Chaplaincy Team, ten minutes' fast walk away; if it's one of the new team members they won't recognise her and will be marching over here in no time. Actually, she would have preferred to be about where he or she is, near her father's old lighthouse, but that's not going to happen.

She sits on the first of the three grassy ledges. It's bad enough. But after a while, those silently tumbling waves below just look like a view from an aeroplane, and she can shuffle herself down to the

The Lighthouse Keeper's Daughter

less-visible second level. From here, she can have her legs straight out in front of her and still feel the ground beneath her feet. But if she pushes herself onto the edge of the seat, and stretches her legs out further and kicks… it might work. She puts the phone by her feet and leans back on her elbows.

'You're going to lose that phone.'

She twists round to see a red-jacketed woman looking down at her with wide eyes. Must have been behind her. 'That's the idea.'

A hand reaches out to her. 'Why don't you come back up here and you can just throw it? Or I'll do it for you – I bowl for the East Dean cricket team, you know.'

'Throwing seems kind of violent. I just wanted to sort of… *let it go.*'

'I'm sure we can think of a better way of doing that,' she says steadily. 'You could… get a new phone and just put this one in a bottom drawer.'

'*No.*'

'Or… I'll buy it for my daughter. She smashed hers during a Facebook row. Youngsters these days forget how to talk to each other.'

Imogen watches the tufts of grass in front of her turn into a watery green blur. 'Not just youngsters.' This isn't going to work. She pushes the phone towards her with her foot, picks it up and turns round to hand it to the woman. Her head reels; she turns back and waits for it to calm down. 'Oh God… can't move. What the hell am I doing here?'

'Crawl up on your all fours, I've got you.'

She's back on the grass and walking back to the car park, arms linked with this woman now introducing herself as Janet.

'So what changed your mind?'

'Forgot it's useful for other things – like booking flights.'

'You've got some messages,' Janet says, handing her the phone.

'*I'm sorry Imogen, I forgot to say that Santi wanted to know how the story ends,*' Pedro has written. Then there's a phrase that probably means something like '*just out of interest.*'

'*It doesn't end. I never finished it,*' she replies, forgetting to write in Spanish.

Jules, Dylan and Ewan have left messages wanting to know how the appointment went.

She calls Jules. 'I'm fine. I'll be home soon. Off to Madrid for a few days tomorrow.' She closes the phone.

'Oh?' says Janet, hearing this.

'I've got some things to do. Thanks Janet, I'm really sorry to have wasted your time.'

Just as she's passing the next car park, there's another tri-tone. Probably another garage, but it's where she pulled in and first heard Santi's guitar. She stops the car. Twitter informs her that @Santi_Montoya is now following her. She stares in disbelief. Then realises it's just a friendly gesture now that it's all over. She could now send him a message, but she won't. Maybe they'll talk tomorrow.

CHAPTER 34

He shouldn't have asked her how it was going to end, but somehow he feels he has a right to know. Has his doing so prompted this visit? He can't refuse to see her when she's come all this way, even if she's apparently also here 'for other reasons'. One of these will be her little red book of course, which she probably doesn't want to trust to the post, but heaven knows what else is drawing her over. Ah well, he can ask her. Something neutral they can talk about.

Hang on, this is Imogen, who used to be the easiest person to talk to in the world, despite their daft language mistakes. He can feel his spirits lifting, so he goes to the bedroom and takes out the novel, reminds himself of the way she sees him as this ignorant, impatient idiot hanging on her every educated word. Okay, later she looks the more vulnerable one, but that's probably just a trick to make the reader more sympathetic. He flicks through some more, then throws it back in the drawer. It's all her, her, her – even if she puts quite a lot of time into this fool.

Back in the living room, he paces up and down – until doing so reminds him of practising the scenes for the audition; the way she watched him, willing him on, then showed him the poem about the guitar... Five o'clock: she must be here by now. What's she doing, making him hang around trying to guess when she might be descending on them?

He picks up the phone. 'Uncle, has she called? I've got things to do.'

'Well get on and do them, she'll ring when she's ready. You could call her, of course. In fact, you could have done that a month ago. Ah. Hang on.'

'What?'

'She's just sent a message asking when it would be convenient to meet you here in the next three days.'

'Well *now*, obviously.'

⁑

Imogen lies on the hotel bed with the Information Pack the English teaching school has given her. It's all set: May the thirteenth for four weeks. Staying in that tiny flat with the balcony overlooking a narrow cobbled street, minutes from all those gardens round the Palace for enjoying the sun. Beyond them, the parks – although they're a bit too near Santi. Something in the diary. Something to get better for. There'll never be a pupil like Santi again, but maybe others can benefit from a little of what she's learnt while teaching him.

After the course, she'll teach English on one of the Brighton or Eastbourne summer courses. Then perhaps when Ollie's at uni, she might teach in Spain. Madrid or somewhere else with good flamenco, plenty of flights, an *apartamento* with a bedroom for Ollie.

Then, then, thens. The abstract happiness of those ahead, and the searing pain of those she needs to leave behind. She looks

The Lighthouse Keeper's Daughter

at her watch, pulls the covers over herself and closes her eyes. Tries out phrases in her mind until they burn a pain through her head, her face, her neck. There must be a migraine pill in her bag somewhere…

><

It's dark. Eight o'clock. Damn, she should have set the alarm. She sits up, swings her legs to the floor and holds on to the bedhead to steady herself. Bloody thing, rattling around in her head; enjoy your last six days, bastard. Five minutes just to get upright; she's never going to make it in time.

><

'I don't know, Santi, she got held up, got a taxi from calle Arenal at half past.' Uncle Pedro pats him on the shoulder.

'It's just like the first time!' His aunt beams, then adjusts her face. 'I mean, in the way she's late and it's raining.'

'You shouldn't have invited her to dinner, Uncle. She's really just coming to collect her things.'

'I thought you were going to be civilized about this? Keep some kind of friendship?'

'We can't send her off into the night on her own without a meal,' Aunt Elena says.

'Well we'll see how it goes. She probably won't *want* to stay, once—'

The doorbell. Pedro and Santi look at each other.

'Poor girl, I better let her in, if you two aren't going to.' Elena bustles past them into the hall.

Then she's there. A little paler – or perhaps he's already grown unaccustomed to her colouring. He kisses each freckled cheek and manages 'It's-good-to-see-you.'

She attempts the Spanish equivalent then settles for a nod.

Her face is the problem: rather than the tearful anxiety he expected, or even hoped for, she's beaming at him uncontrollably – but with just something around the eyes that suggests that she's as surprised as he is that she's doing so.

'Come through, come through,' Uncle Pedro says, taking her coat.

He imagined that she'd be in his favourite soft black top, but she's wearing a short denim dress that she keeps pulling downwards – despite the modesty of the thick navy tights underneath. There's talk of drinks and Aunt Elena is telling him to make a decaffeinated coffee.

Now she's being quizzed about her flight, but it turns out that she's been here since midday – viewing a school that does a month's course in English teaching, and accommodation near the Opera metro. What?

His uncle and aunt also look surprised.

'I will still write when I can, but I will need a more regular pay when I have my own home,' she says in her cumbersome Spanish. 'And I really *like* teaching,' she adds, looking over at Santi.

'Your own home… Does your aunt say you have to leave the lighthouse now?' Pedro asks.

'No, she wants to stay in Jersey with her daughter. But my friend Jules and my half-brother are there now, and having a baby in the summer… I think it will be better if I live in another place.'

'A baby. That's nice for them, after what happened…' Elena says.

'Yes. She thought it was too late, but…'

It's soon going to be too late for *her* to have any more, Santi thinks. But she probably doesn't mind; *books* will be her babies.

'So when are you doing the course?' he asks.

She looks over at him. 'It starts in the middle of May.'

Just when he's supposed to be coming back from New York. As she knows.

'D'you want to come to the studio with me?'

She smiles and nods.

'I've got your papers and notebook there.'

Her mouth falls into a line, a hand going to her face.

She follows him downstairs, takes the sofa as he suggests, while he sits in his uncle's desk chair and swivels round to her. She's looking a bit more troubled, the hand still at her face – more like he imagined – but oddly it's not giving him any satisfaction.

'Did you hear from them yet about the film score?' she asks, now in English.

'We got it.'

'Brilliant! That's great!' She looks over to the computer. 'So...'

'D'you want to hear one of the themes? We're still working on it, but—'

'Please!'

He goes over to the recording desk and switches things on. Sits back in the chair and looks at the ceiling. That saxophone should come up a bit, the guitar needs... How come he hasn't realised until now that it's really very sad.

She looks wrapped up in the music. It fades. 'So beautiful. I love the way it sounds both flamenco and twenties jazz. And it reminds me of when I stopped the car and heard your music for the first time... I felt like the guitar was crying.'

'Yes... Well, there's another theme, more happy.'

'Ah. Is that—'

'Not ready to play yet.'

'Oh.' Then she winces on noticing the pile of papers and the notebook on the desk behind him. Leans on the arm of the sofa, resting her head on her hand as if shying away from them.

He follows her gaze. Their eyes meet.

'Look… I'm so, so sorry,' she says. 'Please don't worry, it's never going to be finished or published.'

'So my uncle tells me. But Imogen, why did you do it?'

She looks at the floor. He can hear his aunt clattering around with plates upstairs, his uncle laughing. Any minute now, Pedro will call for them and he and Imogen will have to sit opposite each other and eat before she's explained herself; it would have been better to meet at his place.

She's still sitting there, head in her hands.

'Come on, I want to know.'

'I suppose I never believed…' she starts.

'Didn't *believe* in us?'

'No! I didn't believe… anything would *happen*! Almost from the start I had to create something, a different Santi that could… that might… Oh, this sounds so stupid.'

'But when you finished your *creation*, you said it had to stop.'

'Yes! Well, *no*, it had to stop because—'

He picks up the notebook and opens it. "It was time to get back to 'real life', it was enough…' You had all you needed.'

'No! The *book* had to stop because everything became real!'

'So…' She's clutching her face again. 'What's the matter?'

'Just a bit of migraine. Might take another pill.' She looks in her bag, swallows something with the rest of her coffee.

'The truth is—'

'The truth is there in the notebook,' she says. 'Look…' She gets up, hanging on to the desk, and takes it from him. He watches her eyebrows pucker. 'Oh God, you know what? I was writing this and then you got back home. What I was going to write was 'This has

The Lighthouse Keeper's Daughter

to stop, time to get back to real life… *which is for once so exciting and real that I can't compete with it here!*"

'But—'

'But *what*? Why can't you believe me? I think you just don't want to now.' She sits down again.

'Because… the novel is all about you.'

'Of course; it's in the *first person*. That's as daft as me complaining that your tracks are *all about* the guitar.'

'But… how can you show what happens, how can you write a story of *comunicación*, with just one of the persons saying about it?'

She nods, with a puzzled half-smile. 'You're absolutely right. I should have made it dual viewpoint.'

'Du… *¿qué?*'

'Used the voice of both characters.'

'You should to have done this, yes. Perhaps you would understand… more of *my* feeling. I too was thinking nothing was going to happen. No chance!' He can't help grinning at the memory of it.

He sees her mouth open in surprise, but then Pedro calls down to them to come up for dinner.

As Imogen starts to go up the stairs, he takes her arm. 'You haven't told me how you were going to finish the story.'

'I didn't have an ending. At the time when I was going to decide, I couldn't write it anymore. I just wanted to enjoy being with you.'

She takes a few more steps, then stops. He waits for her to say something else, but she's just standing there. Perhaps she's waiting for him to repeat that he doesn't believe her – but the thing is, he might be beginning to. They'll talk more after dinner, and tomorrow.

Now she's clutching the bannister and murmuring something.

'What? Sorry, I—'

Very quietly, she's saying something about pain.

'Come and sit down.' He helps her up the stairs and puts her in a chair in the kitchen. His uncle and aunt look angry with him, as if he's upset her. 'She said it's a migraine – seems to have turned into a really bad one,' he explains.

Imogen looks like she's shaking her head. She's holding her cheek. The cheek she's had her hand to since she arrived, Santi realises. Or…

'What is it?'

She doesn't seem to hear him. He asks again, louder, takes her hand, but she looks locked into her agony; there's no reaching her. Pedro is speaking quickly on the phone. Elena has drawn up a chair next to her, holds her, talks to her, until Imogen is sinking into Elena's arms… and then her hand relaxes in his, and they realise she isn't with them anymore.

The Lighthouse Keeper's Daughter

CHAPTER 35

THURSDAY 16TH MAY, 2013
The South Coast, England

'Ah – is for Beachy Head? *Perfecto*. Stop here please.'

The taxi driver studies Santi's face in the driving mirror. 'You want me to pull in?'

'Please.'

The car swerves and comes to a halt, engine still running. 'I thought you wanted—'

'I'll be five minutes,' Santi says, ignoring the concern on the driver's face. He strides up the grassy slope towards the pale blue sky with its weak sun. To his left he can see her father's red striped lighthouse, sitting in a calm sea beneath the colossal cliff. And to his right... there it is. As she said, not pretty. Squat. Grey. Much too near the edge. Had he realised quite *how* near, he would have been very worried about her. But he doesn't have to worry now.

He walks back to the taxi and gets in. It could be the car park where she nudged the stereo and heard his music; where, in a way, he spoke to her for the first time.

'You okay there, mate?'

'Yes. I'm okay.'

'Let's get you to your friends for an early drink then, eh?' The road winds down the hill, passes a few metres from the cliff edge and then, just as it swerves inland, there's a cobbled drive up the next hill to the walled garden of the old lighthouse. 'Must have spotted us – the gate's opening.'

They drive in to the gravelled area of the small garden and are surrounded by a group of people who have left their deckchairs and are waiting while he pays the driver. First of the smiling faces to come forward, as if agreed by the others, is an elderly woman like the one in the *Importance of Being Ernesto*. He holds out a British hand but she kisses each of his cheeks like a true Spaniard and tells him what a delight it is to meet him at last. Then there's a hug and a pat on the back from the freckled half-brother, and a cumbersome one from the pregnant Jules.

'Ollie! I didn't know you were going to be here!'

'Yeah, well I thought I'd have some more Spanish practice for my viva on Tuesday,' he says with a cheeky grin and an awkward hug. 'And this is my dad, Ewan. Finally got him to support Atletico instead of Real, in time for tomorrow!'

A tall attractive guy in a crisp polo comes forward. *Imogen's husband*. A stupid pang of jealousy. '*Hola, bienvenido!*' he says, with an appalling accent. 'You should stay tomorrow night as well and we could watch the derby together – Atletico might actually do it this time.'

'Yes! But I have got to get back—'

'Ever had Pimm's?' Jules is asking, putting a glass of something that looks like a pale sangría in his hand. 'There you go.'

Dylan takes his bag. 'I'll put this in your room. In *her* room, that is. Take a seat, we've managed to lay on some summer weather for you!'

'Thanks but… Can I see the lighthouse? First? I'm sorry but—'

Everyone falls quiet and looks at Dylan.

The Lighthouse Keeper's Daughter

'No, no, I understand. Come on then.'

Santi follows him inside.

'So down here, Dorothy's old bedroom – now ours – and the kitchen and bathroom I was working on when I first met her. And in here…' He opens a door at the end of the hall into a round stone-walled room with baby paraphernalia. 'This is my old room, from when my parents died – exactly eighteen years ago, as it happens. I never had any idea about Imogen until Dorothy told me about her last summer. She asked me to sound her out and keep an eye on her while I did some long overdue changes and repairs to the lighthouse.'

'*Dios mío…*'

'It was hard. Right from the start, I adored her, you know? But I couldn't say anything.'

'I can imagine.'

'Let's go upstairs.'

'Ah! Where Imogen made lots sandwiches for you!'

'Yes! I was always trying to hang around.'

'The views!' Santi goes from one window to another.

'Nothing compared to up here.' Santi follows Dylan up the stone steps to the lantern room.

'*Estupendo!* I think sometimes she worked here.'

'Yes. D'you want to go outside on the…'

'No, I'm ready to see her room.'

They go back down to the living room and open the door into the tower. It's even smaller than he imagined it. A round room with a hidden tiny bathroom under the ledge where the mattress lies just a couple of feet beneath the stone ceiling.

'Some people find it claustrophobic. If you—'

'No, no, I like it. And…' he goes over to a desk with a stripey lamp and looks out of the window towards the father's old lighthouse.

'That's where she had her laptop. Probably where she first tweeted you!'

Santi looks at the desk and imagines her sitting there. Maybe it's the English, but he suddenly feels lost for words.

'I'll leave you to look around a bit. To give you more space, we put her cases of things in the living room. Just come down when you're ready, okay?' He pats his arm and trots downstairs.

Santi sits at the desk. Opens a few drawers. They haven't completely cleared everything out. A pot of those erasable pens. A Spanish dictionary. An older version of her duffle coat. A pair of spotted slippers. Some CDs – ha! – including an unboxed copy of his. And there's a book-size package, with Imogen's name on it.

When his phone tinkles a WhatsApp in his pocket, he grins even before getting it out. He glances at it, then takes photos of the view out to the other lighthouse, the crazy flamenco slippers, his CD. He sends them off without a message.

'Hahahahaha!'

'I love it! And you are right, they are ALL here, even Ollie!'

'Of course! Important visitor!'

'How is your head? Did they take you walking today?'

'Pedro and Elena have been lovely. But I went on my own!'

'NO. You PROMISED.'

'I used the stick. Only as far as VIPS.'

'But if you faint?'

'I'm not going to faint. No stupid blob to press on a nerve now.'

'Yes, but when you were with Esme??? ☹'

'I was just a little under the weather.'

'Ay, that stupid English expression! And did they give you new dates for the course?'

'Seventeenth June. One more month. My balance will be much better by then I'm sure.'

'Good, but we have to see. I must go down to join them now.'

'OK. Forgotten about those slippers – can you put them in one of the bags to come back? ☺. Send them all my love and tell Ols I can't wait to see him.'

'I will. And I'll see if I can find out more about that girl ;-) Talk later.'

':-)'

':-))'

He puts the package and the slippers on top of one of the suitcases in the living room, and looks out of the window while he finishes his Pimm's. Poor Ollie has a folder and a pile of papers by his chair. He wonders how Pato is doing with her revision. He'll call her later and remind her of the dates that Ollie's coming over. So sweet the way she found time to take Imogen out to VIPS last weekend, even if Imogen is now fed up of the vegetarian options there. VIPS. Why would Imogen decide to make her first solo walk to VIPS? The park is the same distance and she loves it there. Or there's her beloved designer stationery shop. But… VIPS. Maybe she just got that far and came back. Or… there was something else around there that she wanted. Without anyone with her. Like the pharmacy next door to it.

He picks up the phone.

'Are you *sure* you're okay?'

'Absolutely.'

'Then what are you doing, going secretly to the pharmacy?'

'Oh God… Why d'you have to be so bloody smart? Um… it was just those few weeks off the pill after the surgery… I can't believe it. But we'll have to! I was going to tell you tomorrow.'

CHAPTER 36

TUESDAY, 16TH MAY 1995
The North Coast, France

**Tues 16th May '95**

Hello again Imogen. May: the time of the year that I always come back to the diary. I suppose it always feels like a time for preparing something. Oh look, it was _16th_ May I started writing again last year. What's so special about 16th May? You'd think it would be the 23rd, the day I left Beachy Head. And you.

Oh Imogen, this was never the plan. We thought Beryl would become closer to Dorothy once I'd gone, that I'd be able to hear about you, see photos. Dorothy would become an aunt in whom you could confide, and she would know when you were old enough to hear the truth, when it would be safe to contact you. But it wasn't to be: Beryl's dislike of Dorothy quickly turned to hatred, as if she somehow sensed that Dorothy had had a part in my disappearance. And then just a couple of years later there's a step-father taking my daughter away from the sea to snobby Surrey – I can't tell you how much that hurt. But worst of all, Beryl – who never wanted change – seemed happy to move house _twice_, as if deliberately severing contact with Dorothy. We no longer even knew where you were. The only consolation was that your step-father's teaching post in a Surrey *private school probably meant that you were having the education that you deserved and I could never have dreamed of for you.*

Once you were eighteen, we considered hiring a private detective to find you. But you'd be about to go to university then, and we worried about disrupting your life. A life that seemed to have taken a turn for the <u>better</u> since I'd gone. What did I have to offer you? And of course there was the possibility that you would reject me and tell your mother - who would go to the police. But I never lost hope that a time would come.

And now it has!

Dorothy was up in London for a show last week, and who should she bump into at Victoria Station but my old fellow keeper Bill, his wife Carole and their now teenage daughter. Dorothy wrote to them some time ago, asking for Beryl's address, and they made out they didn't have it – probably thinking that was what Beryl would want them to do. But in the café they must have softened when Dorothy started talking about you. They said they still exchange Christmas cards with Beryl – and that you have an English degree, a magazine job, a husband and a baby boy! And since they mentioned the name of the magazine you're working for, Dorothy CAN CONTACT YOU!

So this 16th May we're preparing for something very special: YOU. I hope. How can I shift this feeling of not deserving to have you in my life again? It's like the chronic headache I still get after the blow from poor old Vince's anchor; it'll never go away. I made a terrible mistake, I know that now. I love Sophie, and I have a good life here on the farm, if a hard one. But nothing will ever compensate for losing you, and there's no real happiness when it's been bought with the pain of others.

I don't know if you'll want to see me now, but we have a plan. Tomorrow, Dorothy's going to leave a message with the magazine that there's a long lost uncle who would love to talk to you on the *phone and meet you. We'll arrange for you to come and visit us, with your husband and son if you like, have a nice long weekend in Étretat. If you come, I can't believe that what we once had won't still be there, somewhere, and you will <u>know.</u>*

Since we got this idea yesterday, Sophie and I can't think or talk of anything else. We need to calm down! And we're lucky, because it's a beautiful day, Dylan's got an after-school music club, and a friend of ours has lent us this fabulous sailing boat while we're still trying to fix up ours...

So. Imogen. Darling. We'll talk tomorrow.

The Lighthouse Keeper's Daughter

The Lighthouse Keeper's Daughter

ACKNOWLEDGEMENTS

There are three people without whom this book might never have happened. The first is Josemi Carmona, as the idea for this story came from our unexpected friendship, his valiant efforts 'whith' English, and the inspiration of his music. *Gracias de corazón, hombre*. For the space and encouragement to see it through – and his vigorous sounding board – I am, as always, more grateful to Phil than I'll ever be able to put into words. And of course, a huge thank you to Matthew Smith of Urbane Publications, whose energy, enthusiasm and belief has turned this story into a book.

It's been a delight to work with my talented *amigos* David Izquierdo Arispón on the cover image and Marta Rodríguez Cristobal on the corrections to my over-confident *español*. In Madrid, I also want to send *muchísimas gracias* to my *bilingüe*-sister Maggie Left (Margarita Izquierdo) for all her efforts to make me *madrileña*; my great friend Juan del Pozo for his *ánimo* and our *río* of Spanglish *errores*; Silvia (as-Spanish-as-a-tortilla) Wheeler Hill for all those flamenco nights; and Alberto Alonso of Vaughan Radio for having Josemi and me on his bilingual show.

Back in England, I'm profoundly grateful to Rob Wassell for his advice, his '*The Story of...*' books on the Eastbourne lighthouses and Birling Gap, and a magical low tide walk to the Beachy Head lighthouse. I also want to thank Sue Hardy for her wonderful tour of Corbière Lighthouse in Jersey. I benefited from a number of books about lighthouses and keepers, but I'm hugely indebted to the late Tony Parker, whose book *Lighthouse* - in which keepers and their families opened their hearts to him - was a fascinating and invaluable resource. I would also like to thank the lovely Hazel Levene at the Beachy Head Countryside Centre and Andrew Norton of the Royal Yachting Association.

Lastly, a big thank you to the Urbane 'family' and other friends and writers for their encouragement, particularly those that braved early drafts – Sam Mills, Nicola Doherty and, of course, Phil (twice).

Cherry Radford was a keyboard player in a band, a piano teacher at the Royal Ballet School and a post-doc researcher at Moorfields Eye Hospital before suddenly starting her first novel in the middle of a scientific conference in 2009.

Following the publication of *Men Dancing* (2011) and *Flamenco Baby* (2013), *The Lighthouse Keeper's Daughter* is her first novel with Urbane Publications.

Cherry lives in Eastbourne (UK) and Almería (Spain).

She chats about writing and other passions on her BLA BLA LAND blog (https://cherryradforddotblog.wordpress.com), Twitter (@CherryRad), Instagram (@cherry_radford) and her website (http://cherryradford.co.uk).